KT-468-093

BRAINSE CABRACH
CABRA BRANCH
TEL. 8691414

Ice Cold Heart

P. J. TRACY

MICHAEL JOSEPH
an imprint of
PENGUIN BOOKS

WANT MORE?

If you enjoyed this and would like to find out about similar books we publish, we'd love you to join our online SF, Fantasy and Horror community, Hodderscape.

Visit our blog site
www.hodderscape.co.uk

Follow us on Twitter
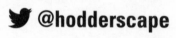 **@hodderscape**

Like our Facebook page
Hodderscape

You'll find exclusive content from our authors, news, competitions and general musings, so feel free to comment, contribute or just keep an eye on what we are up to. See you there!

MICHAEL JOSEPH

UK | USA | Canada | Ireland | Australia
India | New Zealand | South Africa

Michael Joseph is part of the Penguin Random House group of companies
whose addresses can be found at global.penguinrandomhouse.com

First published 2019
001

Copyright © P. J. Tracy, 2019

The moral right of the author has been asserted

Set in 13.5/16 pt Garamond MT Std
Typeset by Jouve (UK), Milton Keynes
Printed and bound in Great Britain by Clays Ltd, Elcograf S.p.A.

A CIP catalogue record for this book is available from the British Library

HARDBACK ISBN: 978–0–241–34582–5
OM PAPERBACK ISBN: 978–0–241–34583–2

www.greenpenguin.co.uk

Penguin Random House is committed to a
sustainable future for our business, our readers
and our planet. This book is made from Forest
Stewardship Council® certified paper.

To PJ – you are always with me.

Prologue

Peter never grew tired of walking the rough forest trails near his home as twilight descended. There was beauty in shadows, especially on a night like this, when a voluptuous full moon was rising in a velvety purple sky. To him, it looked like a mammoth diamond, embellishing a royal cloak.

As he walked, he admired the spires of pines vaulting high above the lower canopy of leafy oak and maple, all casting eerie silhouettes on the forest floor. He delighted in the first firebugs of the season, punctuating the encroaching darkness like tiny restless candles, as they swirled through the woods on their brief mission to mate and die.

Eventually he stopped at the familiar clearing on the crest of a small hill, where the trees opened up to reveal a moon-spangled lake. He heard waterfowl flutter and fuss and squawk in their night-time nests. Bullfrogs were synchronizing in an amorous chorale, and a pair of cats let out ear-splitting yowls, which preceded a union.

It was mating season for just about everything in the forest, but there was also plenty of death afoot. While mating rituals were loud and riotous, the art of death was largely silent. A finely attuned ear might pick up the hushed swoop of an owl's wings as it dove in for a kill, the rustle of a clever fox pouncing through tall grass to take its quarry, and maybe even the faint pad of a larger group of predators, like wolves, stalking a vulnerable fawn. All were stealthy bringers of death, efficient, brutal and without remorse. Yes, death was mostly silent, until the cries of the dying pierced the air. They didn't last long, and there were no sounds after that.

He continued on to the abandoned cabin that had once sheltered hunters during inclement weather. How ironic that it now sheltered the hunted. The door creaked open on rusty hinges and he smelled mold, dirt, shit, blood. He trained his flashlight on the seven dishonest men and women, the traitors, who were huddled in the corner, bound, blindfolded and tethered to the wall. He'd also gagged them, because he had no interest in hearing their lies or their pleas. They still struggled, but very feebly now. Their cries definitely wouldn't last long: he would make sure of it.

He studied the pathetic tableau for a few moments, wondering if he shouldn't take care of things now. None of them deserved the mercy of death, but keeping them here was getting dangerous. Moving them would be even more so.

He heard the distant, guttural rumble of thunder – or had it been an explosion? Either way, it was most definitely a sign meant to guide him. The spirits were speaking to him.

Feeling profound relief and gratitude that he'd been granted direction, he slipped back outside, retrieved the shovel propped against the front log wall of the cabin, and began preparing the grave. It would be a long night of work, but he had the moon to illuminate his efforts and keep him company.

As he shoveled, he never noticed the pair of eyes watching him from the shadows of the forest. It was only when the familiar voice spoke that he realized he'd been entranced by his work to the point of oblivion. Foolish, dangerous, potentially deadly.

'Let's not kill each other, Peter,' the man said. 'It's time to set aside the past and help each other.'

Peter gaped at him. 'How can you ever expect me to set aside the past?'

'Things are ending, you know that, and we can't stay here.'

'I don't want your help. I don't need it.'

'I think you might. I can understand why you don't trust me, so as a gesture of goodwill, I've brought you a gift. I think you'll like it.'

Peter watched a figure emerge cautiously from the forest. From what he could see, he liked the gift very much.

I

Minneapolis detective Leo Magozzi was relishing the early-morning peace of an empty homicide pen. On the days he didn't hitch a ride with his partner Gino, he always made a point of getting to City Hall before anyone else. He'd brew a fresh pot of coffee, check in with any stragglers who were still in-house after pulling all-nighters on a case, then enjoy the solitude and the view of the street from his desk.

When you weren't tangled up in it, there was something oddly restful about watching downtown's morning rush-hour. Vehicles, pedestrians, and light rail trains all swirled together in a chaotic, graceless dance, careening around each other as they forged ahead to their destinations. No matter how messy your mind was, the scene unfolding outside the window was a lot messier, and it brought some perspective that cleared your head. His was already clear this morning, so the view wasn't therapeutic, it was theater, but equally enjoyable to watch. Especially this morning, because he wasn't outside anymore, battling the subzero temperature and congested streets.

A thin veil of snow was blowing over the city, more an ominous mist than proper winter precipitation. The snow-flakes weren't the plump, intricately lacy kind that floated happily down from a warmer sky – they were the bitter, con-stipated pellets that accompanied ungodly cold temperatures.

In elementary school, Magozzi had always been fascinated

Leabharlanna Poiblí Chathair Baile Átha Cliath
Dublin City Public Libraries

by textbook photographs of magnified snowflakes, so dazzling in their beauty and diversity. He imagined that if he looked at one of these pseudo-flakes under a microscope he would see a contorted, angry emoticon with fangs and demonic red eyes.

'It's supposed to be too cold to snow,' his partner Gino Rolseth groused, as he walked into their cubicle, carrying the outdoor chill with him. He was mummified in a huge parka with a funnel hood that was suitable for an Antarctic expedition.

'That's a myth. It's never too cold to snow.'

'Obviously.' He began the long process of shedding his layers.

'That's it?' Magozzi asked with disappointment.

'What do you mean, "That's it"?'

'I mean, where's the fuming tirade over winter in Minnesota? At this point in January, you're usually gnashing your teeth and tipping over desks. You speak for millions of Minnesotans and we count on you to give voice to our grievances.'

Gino rubbed his cheeks, trying to thaw them. 'This is what acceptance looks like, Leo. There comes a time when every warrior must lay down his sword. It's like struggling with a terminal illness – you fight like hell even when you don't have the juice for it, and then you keep fighting some more. And one day it finally settles in, the fact that your destiny is no longer in your control. I've been defeated by Mother Nature and I'm at peace with that.'

Magozzi tapped his pen thoughtfully on his desk. 'It's supposed to be seventeen below tonight,' he goaded him.

'Really? I didn't hear. I stopped watching the weather.'

'We might not go above zero for the next seven days.'

Gino took a deep breath, closed his eyes, then slammed his fist on his desk. 'Goddamnit, Leo! Why did you have to shatter my happy place?'

'Because it hurts me deeply to see you vanquished.'

Detective Johnny McLaren walked into the office in a smart tweed overcoat. It wasn't appropriate for the weather and it definitely wasn't appropriate for McLaren, who could come into work wearing a polka-dot sharkskin suit or a garbage bag without anybody giving him a second glance. His cheeks and nose were pink from the cold and clashed horribly with his carrot-colored hair. 'Who's vanquished?'

'Gino. He gave up bitching about the weather.'

'Who hasn't? There's no point – plus dwelling on it just pisses you off more than you already are.'

'You are looking straight-up debonair this morning,' Gino praised him. 'Did you get kidnapped by a stylist or did Gloria finally convince you to stop Dumpster-diving for your wardrobe?'

'Funny, Rolseth, but the joke's on you. There's a live wire waiting to zap you.' He whistled and twirled his finger around his ear. 'Nutters. Some self-proclaimed psychic who says she's here to report a homicide that hasn't happened yet. She won't talk to anybody but you and Leo. Apparently you two have a lot of street cred with crazy people.'

'How the hell do you know this? You just walked in.'

'Gloria told me. It'll be coming down the pipeline any minute, but I thought I'd give you a heads-up.'

Magozzi thought of their administrator, a big, bold, gorgeous African-American woman who kept Homicide tuned like a Formula One Ferrari and McLaren in a perpetual state of lovesickness. She was the perfect combination of street fighter and benevolent despot, and there was nothing that didn't go through her first. 'Gloria doesn't cotton to bullshit of any kind. Why didn't she kick her out?'

'She desperately wanted to, but the new department regs are cramping her slash-and-burn approach. The lady's ID checked out and she's an upstanding, tax-paying citizen with a successful fortune-telling business downtown, a few blocks from here. And where would we be if we didn't take premonitions seriously?'

'In front of a judge, being gutted by a lawyer from the American Civil Liberties Union and getting the Minneapolis Police Department sued into insolvency for prejudice against charlatans,' Gino snarked.

Magozzi nodded. 'If we don't talk to her, we'll be on Death Row by nightfall. So did you end up getting a new furnace, McLaren?'

'Yeah, and it cost me a bundle. But since you took ten grand off the house's list price, I actually made five off the deal. Better than a night of poker.'

'That kind of pisses me off, you cheap bastard, but you're welcome. When's the house-warming party so I can drink all your beer and revel in the fact that I don't own it anymore?'

'Next month sometime, but you don't have to bring anything, Leo, you already covered that in spades. Rolseth, you're still on the hook. Top-shelf booze is good, in case you're struggling to come up with the perfect gift.'

Gino grunted. 'I'm not struggling, I have a six-pack of malt liquor freezing in my trunk right now with your name

8

on it. I just have to go down to my basement and dig some ribbon and a bow out of Angela's Christmas stash.'

McLaren gave him an appreciative smile. 'Don't worry about the ribbon or the bow.'

'Are you sure? It would be the most expensive part of the gift.'

2

Movies had fixed a very specific image of fortune-tellers in Magozzi's mind: headscarves and kaftans, heavy make-up, unruly, flowing hair, either gray or dyed black, and excessive amounts of jangling costume jewelry. And they always had thick Eastern European accents. But if you passed Blanca Szabo on the street, you would only notice a pleasant-looking older woman in ordinary clothing: slacks, a sweater and a black scarf arranged neatly around her neck.

She was sitting in a chair in the hallway, gaze fixed on the opposite wall, either having a vision or simply resting her eyes. No costume jewelry, just a single, heavy gold necklace with a large amber pendant framed in metal curlicues that undoubtedly held some meaning for the séance crowd.

'Ms Szabo?'

She looked up and nodded. 'Detective Magozzi, Detective Rolseth. I asked for you both because you're known for solving difficult cases. I appreciate you seeing me. I know how busy you are.'

She was so wrong about that. There hadn't been a homicide in almost a month. Some psychic. Although she did have an accent, which was most likely Eastern European, given her name. 'How can we help you?'

'I'm here about a murder. But it hasn't happened yet.'

'That's a pretty difficult job, even for us,' Gino said, but his sarcasm went unnoticed.

'I'm a medium. I communicate with the dead.'

Gino's eyes slid over to Magozzi's. 'Uh-huh. So if this person isn't dead yet, how are you communicating with them?'

'Obviously I'm not communicating with the victim, I'm communicating with spirits. Sometimes they show me things that will happen.'

'I guess that was a stupid question. So you talk to dead people and see into the future. That's a unique skill set.'

Magozzi gave him a subtle jab in the ribs. 'Ms Szabo, our job is to solve murders that have already happened.'

She shook her head and folded her hands in her lap. 'I just want to save her. I'm certain you do, too.'

'You haven't told us anything we don't know,' Gino said impatiently. 'Somebody is going to get murdered. It happens in Minnesota about a hundred times a year. So unless you have some specifics . . .'

'I saw a younger woman, very beautiful. She's in trouble, trapped somehow. She can't move, she can't breathe, but it doesn't feel like drowning. She knows that because she almost drowned when she was a little girl.'

'That's pretty specific.'

'Most of my visions are specific.'

'Great, so how about an identity or a location?' Magozzi asked.

She closed her eyes, presumably channeling one of her imaginary spirit friends. She didn't seem mentally ill, but that term covered a broad spectrum.

'It happens in a room. A nice room, but not a large one,'

she finally said. 'There's a mirror that absorbs everything that happens, but it hasn't revealed its secrets to me yet.'

Damn mirrors were always such uncooperative witnesses, Magozzi thought.

'The woman is terrified, but she's also sad. However, the sadness has nothing to do with her murder. That's all I can tell you.'

'Why did you come to us?' Gino asked. 'If you don't have a specific location or an identity for the victim, what makes you think it's going to happen here? Why not in Canada or Timbuktu?'

'It's a feeling I have.'

'Uh-huh.' Gino clapped his hands together. 'Well, thanks for coming in. We'll start canvassing the city for sad women. This should be a slam-dunk.'

She gave Gino a disappointed look. 'You think I'm a charlatan.'

'It's not personal, Ms Szabo. I just don't believe in magic.'

'I help people. Isn't there magic in that? I bring them closure and peace of mind by being their interpreter for a language Google Translate doesn't have in its database. And what's the harm in that?'

'Like I said, it's not personal. It's just my job is to find the truth, so I have problems with people who manipulate it for personal gain.'

Her dark eyes narrowed shrewdly. 'My clients would disagree with you. You know, there are three types of people who come to me: the desperate, the vain and the curious. The desperate want hope and healing, the vain want to hear good things about themselves and their lives, and the curious either want proof that I'm a fraud, or a reason to believe what I do is real. I make them all happy.'

'I can agree with you there. Sounds like you don't actually buy what you're selling either.'

'You're wrong about that, Detective. I am a true believer and I know what I do is real, even if you don't. I've known it since I was very young.' She gave him a faint smile. 'You and I, we're not so different as you think. We both read people for a living, you in the service of justice, me in the service of well-being.' She stood and laid a card on her vacated seat. 'Thank you both again for seeing me. I hope you can save this poor woman.'

They watched her walk down the hall.

'I guess she put you in your place,' Magozzi said.

'She made a couple interesting points, I'll give you that, but she's still full of crap.' Gino picked up her card. 'Blanca Szabo, Medium and Spiritual Guide. That's all it says. No contact information. How are you supposed to book an appointment?'

'She's a psychic. If you need to get a hold of her, she'll find you.'

3

Petra Juric loved planes, but she hated air travel with a blinding passion. There was something so fundamentally wrong about it. It didn't matter how much you flew, how used to the ever-changing caprices of airport security you were, how many flightways you'd walked down, it was, at its very core, unnatural and eerie and dehumanizing, and travelers' demeanors reflected that the second they stepped into an airport and turned into compliant automatons.

Formerly vibrant individuals surrendered all sense of self-determination and mindlessly wandered polished floors as Orwellian announcements droned in the background; they looked up at the flight boards with ennui-filled faces, then shambled toward security lines with their faces in their phones. They bought bottled water and sometimes a snack, then allowed themselves to be herded like cattle at the gate and unceremoniously stuffed into seats next to strangers they would go to great lengths to ignore.

She rolled her small carry-on through the swishing, automated doors of Chicago O'Hare and felt a blast of warm air, perhaps meant to be an apology for the brittle temperature outside. She was probably being followed, but she didn't care. Airports were some of the safest places in the world.

She endured the indignity of a body scan and a pat-down at security, then headed for the Delta Sky Club, where she was greeted by a cheerful employee named Milly, according to her name tag. Milly made sure her club membership was in good standing and checked her in. 'It looks like your flight is on schedule, Ms Juric, but I'm afraid it's colder in Minneapolis than it is here.'

'That seems impossible, doesn't it?'

Milly gave her a sympathetic nod. 'It does, but anything is possible in January. I hope you have a good flight.'

The Sky Club was soothing, compared to the rest of the airport. It was calm and quiet, mostly populated by businessmen and -women, who worked in silence on their tablets while they waited to be summoned to their flight by the great, all-knowing voice on the PA system. Even phone conversations were subdued. There was food and beverage for the taking, including a full bar, desks, and comfortable furniture for lounging.

Petra helped herself to a bottle of orange juice and selected a seat far from everyone while she waited for Martin. She didn't have to wait long. His hair was the first thing she noticed, the white drift that curtained his brow in a style meant for a much younger man. But his physical decline since the last time she'd seen him was shocking and it made her heart hurt. Maybe she should have been prepared for it, but she wasn't.

His fine cashmere overcoat was far too large for his shrinking frame, his gait halting now, and part of his face seemed frozen, immovable. There was cruel irony in the way his warm brown eyes remained the same, shining with intelligence and the slightest trace of mischief, now trapped in a failing body.

He kissed both her cheeks as he always did, then pulled

her in for a hug, which he'd never done before, but Petra refused to acknowledge it as the final farewell he might have intended it to be.

'It would please me if we could one day meet someplace more agreeable than an airport lounge or my bleak government office.'

She'd always liked his stuffy, formal way of speaking and his curious syntax, which had come from a transient global existence that had begun in childhood. He was the son of a diplomat and an intelligence officer, and had lived in more countries than she would ever visit in her lifetime. It was impossible to tell what his native language was because he spoke so many fluently. 'It would please me, too. We should make a date. That is, if Emmanuelle wouldn't mind.'

He sat down across from her with a raffish smile. 'After forty-two years of marriage, my darling Emmanuelle is always happy to be relieved of me. I don't know what she'll do when I retire.'

Retire. In Martin's case, a fraught word, a euphemism for death from a cruel disease that was gnawing away at his neurological system bit by bit. 'She's going to give you a long list of household chores you've been neglecting and relish every moment as your supervisor.'

'Indeed! In fact, I've seen the list, and it's the most terrifying, insurmountable thing I've laid eyes on in my lifetime.'

Petra stopped herself forcing a smile because Martin would read it for what it was – insincere and unfathomably sad. 'Blanca sends her best.'

His shaggy white brows lifted in delight. 'How is our dear Blanca?'

'The same as always, happy to be living in her spirit world.

We don't speak frequently, but I contacted her when I knew I'd be seeing you.'

'Please send her my warmest regards, and tell her I'd fly to Minneapolis for a reading but I'd like to keep my future a mystery. How were your travels?'

'Difficult. They always are, you know that.'

'I thank you for your honesty.' Martin frowned and leaned forward. 'Are you struggling again?'

Petra was blindsided by the question, and suddenly overwhelmed by guilt. Martin was dying, yet she sometimes envied him that. 'I've never stopped struggling, but I'm fine, Martin, the best I've ever been. Don't look so skeptical.'

'I'll take your words as truth. Don't make an ass out of me.'

The comment was so unexpected, so unlike him, she almost chuckled. 'Never.' She placed a flash drive on the table between them. 'Archived documents we've never seen before and transcripts from all the interviews I conducted. I think there are some promising new leads for some of our cases. Where are you off to next?'

He tucked the drive into his coat pocket. 'I'm going home. I hope you are, too.'

Petra nodded. 'I am. If I have to suffer winter, I'd rather do it there.'

'I agree.'

'I guess that makes us both boring shut-ins.'

'We're just sensible. And there are certainly worse things to be.'

'I wish you wouldn't retire.'

'Time and Fate haven't given me a choice, I'm sorry to say. I've put in a word for you. Several words, actually.'

'For what?'

'For you to fill my position.'

She batted the air with her hand, brushing off the comment. 'I'm just a researcher. An historian.'

'As am I, nothing more. And you are far more qualified than any of the other dabbling, overeducated fools who have cluttered my desk with their feeble résumés. Some of them think the former Yugoslavia is an extinct breed of show dog and the Balkans are mythological Norse gods.'

Petra laughed. 'That's not true!'

'I suppose I'm being farcical, but you would be shocked by the abject failure of some of the most venerated higher institutions of learning. I consider it an outrage and take every opportunity to mock them.' He coughed into his hand and apologized. 'In case this is the last time I see you, let's celebrate with a drink. A vodka! Yes, a vodka. It's always been our poison of choice.'

Petra tried to swallow the sudden dryness in her throat. Emotion was not only a loathsome enemy, it was unacceptable. 'Doctor's orders?' she tried to joke, but her voice was thin.

'Certainly not, but my doctor is gallingly parochial, so I don't listen to him, which gives me great pleasure.'

'Then we'll drink vodka. And toast. To you.'

'To us. To all we've done, and all you'll continue to do when I'm gone.' He reached into his briefcase, withdrew a slim file, and placed it on the table between them. 'I was hoping this would be a gift for you, but I'm afraid it isn't much.'

Petra looked down at the folder and felt her despair amplify. 'Praljik?'

'The only trace of him I could find. His trail went cold

18

eleven years ago, but he was last known in Minnesota. Perhaps it will help.' Martin placed a lumpy arthritic hand over hers. 'I'm sorry, Petra. Go home, rest, you've been working too hard. Look at this later.'

She obeyed and stuffed it into her bag, in the zippered exterior pocket where she deposited all things to be pondered later.

'And please don't be sad for me. I've had the most wonderful life, all the more so because you were in it.'

'I am sad for you, Martin. And I'm sad for Emmanuelle. But, to be honest, I'm sad for myself most of all because I'll miss you so much. I'm a horrible and selfish person.'

'You're neither of those things, my dear. And if you really think about it, like the sensible woman you are, you don't need me anymore. You haven't for two decades.'

'I'll always need you, Martin.'

'Then I'll always be there for you, even when I'm in my grave.'

4

Kelly Ramage assessed her reflection in the dressing-table mirror and liked what she saw. The new pink cashmere sweater was demure, but the way it clung to her lush curves was very nearly obscene: no cleavage necessary to make a statement, not for this girl, who'd been so abundantly blessed by genetics.

She made a few adjustments to her long blond curls so they grazed the rise of her bosom just so, then fastened one of her longer diamond necklaces and admired the small but brilliant pendant that flashed rainbows in the light and drew the eye to exactly the right place in the most subtle of ways. She was pure class, a million miles away from the trailer park in rural Ohio where she'd grown up, and she wouldn't go unnoticed by anybody tonight.

Except her husband, sadly. His interest in her had simply evaporated a few years into their marriage, as if the pleasure switch in his brain had suddenly shorted out. He'd whitewashed her queries about his change in behavior, chalking it up to being overworked, getting older, the burdens and pressures of being a senior partner in one of the largest accounting firms in the Midwest. Unconvinced by his excuses, she'd spent endless hours fretting about what had gone wrong. Was the downward trajectory of their marriage somehow her fault? Had he taken a lover? Was he secretly gay? But eventually she'd come to the simple conclusion that he'd misrepresented himself during their courtship; everybody did it in the beginning to one degree or another. She'd been a prize, still was, and guys like Todd Ramage didn't get bombshells like her without pretending to be something they weren't.

Her mother, well aware of her only offspring's restless spirit, had warned her about marrying so young, especially to an accountant seventeen years her senior. 'The world is a big place, Kelly, and you won't be happy with an average life until you see some of it. And look at you – you belong in Hollywood, not in some suburb married to an account- ant almost old enough to be your father. Give yourself some time to explore. Don't settle or you'll regret it.'

Those words had been wise, spoken by a woman who'd settled and regretted it bitterly. But, headstrong as she was, she hadn't listened to her mother, because the words hadn't resonated with her at the time. Todd had just made senior partner, and with that came a stake in the firm, so there was money, more than she'd ever dreamed of. That in itself was a powerful aphrodisiac for a girl who'd grown up desperately poor. And equally arousing was the way she'd been able to turn her shy, considerate lover into a lustful, adventurous one, who'd ravished and worshipped her in the ways she craved, the ways she deserved. But it had all been for show. A trick to woo his trophy to the altar, only to neglect her later.

She heard the front door open downstairs, then the pre- dictable plod of Todd's footsteps as he walked into the foyer and placed his briefcase on the bench by the door. He would sit down, take off his shoes, put on his suede slippers, then pad to the kitchen to greet her. Except she wasn't in the kitchen tonight, she was in the bedroom, checking out her boobs and making sure her hair, her clothes, her jewelry were absolutely perfect for the night.

'Kelly?' he called.

'Be right down.' She pursed her glossy lips at her reflection, then grabbed her tote bag and skipped down the stairs in the stiletto-heeled boots bristling with silver studs she'd bought with the sweater. The two things didn't belong together, but that was part of the fun, keeping people guessing, keeping them intrigued. A fuzzy sweater and fuck-me boots. What a conundrum.

When she breezed into the kitchen, Todd was munching on the cheese and crostini she'd laid out. Of course he'd chosen the bland, boring Cheddar instead of exploring the more exotic cheeses. His mild gray eyes lifted and, for a moment, she thought she'd surprised him, maybe even inspired a little lust. He would take her in his arms, kiss her neck, call her his goddess like he used to . . .

'You look nice.'

No lust there, not even close. She didn't look nice, she looked smoking hot, and she'd have got more of a reaction from a priest. 'I went shopping yesterday. You like?' She did a slow pirouette, giving him ample opportunity to admire her buxom profile.

'You don't normally wear pink. It's a good color for you. Are you going out?'

Even though she was used to the disappointment, the rejection, the dismissal, it still stung. She really had been madly in love with him once, and in spite of everything, she still had deep feelings for him, even though she wasn't *in* love anymore. 'Eleanor and I are going to an art opening in Minneapolis.'

'That's nice. Who's the artist?'

'Rado.'

Todd actually looked intrigued. 'He's the "syzygy-of-art-and-technology" guy, right? The one who never shows up at his openings and only accepts bitcoins for payment?'

'Yes. I didn't think you were interested in art.'

'I'm not. I just read about him in some magazine. The article said his only talents are drumming up controversy and exploiting the mystique of anonymity.'

'It's all part of his work.'

'He sounds clever, I'll give you that. Any artist who gets a spread in a national magazine is doing something right, even if they did lambast him.'

Kelly checked her watch impatiently. 'I have to go, Todd. I promised Eleanor I'd pick her up at seven. We're grabbing dinner after the show, so it'll be a late night. Don't wait up for me.'

Todd gave her a stern, disapproving look, so unexpected it spurred her heart into a panicked rhythm. Was he actually suspicious? Did he even care enough to be suspicious?

'It's going to be deadly cold out there tonight, Kelly, the coldest night of the year, they're saying, and it's already snowing. If you have drinks at the gallery or dinner, even just a couple, I'd feel a lot better if you stayed at Eleanor's. It's a long drive back here from Minneapolis and there's no reason to take any chances.'

Kelly blinked at him, relieved by his response, confused by his sudden paternalism, but more than happy to capitalize on it. 'You're absolutely right, Todd. I wasn't even thinking about the weather. I'll see you in the morning, then. I'll be home before you leave for work.'

He gave her an uninspired peck on the cheek. Another disappointment. 'Have fun. Give Eleanor my best.'

'I will,' she promised, allowing herself to feel the exquisite buzz of wicked, delicious anticipation and just the perfect edge of fear. She was such a naughty girl.

5

Magozzi was reading aloud from a leather-bound Shake-speare anthology and his audience of one was captivated by the performance. His daughter was only five months old, but she clearly recognized talent when she saw it – her awe was reflected in her big, wondering blue eyes.

Grace MacBride's charming, stub-tailed dog Charlie didn't count as audience because he was sound asleep, snoring loudly, but Magozzi didn't take offense – the excitement of having a new charge to watch over drained most of his energy by the end of the day.

Elizabeth let out a wet gurgle, and since no vomit fol-lowed, he took it as encouragement to continue his reading with even more bravado. 'What, ho, Pisanio! The king my father shall be made acquainted of thy assault . . .'

He suddenly noticed Grace standing in the doorway of the nursery. *Really, Magozzi? Shakespeare?* her cool, skeptical look communicated.

'Grace! Elizabeth and I are just having bedtime-story hour. I offered her a nightcap, but she declined.'

'I had no idea you were so enthusiastic about the classics.'

'I wasn't until half an hour ago. I thought I could bore her to sleep, but Shakespeare's really growing on us. There's a certain cadence to his writing.'

'So I've heard.' Grace was trying hard not to smile, which

Magozzi found adorable. 'There's a certain cadence to Dr Seuss, too, which is probably more age-appropriate.'

'Nonsense. Elizabeth is a highly advanced child as evidenced by her emphatic love of *Cymbeline*, which is a very deep track in the Shakespeare bibliography. All the other kids her age are still on the lightweight stuff, like *A Midsummer Night's Dream*. Why do you have Shakespeare in the nursery?'

'Harley gave it to me. He's rearranging the English literature section of his library and he had extra copies.'

'Please tell me he didn't give you Chaucer, too.'

'He tried, but I politely declined.' She knelt down and patted the wiry fur on Charlie's head. He snuffled, opened his eyes and licked her hand before dozing off again. 'You managed to bore Charlie to sleep.'

'*Cymbeline*'s not for everybody.'

When Elizabeth started fussing, Grace took her in her arms, rocked her gently, made some cute faces, stroked her forehead. Magozzi wanted to take credit for at least some of Elizabeth's beauty, but seeing mother and daughter together, it was clear whose DNA reigned victorious. She and Grace looked like identical twins separated by a generation, with the same dark hair, creamy white skin, and startling blue eyes the color of the Caribbean Sea. Grace didn't possess a single baby picture of herself because she'd never had a family, but Elizabeth was a living, breathing one.

Magozzi watched her, wondering if it was difficult for Grace to comprehend the abundance of joyful emotions that had pushed their way into her psyche after their baby had been born. The dark, scarred former fugitive she'd once been didn't reconcile with the happy mother she was now, which was amazing to behold.

But, still, it was strange to see the former Grace fade away slowly, day by day, as if some cosmic artist was clearing his canvas to make room for a new vision. The only lingering artifacts of the person she had been were her universal distrust of anybody outside her small inner circle and her obsession with security. Those traits might diminish with time, but they would never fully relinquish their hold on her, which, in this world, was probably a good thing.

'I'm thinking of taking the day off tomorrow so we can head to the lake early, hibernate in front of the fire for the weekend. Gino and I are currently obsolete anyhow – there hasn't been a homicide in Minneapolis for almost a month. It's too cold to kill in January, which is the only good thing about it.'

'You just jinxed yourself.'

'You don't have a superstitious bone in your body.'

'Statistically speaking. Sadly, a month is a long time without a murder.' She lowered Elizabeth into her crib and dimmed the lights. 'Apparently, you and Bill wore her out. She's already sound asleep.'

'Monkeewrench wore her out. Annie and Harley fight over her all the time and Roadrunner keeps trying to put her on a tricycle, hoping it'll imprint enough so she'll ride the Tour de France with the men one day.'

'You know none of that is true. At least, not entirely.'

'Funny a bunch of computer geniuses aren't pushing code on her already.'

'She can write code in her sleep. She's probably doing it right now.'

Magozzi chuckled. Grace's best friends and partners in Monkeewrench Software were the most doting, cherishing extended family any child or parent could hope for. And in spite of all their eccentricities, or maybe because of them, they were the greatest babysitters in the world. 'I'm jealous you get to take her to work.'

'Elizabeth is like a cat – she sleeps most of the day.'

'I'm still jealous. I'm Italian, I have jealousy issues.'

Grace smirked at him. 'She's a little young to spend a day in Homicide. Come on, let's get some dinner.'

Magozzi followed her into the kitchen, watching her silky black hair swish across her back. She was letting it grow out again and it was almost the same length it had been when he'd first met her, back when she and the rest of Monkeewrench had been murder suspects. How times changed. 'So what do you say about heading to the lake tomorrow?'

Grace ladled a delicious-smelling stew into big bowls. 'It sounds wonderful, but I need the morning to work, maybe longer.'

'New project?'

'Bit Monster just hired us to rework their security platform.'

'Is that a gaming company?'

'No. It's one of the largest cryptocurrency exchanges in the world.'

'You mean like bitcoin?'

'That, and over a thousand other currencies like it. And counting.'

'You're kidding. I thought that whole thing was on the way out.'

'It's not mainstream, and it may never be, but it's here to stay as long as there's money to be made.'

'Who makes money off it?'

28

'A small percentage of investors who understand its volatility and know what they're doing. Exchanges make a bundle, too, and so do criminals. Bit Monster was hit with a cyber attack last year and lost almost four hundred million dollars . . .'

'Four hundred *million*?'

Grace nodded.

'How is that even possible?'

'The cryptocurrency landscape is the new Wild West and a criminal hacker's paradise. It isn't centralized or regulated and transfers of funds are largely anonymous. That's why they need a security fix. We're doing a forensic analysis of the attack now so we can find the weaknesses in their system. And, hopefully, who was behind it.'

'If they lost that much money and they're still in business that really says something.'

'I told you it could be lucrative if you know what you're doing. But it's a fool's errand for the rest of us.'

Magozzi was still trying to comprehend that many zeroes as he dipped into his stew. It was the best thing he'd ever tasted, with the exception of everything else Grace cooked. The kitchen was where she went to relax, whether it was here, at the lake, or at the Monkeewrench office housed in Harley's Summit Avenue mansion. It didn't matter if she had an appreciative audience waiting for food, she just cooked when she needed to re-center herself and they were all the grateful beneficiaries of her kitchen therapy.

Beauty, brains, astounding culinary skills – every day he felt like the lucky guy who'd pulled Excalibur from the stone. 'From your brief but dour synopsis on cryptocurrencies, I hope they're not paying you in them.'

'Not on your life. Bit Monster offered and we all walked out of the meeting. They reconsidered.'

'I'm glad to hear you all chose a peaceful negotiation and didn't pull your weapons.'

Grace gave him a faint smile, those Caribbean-blue eyes flashing a little mischievously. 'I thought about it, but gangster's not my style anymore. That goes away when you have to excuse yourself from a high-level meeting to pump breast milk in the employee bathroom.'

Harley Davidson had temporarily abandoned the Monkee-wrench office on the third floor of his mansion and was sitting in the darkened media room, listening to Erich Korngold's *Die tote Stadt* – The Dead City – at concert volume. It wasn't a particularly impressive twentieth-century opera, but 'Marietta's Lied' was one of the most spectacular arias ever written in any century. As the soprano's paean to love everlasting crescendoed in tonal purity, he closed his eyes and let the music transport him. When the track stopped abruptly, he bolted in his seat and spun around.

'Harley, you've been in here for almost an hour,' Roadrunner complained from the doorway.

Roadrunner was six foot eight and as thin as he was tall. Backlit by the hall sconces, he looked like a silhouette of whip licorice. Even in the dead of January, he wore one of his competition Lycra biking suits, because the crazy son of a bitch rode one of his bicycles no matter what the weather was. He didn't even own a car.

'Goddamnit, Roadrunner, you just ruined the best part. Hope itself was just about to soar heavenward even as true love must die.'

'What the hell is wrong with you lately? Why aren't you in the wine cellar decanting something, like you usually do on your work breaks?'

Harley raised his glass. 'Because I'm drinking an Austrian white, which doesn't require decanting. You can't listen to Korngold without Grüner Veltliner.'

Annie Belinsky sauntered in behind Roadrunner on spike-heeled boots, her magnificently generous figure draped in blond mink that matched her bobbed hair and metallic lipstick. 'I'm with Roadrunner. Your mind's not right, Harley.'

There was barely a lingering trace of her Mississippi drawl, but the Deep South phraseology clung more stubbornly. Of all her plentiful charms, Harley found that one especially endearing. 'I can't imagine what you're talking about.'

'Of course you can. First of all, you cleaned out your precious library, then you went off Bordeaux, and now you're drinking white wine and getting all maudlin listening to depressing music alone. That's just a fancy version of a slow hillbilly suicide.'

He gave her a devious smile. 'It's not depressing, my delightful Southern cream puff. It's uplifting and joyful, just like you, wrapped up in that mink.'

Roadrunner snickered and Annie rolled her eyes to the ceiling. 'Oh, dear Lord, you are very nearly a lost cause. If it wasn't eleven at night, I might express my concern for your deteriorating mental disposition, but I have to go home. And so does Roadrunner. Grace will be here early in the morning before she and Magozzi head to the lake and we have a mountain of work to do on Bit Monster.'

'Bit Monster's going to be a piece of cake. I already have some great ideas.' Harley pushed his tattooed, muscled bulk out of his chair, his leather biker's jacket creaking as he moved, his jack boots thudding heavily on the aisle's plush carpet as he negotiated the pitched floor toward the exit. 'I'll walk you out.'

Annie touched Roadrunner's arm. 'My driver's waiting out front, sugar. Let me give you a lift. It's insanely cold, it's snowing, and you can*not* bike home in this weather.'

'I'll be fine. It's not that far, and I can do it in my sleep.'

'It's eight miles as the crow flies and you'll freeze to death before you get to the parkway.'

Harley raised a brow at Annie. 'And you're worried about my mind, not his? For Christ's sake, Roadrunner, throw your bike in the back of my Hummer. I'll get you home in five minutes.'

'No, it's good training.'

'For what?'

'For handling extremes.'

'You're a sick bastard, you know that?'

Roadrunner shrugged. 'You've got your opera, I've got my bike.'

'I think both of you should be institutionalized,' Annie sniped, stalking away.

6

When the doorbell rang, Kelly's heart started slamming against the wall of her chest. It seemed so odd because the rest of her body felt slow and gooey and molten, like a chocolate chip in a cookie just out of the oven. It was a silly thing to think, but it somehow seemed profound, like something she should write down.

She'd never taken Ecstasy before, but it was the most intensely wonderful thing she'd ever experienced, this epic, brilliant infusion of pure bliss. She had the dreamy sense of floating to the door to let James in, and had no doubt that this would be the best night of her life, something she would want to relive over and over again.

He looked like the pictures he'd sent, but he seemed even more mysterious and dangerous in person, more filled with dark promise than she'd imagined he could be. He walked in without a word, closed the door, took her chin in his gloved hand, and stared deeply into her eyes. His were vivid green, a color she'd never seen before, but all the colors everywhere seemed sharper and brighter as endorphins flooded her brain. It was as if colors hadn't existed at all until now.

'Kelly,' he finally said. 'Have you had a good night so far?'

'I waited for you, but you never showed up.' She pouted.

'You're wrong about that. I was there, in both places, watching you. You just didn't see me.'

Kelly felt her mouth form an amazed O. 'You were?'

'I was, and it was very exciting for me. Was it for you? The anticipation, the uncertainty, the unknown?'

She nodded and her head felt buoyant, like it might lift off her neck and take flight.

'I thought it might be. Pleasure is always more rewarding when it's delayed.'

'I don't want to wait anymore.'

He chastised her with a look. 'I wasn't happy that you changed plans at the last minute, Kelly. I had a perfect place picked out.'

'This is more perfect.'

'You don't know that, because you don't know what I had in mind.' He clucked his tongue in disappointment. 'You're such a naughty girl. And you know what happens to naughty girls.'

She dropped to her knees dramatically, because that was how they'd scripted it. 'They must be punished.'

'I'm afraid you're right.'

'I deserve to be punished.' She watched in detached fascination as he pulled a pair of handcuffs out of his coat pocket.

'Did you do what I told you to?'

Kelly nodded obediently. 'I took it.'

'That's good. Maybe I'll spare you for obeying.'

'I don't deserve mercy.'

He smiled. 'You might be right about that. Shall we see?'

She led James to the bedroom and he stood at the foot of the bed, commanded her to take off her clothes and lie down on her back. She eagerly complied with his wishes, she was going to be a good girl now and accept her punishment.

She felt a thrill when she heard the handcuffs ratchet closed on her wrists, tethering her to the iron spindles of the headboard, felt an even greater thrill when he leaned over her, his breath warm and wet as he tied a blindfold over her eyes.

As ecstatic as she was, the panic didn't set in until she felt the sharp lashes on her stomach and thighs and heard a strange, low chuckle as James grabbed her ankles. This wasn't what they'd talked about, what they'd agreed on, and she knew, she *knew*, that something wasn't right.

'Red!' She said the safe word forcefully, but he hadn't heard her, because he was wrapping something heavy and rough around her ankles. 'RED!' She screamed it this time, flailing against the rope, trying to kick it loose. And then there was a dull thud and a burst of pain as something hard connected with her skull. She cried out, then started whimpering as she felt her ankles being tied to the footboard of the bed, rendering her completely helpless.

'Please, please, no, this isn't how it was supposed to be. Not what we talked about.'

'I think we're done talking for now, Kelly.'

She heard a loud screech – tape being torn from a roll? – and then something sticky and unyielding was covering her mouth. She tried desperately to breathe through her nose, but she wasn't getting enough oxygen, and the more she struggled, the dizzier she felt.

She knew there was worse to come, knew it with a terrible

certainty, so she let her mind find Todd. Dear, sweet, boringly considerate Todd, telling her that he couldn't do these things to her because he loved her and people didn't debase the things they loved.

I'm sorry, Todd. You were so good to me. Too good.

7

Petra was sitting on the window seat in her living room, sipping more vodka – well, maybe a little more than sipping – while she watched delicate snowflakes drift dreamily down from a dark sky, as dark as her day had been, as dark as most of her life. When they entered the golden halo of the street lamps on their descent, they winked and sparkled like fireflies. But then they landed on the salted sidewalk and died prematurely, their unique, fragile beauty extinguished just like that.

Her mind suddenly made the perilous trek back in time and she remembered the pristine snowy farm fields of her childhood, uncorrupted by salt, shovels, plows, or the grime of the city. Those fields spread as far as the eye could see, a soft ermine blanket that kept the earth warm until spring. She used to ski those fields for hours, her yellow Labrador Mirna bounding in the snow beside her, tongue lolling, steam from her breath wreathing her sweet face . . .

No! Don't go there! Don't you dare go to where the bodies are.

But she couldn't keep her thoughts from racing back in time, and soon she felt a prickly, incipient panic start to take deep root, like it did sometimes, even now after so many years and so many vodkas. It was the kind of panic that devoured any sense of control and brought chaos and misery if left unchecked. It happened less and less as the years marched toward her fortieth on this planet, but the intensity of her memories hadn't diminished. Neither had the agony they brought, or the fierce anger she felt because her fondest reminiscences would always be off-limits to her, forever desecrated because they were inextricably linked to evil. To Peter Praljik.

Episodes like these usually faded as quickly as they flared, but this one was intensifying, so she ran to the bathroom and fumbled the cap off an orange bottle of lorazepam. She dry-swallowed two and leaned against the sink, waiting until the attack ultimately surrendered its hold to the pharmaceutical that suppressed her central nervous system and kept the horror at bay.

Escape. That was all she'd ever wanted to do, but anywhere she went in the world, the memories would always be with her, and she was afraid they would follow her into the afterlife. She didn't believe she would go to Hell when she died but, come to think of it, what would it matter if she did? She was already there. She had been since she was eleven years old.

Finally, a dazzling euphoria started to soften her from the inside out, loosening her limbs and settling her heart and breathing into a normal rhythm. It was almost midnight and she felt a seductive urge to sleep, but knew she didn't dare, not just yet, because her dreams wouldn't be safe. She needed to scrub her mind. She would take a walk, just like she always did when the flashbacks occurred. She would make new, good, memories of snow to fortify the ones she'd already created since she'd been in Minneapolis. Or maybe she'd just keep walking until she found the end of the earth.

It was a brutally frigid January night, so she dressed in her warmest clothes, but it didn't take long for the wicked temperature and brisk wind to penetrate the layers of goose down, fur and the more modern insulating fabrics she wore beneath them. But the deadening cold felt good as it seeped first through her skin, then into her bones. Numb body, numb mind.

Her neighborhood nipped the skirts of downtown Minneapolis, and tonight it was quiet and beautiful, slumbering peacefully as snow gathered on window panes and frosted the bare branches of trees and shrubs. It amazed her that she could still see beauty for all the ugliness there was in the world and in her past. Or maybe that was why she saw beauty where others might not.

The houses were all dark except her neighbor's at the far end of the block. She didn't know who lived there or what they did for work, but the lights always seemed to be on, whatever time she passed. Occasionally she glimpsed a shadow, some movement behind a small crack in the blinds that were always closed, but she'd never seen anybody come or go, had never seen a vehicle in the driveway. She paused at the front walk tonight, wondering if this person was a ghost, like she was. It was comforting, imagining someone as alone as her.

Petra took a startled breath when a fat-tired bike with a flashing headlight rounded a bend in the road and headed in her direction at reckless speed. The rider was a tall, thin man, and was clearly an idiot: who went biking at midnight in the middle of January, while it was snowing, no less? She suddenly realized what a stupid thought that had been. Who was she to pass judgment? She was out here walking, which was equally foolhardy. The man probably thought she was an idiot, too, which at least gave them common ground.

She waited for him to pass, but he slowed down instead. Tranquilized as she was, it didn't trouble her as it would have normally. She was totally calm and fearless, almost giddy, impervious to bad thoughts or bad deeds. Her mind simply flashed through the many evasive or defensive actions she could take if it came to that.

Suddenly, there was a sharp scraping sound, tire on ice, and she saw the rear wheel of the bike fishtail. To give the man credit, he didn't fall, just hopped gracefully off the bike before it went down. He stared at it for a moment, as if it had betrayed him, then gave her a quick, sheepish look before righting it again. 'That was embarrassing.'

'Not really. It's icy.'

He gave her a curious look, then averted his eyes, which were large and a pale, glacial blue. This one was shy and awkward, even though he was a grown man.

'Uh . . . can I help you?' he finally asked.

What a strange question. 'I might ask you the same thing.'

'I meant . . . you were stopped in front of my house, looking at it. Not that there's anything wrong with that,' he added hastily.

'This is your house?'

He nodded.

'Then we're neighbors – I live down the block.' She gestured behind her. 'I've always wondered who lived here, and now I know. It's a very nice house. I was admiring it. My name is Petra Juric.'

'I'm Roadrunner.'

'A nickname?'

'It's my only name.'

'I guess when you have such a good name, you only need one. We all have something to run from, don't we? It was nice to meet you, Roadrunner. Maybe I'll see you around again.' She tugged her sable hat further down on her head and continued walking into the windblown snow.

'Don't stay out long,' he called after her. 'The weatherman said ten minutes to frostbite on exposed skin.'

She didn't answer, just kept walking until she reached the edge of the neighborhood, then started looping back and forth, north end to south end. When she finally grew tired, she detoured to the little park overlooking the Mississippi River. Her face and lips were numb and she felt ice crystals weighing down her eyelashes. Her fingers and toes were aching and the frigid air was starting to burn her throat and lungs. Her gait had become lethargic and careless and she knew it had been foolish to walk for so long.

Ten minutes to frostbite, the tall, thin Roadrunner had said, and she must have been walking for half an hour at least. How long until hypothermia? He hadn't mentioned that. But she didn't have the good sense to worry about it.

She sat down on a bench that faced the frozen river and the brightly lit Father Hennepin Bridge that spanned it. On the opposite bank of the paralyzed snake of great water, the lights of downtown Minneapolis spangled the night, winking like terrestrial stars. It was a breathtaking view, even more so in winter than summer. She closed her eyes, thinking it wouldn't be so bad if this was the last thing she ever saw.

*

Roadrunner was perched on the hearth in front of a toasty fire, rubbing his hands together nervously. For the first time since he'd lived in this house, he had the blinds on the front windows open so he could watch the street. He'd seen the woman before, walking the neighborhood at all hours, in all weather, but until tonight, he'd never been close enough to see the V-shaped scar on the left side of her face or the solemn eyes, so dark they looked like disks of onyx. She'd smelled of alcohol, but hadn't seemed impaired. But there was something troubling about the way she'd so cavalierly strode away into the cold, snowy night, as if she had no intention of coming back.

Roadrunner checked his phone again. The temperature was minus twelve Fahrenheit and falling steadily along with the snow. A strong wind had picked up and it was rattling the windows and crying in the eaves. And Petra hadn't walked by yet. Almost thirty minutes had passed.

He felt embarrassed for fretting. She was an adult who had her own life and an agenda for the night that was none of his business. She'd probably been on her way to visit a friend in the neighborhood or have one last drink in the little hotel at the end of the street.

Ten minutes later, he found her lying on a park bench, her lips tinged with blue.

8

Todd Ramage filled his travel mug with coffee, knotted his tie, and tried Kelly again. He'd already left multiple messages and texts, and every minute that passed without a response, the knot of dread in his stomach tightened. His mind kept repeating the most sensible explanation over and over, like a protection spell – she and Eleanor had gotten a little tipsy over dinner, had a couple more glasses of wine when they got to her house, and Kelly was sleeping in after a late ladies' night. She'd wake up with a headache because she didn't drink very often, and call just as soon as she turned on her phone.

But the negative side of his personality, perhaps the most dominant side, looked out at the snow that had accumulated overnight. It wasn't much, but according to the road reports, there had been hundreds of spin-outs and accidents because it was too cold for the road chemicals to melt the ice that lay beneath the fresh snow. And Kelly might be one of those accidents.

He called the office to let them know he'd be late, then went to the den and started to rummage through Kelly's desk. He didn't know Eleanor's number, but Kelly kept a handwritten log of all her passwords and phone numbers in a notebook with a cute kitten photo on the front cover, just in case something happened to her phone.

In spite of his distress, a smile tugged at his mouth when

he looked through Kelly's precise, rounded script, meticulously organized into categories. She had websites and passwords in one section, phone numbers in another. A third contained significant dates. He saw their June anniversary circled with a big heart, which was a woeful reminder that he hadn't been very attentive lately. In fact, he'd been a downright bore, consumed with work, new clients, a possible merger with a west-coast firm, and all the rest of the interference life brought in middle age. Time passed too quickly – and why was it the most important things got the least consideration?

Because you take them for granted. You assume they'll always be there because they always have been. You grease the squeaky wheels, plug holes in the dinghy while the yacht floats away.

He would change things, starting today. He'd buy Kelly roses, then take her out for a lavish dinner at her favorite Italian restaurant. He wouldn't raise a brow when she ordered the overpriced langoustines and porcini risotto with winter truffles. Over tiramisu and espresso, maybe even some Sambuca, he would tell her they would finally be taking her dream trip to Costa Rica for their anniversary this year. It wasn't too late to turn back the clock and cherish his goddess.

And what if you're too late?

Todd shook away the evil, unbidden thought and finally found Eleanor's mobile number. The phone rang seven times before finally he heard a sleepy, rough voice say hello.

'Eleanor?'

'Who is this?'

'It's Todd. Todd Ramage.'

He heard bedclothes rustling. 'Todd?'

'I'm sorry to bother you so early, but I'm trying to reach Kelly. She's not answering her phone. Will you check to see if she's still there?'

'Where?'

'At your house. She said she was leaving early this morning and I'm worried sick about her. The roads are terrible.'

There was a long silence before she spoke again. When the words came, they were blurry, formed by lips that hadn't limbered up yet. 'I didn't know she was staying. Of course, she has my key, she's always welcome . . .'

'What? What are you talking about?'

'I'm in San Diego. I've been here all week.'

He felt a sudden burning heat spread through his stomach and suffuse his arms and neck and face. 'You didn't go to the art opening with her last night?' he asked stupidly, because he already knew the answer. Of course Eleanor didn't go to an art opening in Minneapolis last night because she was in San Diego, had been all week. There was obviously some misunderstanding, and it would all make sense once he talked to Kelly . . .

'Todd, tell me what's going on.'

Everything's all right, he told himself, trying to keep his breathing slow and even so his voice wouldn't shake. 'Kelly told me you were going to the Rado opening with her. She was going to stay with you because of the weather and she said she'd be home before I left for work but she's not and I can't reach her and I'm . . .'

Worried? Panicked? Terrified? The rest of his words dissolved on his tongue before he could give them voice.

Eleanor sounded wide awake now. 'If she was in the city last night, I'm sure you're right. She decided to stay because of the weather. Let me call my neighbor Roy and have him check, okay? I'll let you know as soon as I hear back from him.'

'Thanks, Eleanor.' He hung up and didn't let his thoughts go any further.

Royston Wade shuffled across the snow-covered street, head bent against the bitter wind. Damn weather wasn't fit for a polar bear. He should have gone to Arizona with his wife after Christmas, but he'd been stupid enough to postpone his retirement for six more months. He'd get cut loose this July and, by God, he was never going to spend another winter in Minnesota. This year, he would leave for Arizona in October and not come back until May.

He walked up Eleanor's driveway and stopped beside the black Mercedes SUV. It was the vehicle she'd asked about, the one that belonged to her friend Kelly. A good two inches of snow covered the roof, which meant it had been parked there for a while. He hadn't seen the car or noticed any activity here last night, but he'd gone to bed early with a double pour of Kentucky bourbon and his latest copy of *Popular Science*.

He walked up the front steps and rang the bell, just like Eleanor had asked him to do if the vehicle was still in the driveway. When there was no answer, no sounds coming from inside, he rang the bell again. 'Mrs Ramage?' he hollered, over the wind. 'I'm Eleanor's neighbor, Roy. She asked me to come over and check on you.'

Again, no answer. He rang the bell a couple more times, then knocked hard on the door. Eleanor said she might be asleep, but he sure as hell wasn't going to use his key, let himself in, and scare the daylights out of a strange woman.

Still, he was starting to feel uneasy. Eleanor had sounded worried, and what if her friend was having some kind of a medical emergency?

He knocked again, then tested the knob and took a sharp breath when the unlocked door creaked open. That wasn't right. Everybody locked their door in the city – at least, they should, especially a woman alone. Hell, he even kept his door locked during the day when he was at home. Nowadays, you couldn't be too careful, with home invasions and crazies roaming around robbing people in broad daylight.

He craned his head and listened, but still didn't hear any sounds coming from inside: no TV, no movement. 'Mrs Ramage, it's Eleanor's neighbor Roy,' he repeated loudly, then stuck his head through the door.

He recoiled instinctively when a strange odor hit him. It was faint but it was there, bad and wrong. When rational thought finally caught up with his reptile brain, he stumbled backward, almost slipping off the top step. His legs started shaking as he hurried back to his own house as fast as they would carry him. Whatever medical emergency she might have had, he was far too late to intervene.

9

Any homicide was a gruesome parody of intimacy: personal for the killer, personal for the victim, personal for the cops investigating it. It was a grim commentary on the nature of his job and his years working it that Magozzi had somehow learned to separate himself from murder victims in the interest of self-preservation. When he walked onto a scene, he saw a knifing or a shooting or an assault; he saw blood, bruises, broken bones; and beyond, heartbreak and tragedy that had to be kept at arm's length. In order to be effective, you had to focus on the minutiae of each crime instead of the big, sorrowful picture of a prematurely terminated life. That was the only way a homicide got solved.

But this scene was different and he knew it would probably actively haunt him for the rest of his life. The rage he felt, the sorrow, the disgust over what humans were capable of was almost impossible to put away. This wasn't the grotesque horror of a serial killer carving up a body and scattering the pieces, like a spoiled kid dumping a jigsaw puzzle on the floor. But it was sick and deeply disturbing in its own special way.

The victim's wrists were manacled to the bed frame with handcuffs, her ankles tethered to the footboard with rope. She was naked, her legs spread wide, her entire head encased in duct tape – a common household product put to hideous use. It was turned to the side, probably blindly looking for escape even as she suffocated. Her skin was black in places where the blood had been shunted by her restraints, ghastly pale in others.

There were welts across her stomach and thighs but no bleeding anywhere. A bruise circled her neck, but there was no immediate sign of the ligature that had caused it. The honey-blond hair that wasn't trapped beneath tape was the only thing that looked healthy and alive.

Gino was breathing shallowly out of his mouth. 'Jesus Christ,' he finally said.

Magozzi felt the fragile barrier of detachment from the victim collapse. This pitiful, violated thing had been somebody's baby once. Somebody's Elizabeth. He shook his head fiercely, chasing his daughter out of his head.

'Don't go there,' Gino said sternly.

'I'm trying not to.'

'Your daughter doesn't belong here. Let's get that straight right now.'

Gino understood – he had a smart, beautiful daughter named Helen, who was looking at colleges now, and a much younger son named Noah he still referred to as 'The Accident', because he had been. Magozzi had always privately wondered how his partner had been able to separate his work from his life, and now he was going to have to figure it out for himself.

'Yeah. Thanks.' He turned away and saw a tote bag sitting on the dresser, fine leather embossed with the repetitive pattern of a high-end designer's monogram. A large sunburst mirror hung on the wall above the dresser and he thought of Blanca Szabo. She was right about one thing: this mirror had seen everything, but it wouldn't share its secrets with him, just like the mirror in Blanca's vision hadn't shared with her.

She can't move, she can't breathe . . .

A skillful con by a devout practitioner. Psychics painted pictures with broad brushstrokes, keeping their prognostications as vague as possible. There was a fifty-fifty chance that whatever they said would hit some sweet spot. Still, her words shadowed his thoughts.

Gino was obviously tracking in the same direction. 'We need to talk to Blanca again. She's not a psychic, but she could be a killer. Crazy attention-seeker goes to the cops, feeds them some details of a crime, then goes out and commits it.' He stopped, catching Magozzi's eye. 'What? You're looking at me like I'm the one who's nuts.'

'Blanca Szabo didn't do this anymore than she can see into the future.'

'Yeah, I guess that's kind of a stretch, even for me, but still, she might know something. Even if it's something she doesn't know she knows.'

'We'll talk to her again.' Magozzi gloved up and started going through the contents of the handbag, a temporary distraction from the horror on the bed. 'Wallet full of cash and credit cards. Keys to her car. Driver's license belongs to Kelly Ann Ramage. Five-five, one twenty-five, long blond hair in the photo.'

He showed the license to Gino, who nodded. 'Matches the registration on the Merc in the driveway, matches the homeowner's and husband's story and description. It's her.' Gino walked around the bed and pointed to the pile of women's clothing and provocative black lingerie on the floor. 'A planned hook-up that went really, really wrong?'

'Seems like it. Doesn't read random stranger attack. No sign of breaking or entering, no disturbance in the front of the house, and if it was a robbery, they would have taken her Louis Vuitton and her eighty-thousand-dollar SUV.'

'If this started out as consensual before it got out of control, there should be prints all over the place.'

'We can hope.'

Gino shook his head and looked away for a moment. 'I'm afraid to see what's under that duct tape.'

'We're going to have to wait for the autopsy to find out. No way the ME is going to remove it in situ.' Magozzi reached the bottom of Kelly Ramage's tote and pulled out the latest model of iPhone, which would, of course, be obsolete by the end of the year. 'Point of contact with the twisted bastard who did this is probably right here. This might be our golden ticket.'

'Almost guaranteed. What did we do back in the old days when people still had belly buttons instead of umbilical cords attached to their phones?'

'Those were sweaty, hard-working days.' Magozzi turned on the phone and it came to life with a familiar chime. 'It's locked.'

'Of course it is. By the look of things, she was a married woman leading a double life.' Gino walked into the adjacent bathroom and Magozzi followed. They found a small travel kit open on the vanity, the kind you put your cosmetics and toothbrush in, except this held a very different assortment of personal products: condoms, a variety of lubricants, a vibrator, and a small plastic bag with three pills in it. They were green with smiley faces printed on the front.

'Ecstasy,' Gino said. 'The start of the party was planned, the ending wasn't.'

Magozzi looked under the vanity and pulled out a small stainless-steel trash can. There was a clean plastic liner and a single crumpled tissue with lipstick on it. Kelly had freshened up for her visitor, but hadn't gotten any further than that. 'None of the personal stuff looks like it was used, and there's nothing in the bedroom either. No condoms or condom wrappers, no tubes of Joy Jelly, no ligature, no whip.'

Gino shrugged. 'Maybe he tried to clean up when he realized he killed her.'

'Or maybe torturing and killing her was his plan all along and this was never about sex.'

'Tough to prove intent. I don't know shit about bondage and S&M, but maybe this is how it goes. Torture is the foreplay and the rest got cut short when this asshole wrapped her head in duct tape and forgot she had to breathe.'

They did a tour of the rest of the house, kitchen first. It was spotlessly clean, the dishwasher empty.

'No half-full glasses of wine covered with fingerprints and saliva,' Gino sulked, picking up the sponge perched on the stainless lip of the sink. 'Bone dry. Nobody washed up last night.'

'I don't think it was that kind of date.' Magozzi opened the refrigerator. It was mostly empty, except for the usual condiments, what you'd expect from a homeowner who was planning to be out of town for a while. There was a bottle of popular French champagne in the door, priced at the low end of the spectrum, but still costly for 750 milliliters of grape juice.

'This stuff is overrated and overpriced. You can do much better with a smaller producer or a Crémant de Bourgogne,' Harley had told him, while instructing him on the finer points of bubbles. Magozzi hadn't understood most of what he'd said, but he'd certainly enjoyed the experience immensely. 'Maybe the killer brought the champagne and left some prints on the bottle.'

'That would be dandy.' They both started when they heard shouting coming from the front of the house. Outside, two of the uniforms who had been working the neighborhood canvass were restraining a hysterical man. Middle-aged, salt and pepper hair, nice suit, no overcoat. 'That's my wife's car!' he shouted into the wind. 'I need to get in there!'

'Shit,' Gino muttered.

IO

Todd Ramage was sitting in the back of their sedan. Magozzi, Gino and the other officers on site had finally talked him down from his mania, and now he was staring like a zombie, either unaware or uncaring that tears were rolling down his cheeks in a slow, steady stream. 'Are you sure it's Kelly?' he finally asked.

Well, no, they weren't sure, not a hundred percent, but they *knew*. And so did he. 'I'm afraid it's likely, sir. We're very sorry.'

'I was going to take her to dinner tonight and surprise her with an anniversary trip to Costa Rica.' He let out a pained, strangled sound. 'You need me to identify her, don't you?'

Magozzi thought of the duct tape and winced. 'Eventually, sir. For now, you could really help us out by telling us your story. Starting with the last time you saw your wife.'

He looked out of the window at her Mercedes, then focused on his lap, where his hands were clenched in tight balls. 'Last night. I came home from work at five and she was dressed up. She looked beautiful. She's a very beautiful woman.'

No past tense, not yet, Magozzi thought grimly. It would take a while for the language to catch up with reality.

'She said she was going out with her friend Eleanor. Eleanor Dray. This is her house.'

'We know.'

'But I found out this morning that Eleanor's out of town. She's been out of town all week. Kelly lied to me.'

'What did she say her plans were?'

'She was picking up Eleanor at seven and then they were going to the Rado show.'

'What's Rado? A band or something?'

'It's the name of an artist she likes. He had an opening last night.'

'What about after the show?'

'She told me they were going to dinner. I suggested she spend the night with Eleanor because of the weather. It had already started to snow fairly hard, and it was so cold. We live in Stillwater and that's a long, dark drive to be making on bad roads. If I hadn't suggested it . . .' He let out an agonized sigh.

'Did you have any contact with her last night after she'd left your house?'

'No. She just told me she'd be home before I left for work this morning. When she wasn't, I called Eleanor and . . . I guess you know the rest.' He took a deep breath. 'Detectives, tell me what happened to my wife. I have a right to know.'

'You do, and as soon as we process the scene, we'll be able to tell you more.'

He lowered his head and pressed the heels of his hands against his temples. 'She had a lover and he killed her. That's what happened, isn't it? And if anybody knows anything about it, it would be Eleanor. She was Kelly's best friend.'

'We'll speak with her, of course, but there are other

possibilities right now.' There really weren't, at least in Magozzi's opinion, but he felt that Todd Ramage deserved a small act of kindness.

'Did you suspect your wife was having an affair?' Gino asked.

'No, absolutely not. Not until now. Why else would she lie to me?'

'We'll get answers, sir,' Magozzi reassured him. 'And justice for your wife. It just takes time. You arrived shortly after we did, and Crime Scene isn't even here yet. There's a lot of work to be done.'

'She lied to me,' he repeated, but he was speaking to himself this time.

Gino asked, 'Sir, does your wife have a personal computer at home?'

'Yes, of course.'

'We'll need to take that.'

'Anything that helps you find her killer.'

'I'd also like to ask that you don't try to log into her computer, as tempted as you might be.'

He blinked at Gino in the rearview mirror.

'To ensure everything is just like she left it. We don't want to risk any kind of interference that could hamper the forensic analysis of her hard drive.'

Magozzi looked in the side mirror and saw the Bureau of Criminal Apprehension van pull up to the curb. 'Sir, do you have somebody you can call? Friends, relatives, someone who can sit with you?'

He nodded.

'Call them and go home. We'll stop by later.'

He reached into his suit pocket and pulled out a

business card. 'I can't go home right now. I can't be there. Call my cell when you're coming. I'll meet you there.'

'We will, sir.' He looked down at the card. Senior accountant and partner at Schlenner, Cole and Ramage. Magozzi didn't make enough money to need an accountant, but he recognized the name of the firm.

Gino let him out of the car and led him to his own while Magozzi got out to meet Jimmy Grimm, the BCA's head tech. He was dressed like any savvy Minnesotan braving extreme cold, in a thick, hooded parka. 'Glad to see you, Jimmy. You're not suited up.'

'Hell, no. In this kind of weather, I wait to get the lie of the land before I start prancing around in my whites. It's still eight below zero. Did you know that?'

'No, and I wish you hadn't told me.'

'It's bullshit,' he muttered, his woolly brows shuttering down on his eyes, as if to keep them warm. 'Fill me in.'

Magozzi let out a frosty puff of breath that disappeared into the frozen air as soon as it came out of his mouth. 'BDSM scenario.'

'As in bondage discipline?'

'And sadomasochism, yeah. We're looking for one warped son of a bitch.'

Grimm jerked a thumb toward Todd Ramage's car, also a Mercedes, but a high-end sedan. 'Who's Gino talking to?'

'The husband of the victim. She told him she was going to an art show with her girlfriend and spending the night with her here, but the girlfriend's been out of town all week.'

'We're all one decision away from calamity.' Jimmy glanced at Todd Ramage again. 'Any chance the husband is good for it?'

'No way.' Magozzi pointed to the SUV. 'Pay close attention to the vic's car. Maybe she drove her killer here.'

'Wouldn't that be perfect? The killer makes his escape in an Uber after he does his dirty work and, bingo, you've got all his information through the app.' Jimmy looked at the jumble of footprints on the snow-covered sidewalk leading up to the house. 'Tell me about this mess.'

'It was like this when Gino and I got here. They belong to the neighbor who did the welfare check and the first responders. And us. No other prints anywhere around the house. Of course, that doesn't mean much – whatever prints the killer left are buried in fresh snow.'

Jimmy knelt down and sifted some snow through his gloved fingers. 'It's dry, and there isn't much of it.'

'Does that mean something?'

'It might mean the prints are buried, but not gone. The impact of a boot or shoe compresses the snow and the friction raises the temp just a little. It was way below zero last night and windy, so the prints would have set up immediately. There could be a perfect ice cast under this snow.'

'So maybe this shitty weather is good for something?'

'There's an extremely slim possibility, but I'm trying to be creative.'

'That's better than nothing.'

'Not necessarily, because it might be exactly that. Nothing. Let me gear up, then take me inside so I can do my thing.'

'Is Anant coming?'

'On his way, but it could be a while. He's stuck in a snarl on Crosstown.'

11

Dr Anantanand Rambachan was an imposing man, even taller than Roadrunner's six foot eight inches, but hewn from more solid genetic material. He had probing brown eyes and a smooth, solemn face that suited his vocation: when your job was interpreting for the dead day after day, there wasn't much opportunity to forge smile lines. His presence and wisdom were intimidating in equal measure, but Magozzi and Gino had worked with him long enough to know the man beneath – humble, compassionate, and delightfully human.

He shook their hands warmly. 'Detectives, it's been a long time since I saw you both. And may I offer many congratulations on the birth of your daughter, Detective Magozzi? I always thought that fatherhood would suit you well, and I see I wasn't mistaken, as you're looking very well in spite of these terrible circumstances.'

'Thanks, Dr Rambachan. I should have thought to do it sooner.'

'I think your timing was perfect.'

'And how about you, Doc?' Gino asked.

'I'm very well, thank you.'

And so the pleasantries went, an enjoyable prelude that postponed the miserable task at hand. After a lot of prodding, Anant had modestly shared that he was slam-dunking his intramural basketball team into championship position and his daughter had recently been awarded a Rhodes scholarship. Good things for a good man. At least the cosmic wheel was rolling in the right direction for somebody.

But they were all business now, Anant leaning over Kelly Ramage's body as he did the preliminary assessment, which confirmed what they already suspected from prima facie evidence: she had died last night or early this morning, most likely from suffocation, there were no obvious signs of sexual activity aside from the body position, and the details of her death would have to wait until the autopsy.

Magozzi's eyes kept straying to the waiting gurney and the folded body bag on top – ugly, ominous things that didn't belong in anybody's bedroom doorway. 'The bruise on her neck doesn't seem like a violent crushing injury, more like it was part of the ritual, but not meant to kill her.'

'That is a reasonable initial impression but, of course, this young woman is keeping her secrets for now.'

'We think she may have ingested MDMA. It's dyed green.'

'Thank you for informing me, Detective. If I see staining on her tongue or residue in her stomach, I'll know what it is long before Toxicology comes back.' Anant straightened to his full height, which made the small room seem even smaller, and gestured to the duct tape with a doleful expression.

'I know of two other cases where victims' heads were wrapped in this dreadful manner. They're old cases now, and both were men.'

'Was it sexual?'

'It was.'

'So this isn't unusual?'

'Oh, it's very unusual. Very dark indeed. Both were deemed unfortunate accidents.'

Gino sighed and turned away from the body. 'That's what we're thinking here, but intentional homicide isn't out of the question. It's going to be tough to prove under the circumstances, though.'

'I hope I'll be able to help you.'

Gino and Magozzi watched silently as Anant began the more meticulous examination of the body, accompanied by copious note-taking and photography before they released her from her bonds. He spent a long time examining her wrists and ankles.

'There is tissue damage, deep abrasions,' he finally said. 'Deep enough that there was some significant subcutaneous bleeding.'

'She was fighting.'

Anant nodded solemnly, but made no further comment.

Eventually, he and his assistant began gently to maneuver Kelly into the body bag. He held up his hand abruptly when he saw the blood on the pillow and very delicately turned her head to face front. On the left side, there was a tiny gap in the layers of duct tape, just enough to expose bloody hair.

'He knocked her around. She was definitely fighting,' Gino said quietly.

The ratchet of the bag's zipper closing was a terrible, final sound.

12

After Anant had left, Magozzi and Gino walked through the entire scene again with Jimmy, then checked in with Royston Wade and the officers who'd conducted the neighborhood canvass. Both were a bust – nobody had noticed Kelly Ramage's car in the driveway last night, let alone seen or heard anything unusual.

It wasn't surprising – this was weather for hibernation and everybody did it: it was primal instinct. Once you were safely inside, you closed the curtains against the cold and hunkered down in your warm cave, fantasizing about spring and the first backyard cookout, both of which were still months away. Very few people window-gazed on a frigid January night – it was too depressing.

The autopsy would take place tonight. The crime lab would get to work processing evidence immediately, so their primary focus now was pursuing their most important leads: the iPhone, any surveillance footage from the art gallery, and Kelly Ramage's home computer. The fact that she had most likely arranged the meet with her killer was reason to be cautiously optimistic, but Magozzi knew better than to expect a swift conclusion in any case, no matter how straightforward it seemed.

It was past morning rush-hour by the time they left Eleanor Dray's house, but the traffic was still horrendous as they inched their way back to City Hall. They'd already passed six accidents, all SUVs driven by urban cowboys or cowgirls, who had erroneously believed their four-wheel-drive mounts made them impervious to ice. Four-wheel-drive might help you get out of the ditch, but it was impotent against the errant patch of ice that would put you there.

'You'd think by January people would know how the hell to drive in winter,' Gino complained irritably, tapping an arrhythmic paradiddle on the steering wheel.

'Some people don't figure it out until May.'

'We're burning up precious time here. If we ever make it downtown, I'm going to park in front of City Hall and make some calls while you run Kelly Ramage's phone to Tommy Espinoza. Make it fast and gather any legit edibles you can on your way out. Angela gave me a smoothie for the road this morning, but a man can't live on liquefied fruit. Plus, they're disgusting. I dumped it once I got out of her line-of-sight.'

The mere mention of food, even a dreaded smoothie, elicited a loud, angry pang in Magozzi's stomach, reminding him he hadn't even had time to grab a piece of toast this morning. But what troubled him more was that Gino's wife had made him a smoothie. She was the unapologetic, uncontested queen of gooey, saucy lasagna and cannelloni and all magnificent Italian-American things that probably shortened your life with each bite. She didn't care that her husband had a modest front porch that hung over his belt, because food was her ultimate expression of love. 'What's wrong with Angela? Is she sick?'

Gino actually chuckled. 'Helen has been corrupted by the food guilt police at school – they're everywhere. Now she's corrupting Angela with impassioned homilies about clean living and healthy choices. The kid lives on goat-milk yogurt and seaweed nowadays, and if that isn't an eating disorder, I don't know what is. When I was her age, the only things that passed my lips were cheeseburgers, pizza, and Mountain Dew, and I survived to tell about it.'

'It was a different era. And we were stupid.'

'Kids are supposed to be stupid and delusional about their own mortality. It's a beautiful time in life.'

'She's worried about your mortality, not hers.'

'She shouldn't be worried about anything right now, except getting into the college she likes and having a good time. I think there's a global conspiracy to guilt-trip the fun and careless genes out of kids and turn them into fearful, hysterical doom-mongers. Life kicks your ass soon enough – give the poor things a little time in oblivious paradise.'

'Seems like a sensible life philosophy.'

'Damn right it is. Plus, you need fat for your brain to work right and to process protein, I keep telling her. Do you know why the Donner party died?'

Magozzi had to reset his mind back over a century. 'They got stranded in winter and died of starvation.'

'No, they died from protein poisoning. They were half dead from starvation when they finally got desperate enough to eat their completely dead friends, but their friends didn't have any fat left on them. Look it up. Protein poisoning is a thing.'

'So if we get stranded on the way back to City Hall, I should carve you up right away?'

'Definitely. Cannibalism isn't a choice, Leo, it's a survival skill, but you have to go all-in at the beginning.'

'Please tell me you didn't have this conversation with Helen.'

'We didn't get to the cannibalism part.'

'I suddenly lost my appetite. I can't imagine why.'

'I haven't. It's Friday. McLaren usually brings donuts on Friday. He also keeps a bottle of Scotch in his desk drawer, so shake him down for whatever he's got, just as long as it has calories.'

13

Hennepin County Medical Center was a Level I trauma hospital in the heart of downtown Minneapolis. Roadrunner had been there a few times before, and it didn't seem like a place where any of the staff ever had a chance to catch a breath. That morning it was almost as busy as he'd ever seen it, and the fifteen-minute wait at the gift shop gave him plenty of time to reflect on the wisdom of his presence there. If it had been a sixteen-minute wait, he would probably have talked himself right out of the door.

Coward! Cowardly little shit! That's right, you run as fast as you can, I'll still catch up with you . . .

He shook his head to clear the dark track his mind had taken and hesitated at Petra's door, not sure what the etiquette was for entering a stranger's hospital room. Did you knock? Announce yourself and just walk in? It suddenly occurred to him that there was no etiquette because you didn't visit people you didn't know when they were in the hospital. But he'd probably saved Petra's life, and he hoped that made it slightly less weird.

With a deep breath, he pushed open the heavy door. The privacy curtain was partially closed and he heard nothing but the hum and beeps of medical monitors behind it. He looked down at the vase of yellow daisies he was clutching. He suddenly decided it was wrong to be here, wrong to intrude, wrong to be bringing flowers. He'd leave them at the nurse's station with a note . . .

'Come in, Roadrunner,' he heard Petra's voice and caught the faintest ghost of an accent, which he hadn't noticed last night.

He hesitated, then peered around the curtain. She was sitting up and, without the multiple layers of outerwear, he realized she was just a tiny thing, dwarfed by a hospital bed designed to accommodate all sizes up to very large. Her hair was as dark as her eyes and it fell in thick waves to her shoulders. The V-shaped scar was strikingly pale against the red of her cheeks. Wind burn, cold burn, but no frostbite. 'How did you know it was me?'

'Because there's nobody else to visit me.'

The accent was gone. Maybe he'd imagined it.

She waved him in. 'Please.'

Roadrunner hesitated, then walked in and placed the daisies on a table by her bed. Her eyes went to his badly gnarled hands, and even though the injuries were ancient, they burned under her gaze. He quickly tucked them behind his back. 'I'm glad you're okay.'

'I would be dead if you hadn't found me when you did. That's what the doctor said. Have you ever saved a life before?'

He shrugged, not sure how to answer. Monkeewrench had saved many lives with their work or, more accurately, prevented death, so there was no way definitively to quantify it. 'Indirectly, I guess.'

'There is nothing indirect about saving a life, however you do it.'

'Have you?'

'A few times,' she said, without conceit. 'You have a bond forever. It can't be broken. Have you ever died before?'

Roadrunner gaped at her and started to wonder if maybe Petra wasn't in full possession of her faculties.

She searched his face. 'No? I have, but I was brought back. They always talk about seeing light, don't they? But I didn't. I didn't see anything.' She reached out and touched the flowers. 'I love daisies. Especially yellow ones. When I was a child, there was a whole field of them behind our house.'

Roadrunner's eyes darted nervously around the room, taking stock of his surroundings. Equipment monitored her vitals; an IV fed into her arm. There was a sink, a sofa and two chairs, and a rolling tray with a half-drunk cup of tea, an untouched bowl of oatmeal, a banana. The conversation was too intense and unsettling, and this environment suddenly seemed far too intimate, everlasting trauma bond or not. 'I should go and let you rest. I just wanted to check in on you.'

'I appreciate it. I hope you didn't bike here.'

'I took an Uber.'

She fixed her onyx gaze on him. 'I wasn't trying to kill myself, if that's what you're wondering.'

'No, I wasn't,' Roadrunner lied.

'But if I had died, I wouldn't have minded. I was having very nice dreams.'

14

Tommy Espinoza was a detective, but he was also MPD's chief computer geek, and he was a brilliant one, which explained why he had an office while the rest of them had to slum it in the Homicide cube farm. The rationale was solid: his work demanded uninterrupted focus, and he couldn't achieve it without privacy and silence. They were all jealous as hell, but Tommy was such an asset and a mensch besides, nobody could muster any resentment toward him.

His door was partially open, so Magozzi gave it a rap and let himself in. He was hunched in front of his computer, his eyes reflecting whatever was flashing on the monitor. 'Are you gaming on the state's dime, Tommy?'

He pushed back from his desk and dipped his hand into a bag of Cheezy Puffs. 'No. I'm trying to find a house-warming gift for McLaren. What did you get him?'

'A new furnace.'

'Nice.'

'He has top-shelf booze on his wish list.'

'I was thinking blow-up doll. I know he thinks Gloria's finally going to take the bait, but I'm not holding my breath.'

'I don't know, I'm not counting him out yet. Tommy, we need you to unlock a phone.'

'Is it an iPhone?'

'Yeah.'

Tommy rubbed his hands together briskly. 'You're in business. We just got a GrayKey.'

'What's that?'

'It unlocks phones. Remember when the feds paid that Israeli company nine hundred grand to unlock the San Bernardino bomber's iPhone when Apple refused?'

'No.'

'Well, they did, but those days are over.' He fondly patted the small gray box on his desk. 'This little honey only cost thirty grand.'

'Is that all?'

'It's a bargain at twice the price. Unlimited unlocks and it doesn't even have to be connected to the Internet to do it.'

'Great. I think.'

'If you're worried about slippery slopes, don't. They're everywhere, my friend.'

'How long will it take?'

'Depends. A couple hours, a couple days.'

'Can you get on it right away?'

'Sure. What's your case?'

'A really ugly bondage scenario. Married female victim with a secret life. Her head was wrapped in duct tape.'

Tommy scowled. 'Jesus.'

'If you get into that phone before we're back, go through everything – calls, emails, texts, pictures, websites she visited.'

'You got it. Do you have any leads?'

'We have a few places to go.'

'Where's Gino?'

'Waiting for me in the car and he's starving. Do you have any food?'

Tommy tossed him an unopened bag of Cheezy Puffs.

'Thanks. Did McLaren bring donuts this morning?'

'He's not in yet. Says he's stuck behind a jack-knifed semi on I-94.'

'I believe it. The roads suck.'

Magozzi made a detour to the Narcotics Division and found Ty Overgaard hunched over his computer, muttering a colorful string of expletives. He was a gaunt, rangy man with long hair and neck tattoos, perfectly suited for undercover work because he could easily transform into an exemplary dirtbag. Looking at him, you'd never guess he was a happily married man and the proud papa of three pre-school kids.

'Computer troubles, Ty?'

He looked up and the flesh of his hollow face lifted as he smiled. 'Hey, Magozzi, what's the news from Homicide?'

'We finally got one this morning.'

'Nothing like job security. What can I do for you?'

'We found some X at the scene. Green, smiley faces. Have you seen any around?'

'No X, not for a long time. But there's so much heroin and fentanyl on the streets now, shit that doesn't kill isn't even on our radar anymore. I'll ask around, though. I'm dealing with a pain-in-the-ass snitch, who moves other synthetics and steroids. Maybe he knows something.'

'Thanks.'

'I'll be in touch. See you at McLaren's housewarming?'

'Wouldn't miss it. Espinoza's bringing a blow-up doll.'

*

On his way out Magozzi called Grace. So much for an early weekend escape to the lake. Sadly, that was off for the foreseeable future. He thought of last Saturday's brief January thaw when Grace had bundled Elizabeth up in a puffy pink snowsuit and they'd brought her outside to see snow for the first time. He'd stayed back to take pictures while Grace carried her down to the frozen lake, and his throat had grown tight seeing the single set of footprints in the snow. One day soon there would be two sets of footprints, and years down the road, that second set of footprints would walk away in their own direction.

Her voice startled him when she answered. 'Hi, Grace.'

'Magozzi, how's the case?'

'Disturbing. And it's going to be all-consuming for a while. I'm sorry.'

'Don't be sorry for doing your job. I don't think I've ever heard you specifically say a case was disturbing because they all are.'

'True, but this is dark in a new way we haven't seen before.'

'Can you tell me?'

Magozzi did, and when he was finished, he heard Grace utter a soft, melancholy sigh. 'I'm sorry. Let us know if we can help you.'

'Thanks. What's Elizabeth doing?'

'I think she's trying to have a conversation with Charlie, but there's a language barrier.'

'Don't let those two fool you. I'm sure they're plotting a global coup to seize absolute power.' Magozzi was suddenly feeling terrific, because life seemed normal again, at least until he saw the looming front doors of City Hall.

Beyond them was a morgue where Kelly Ramage's body lay, waiting for justice. 'I'm sorry, Grace, but I have to run. Gino and I will try to stop by the office later.'

'We'll be here.'

'Give Elizabeth a kiss and make one of my stupid faces at her. She'll understand.'

15

Gino was idling on the curb in front of City Hall. White clouds of vapor chuffed out of the sedan's tail pipe, then froze instantly on the street, compounding the already treacherous driving conditions. Black ice, they called it, a phenomenon that existed only when it was outrageously cold. You couldn't see it happening, you couldn't see it when you were driving, but it was there, glazing the streets and highways into one giant hockey rink. Black ice. A Minnesota treasure.

Magozzi climbed in and tossed the bag of Cheezy Puffs on the console.

'My God, I could weep. What did Tommy say about the phone?'

'He said no problem, he's got a new toy. Did you get a hold of Eleanor Dray?'

'Yeah. She's a dead end. According to her, there's no way Kelly was cheating on her husband. She was adamant, even when I pointed out that she lied about being with her last night.'

'Some secrets you keep.'

'In this case, the kind you die with,' Gino muttered. 'I called all the local cab companies, but nobody dropped or picked up a fare last night at Dray's address. Same with Lyft and Uber. My only good news is I found the gallery that hosted the Rado show last night. Are you ready to see some art?'

'I'm ready to see some surveillance footage.'

'Do you think Kelly Ramage actually went?'

'None of the neighbors saw anything at Dray's house last night, not even a vehicle, not until this morning, which means she got there late, after everyone was hunkered down and probably asleep. I'm hoping she met up with her killer at the gallery.'

'Seems a little weird to go to an art show when you have other plans.'

'If she had some kind of a relationship with her killer beyond a one-time hook-up, it wouldn't be so weird. Whatever your proclivities, it can't be all bondage all the time, right?'

'I wouldn't know.' Gino pulled into traffic and almost grazed a lumbering city bus. The bus driver flipped him off and Gino responded in kind. 'Asshole.'

'To be fair, that was mostly your fault.'

'It was totally my fault, but he didn't have to flip me off. My day was already ruined the minute I answered the phone this morning, and he just made it worse. And I just made *his* day worse. We're all just evil little tribes, profanely gesturing our way toward collective misery.'

'You are having a bad day.'

'And you're not? I'm going to have nightmares for the rest of my life. And you know what doubles the suck factor about this? When the circumstances of Kelly Ramage's death get out, that poor woman is going to be judged. People will tsk-tsk about high-risk behavior, like she was asking for it. Her husband thinks he's already at rock-bottom, but he has no idea what's coming at him.'

'You're probably right. That's really depressing.'

'It gets worse. Big-time accountant at a big-time firm? He's going to be radioactive, which really pisses me off, because his wife is a victim, so he's a victim, and they're both going to be treated like pariahs.'

'If people heard that perspective, they'd be shamed into human decency against their will.'

'That's the worst part, having to shame people into decency.'

Magozzi tore open the bag of Cheezy Puffs and handed it to Gino. 'You need a therapeutic dose of orange food coloring. It's a mood elevator. Once you partake, all will be right with the world.'

Gino made a turn onto Washington Avenue, then shoved some neon extrusions into his mouth. 'I tracked down an address and phone number for Blanca Szabo, but she's not answering. I figured we'd stop at her shop on the way to the gallery, do a quick bash and pop, put her under the Klieg lights if we need to, then either eliminate her or put her on the person-of-interest list.'

'Good idea.'

'Did you let Grace know your day off at the lake isn't going to pan out?'

'Yeah. It's okay, they're busy working, too.'

'What's the latest?'

'Security for a cryptocurrency exchange that got fleeced for four hundred million last year. Bit Monster.'

'I heard about that. One of the biggest heists ever.'

'Where did you hear about it?'

'Helen. All seventeen-year-olds exist in a digital time-space warp, which is probably where she got her healthy-food obsession. They know everything that happens there and almost nothing that happens in reality. My grandkids are going to be malnourished robots. And maybe cyber criminals.'

16

Blanca's place of business was a small, unmarked storefront, save for the unobtrusive placard in the window that simply said 'Medium and Spiritual Guide'. A hanging sign on the inside of the door said the shop was closed, but the door was unlocked and made an eerie creaking sound as Magozzi pushed it open.

The interior was dim and redolent of incense, candle wax, and an undercurrent of antique mustiness that probably emanated from the jumbled collection of old furniture and the threadbare rugs and tapestries that adorned the floors and walls. The dominant feature of the room was a velvet-draped table with a large crystal ball set in a dragon-claw stand. Doorways were draped with exotic fabrics and beaded curtains, and every flat surface was crammed with stacks of dusty books, mystical-looking objects, and even more crystal balls. Apparently you could never have enough. The woman herself wasn't a Hollywood cliché, but her shop had the look and feel of a B-movie set.

'Ms Szabo?' Gino called out. 'It's Detectives Rolseth and Magozzi. Can we have a word?'

No answer.

'Ms Szabo?'

Still no answer.

Gino walked further into the crowded space and pushed aside a curtain of multi-colored beads, revealing a living area filled with more mystical ephemera. There was a bed, a microwave, a hotplate, and a small sofa. 'Looks like she lives here, too.'

'Makes sense – downtown rent costs a fortune. Ms Szabo?' Magozzi called again.

'Maybe she stepped out for coffee or a magic potion.'

'Without locking up?'

'She doesn't strike me as the type who's real concerned about worldly goods. Plus, I don't see a whole lot here to steal, unless you're into creepy figurines and crystal balls.' Gino walked to the back of the shop where there was another doorway, this one covered with heavy brocade curtains. He parted them and they walked into a utility room jammed with more old furniture, dilapidated cast-offs languishing in hoarder Purgatory.

Aside from the furniture, the rest of the space was empty, with exposed pipes, ceiling-mounted ductwork, and a furnace that had seen better days. There was a small tool box and a ladder in the corner, and it looked like somebody had spent some time trying to tape a leaky fitting, but water was still dripping in soft, steady plops onto the cement floor and was starting to spread.

Magozzi pointed to a roll of duct tape on one of the ladder's rungs. 'That stuff can kill well enough, but it can't fix a bad pipe. Blanca's deadbeat landlord is in a world of hurt if they don't get somebody who knows what they're doing in here fast.' He gestured to the walls mottled with black. 'Mold. It's all over.'

'Yep, this is pretty much a biohazard.' Gino walked further into the room, skirting around a table stacked with chairs, then recoiled and took a few quick steps backward.

79

'What? Oh, shit.' Magozzi stared down at Blanca's life-less form, face down on the floor. Her neck was at an odd angle, as if she'd fallen from a height, probably the ladder. He knelt down and checked for a pulse – you had to, even when you knew the victim was dead. It always took effort to resist the urge to do anything more, as futile as it would be. Even in accidental deaths, you had to preserve the scene as you found it until the circus arrived and recorded everything. 'She's starting to get cold. This didn't happen that long ago.'

'Her landlord's got a lot more to worry about now than mold. Her relatives are going to end up owning this dump when the lawyers are finished.' Gino shook his head. 'Poor lady.'

'McLaren and Freedman are next on the roster. Get them in here. We'll bring them up to speed on everything and they can take over. The clock is ticking on Kelly Ramage.'

17

Grace was in the third-floor Monkeewrench office in Harley's mansion, rocking the elaborately carved Victorian cradle he'd procured from a European auction house. According to the piece's provenance, it had been crafted for an Austrian prince, and Harley had deemed it the only vessel outside a museum worthy of Elizabeth.

There was no point trying to dissuade Harley from showering the baby with priceless gifts, but when she got older, Grace would have to put an end to the excessive spoiling. In the meantime, she didn't see the harm in letting him embrace the role of benefactor uncle. Monkeewrench Software had made them all equally wealthy, but Harley's greatest joy was spending it on the people he loved and it seemed cruel to deprive him of the pleasure.

She listened to the customary background noise of Annie's and Harley's squabbling, this morning over the approach to the Bit Monster job. Neither of them lacked strong opinions on anything, and they almost never aligned. Agreement between them would be cause for concern.

'A ground-up renovation of Bit Monster security is *not* what we were hired to do,' Annie huffed. 'They have a very respectable framework. It just needs some patching and modifications. There's no reason to throw the baby out with the bathwater and write something entirely new.'

'That's where you're misguided. I think the hack last year might have been an inside job, so the only way to give Bit Monster iron-clad security that protects them from the inside and the outside is to start over with our own software. Something totally unfamiliar to the bad guys, something so smart it can't be compromised. We can booby-trap it with a virus that will trace anybody who tries to hack them again and it will lead us right to their front door. Pretty brilliant, right, Grace?'

Grace folded her lips on a smile. 'It's a very good plan, but Annie's right. We weren't contracted for ground-up reno, which would cost a fortune and take at least a year. They need help now. That's why they called us.'

'We can't cut corners on this – it's our reputation on the line.'

'I know. So why don't you just put the booby-trap in our modifications?'

Harley blinked at her, all his bluster defused. 'That's a different way to look at it.'

'Do you really think it's an inside job?'

'It's a damn good possibility. I've identified two sketchy characters associated with the organization: one of the founders has a past fraud conviction that was overturned, and another private equity guy who helped get Bit Monster off the ground. He's not part of Bit Monster anymore, but he's the most suspicious – his CV says he's a finance guy out of Switzerland, but that's bullshit. He doesn't exist outside a flimsy digital presence that dead-ends at a Balkan ISP. Which really sucks, because Eastern Europe is filled with more criminally inclined computer brainiacs than the rest of the world put together.'

'That is suspicious. Do you think one of the Balkan Mafias infiltrated Bit Monster at the beginning?' Grace asked.

'For all we know, a Balkan Mafia is running the whole show. Cryptocurrencies are unregulated and moving them around is virtually untraceable. There's nothing better if you're a dark-sider, and what an awesome cover . . .'

Annie shot an intimidating glare at Harley. 'Are you being serious?'

'God, of course not. Criminals aren't going to hire us to stop them. Besides, Bit Monster is a publicly traded company. Cryptos might not be regulated, but the NASDAQ is. Hey, does your Bulgarian ex-boyfriend still work for Interpol Cybercrime?'

'To be clear, he was never my boyfriend, just a brief dalliance.'

Harley grinned wolfishly. 'Whatever. Does he?'

'I wouldn't know.'

'Well, if you're still on speaking terms with your transitory boy toy, dust off your black book and get him on the phone. Interpol might have some information we can use that we won't get through the regular channels.'

She eyed him imperiously. 'My black book doesn't get dusty.'

Roadrunner suddenly came through the office doors, uncharacteristically tardy, out of breath, and red-faced from the cold. Charlie jumped up from his sentinel's position at the foot of the cradle and greeted him with a soft, fond bark. 'Hey, buddy, hey, everyone. Sorry I'm late.'

Annie spun in her chair and probed him with a flutter of rhinestone-studded lashes. 'We were wondering what happened to you, sugar. If you don't mind me saying, you seem a little bee-stung this morning.'

Harley rolled his head around and put his feet up on his desk. 'Yeah, what the hell is up? The latest you ever get here is seven a.m. It's damn near lunchtime.'

Roadrunner ignored the query and tiptoed over to Elizabeth's cradle. 'She's sleeping? With all this noise? I could hear Annie and Harley from the first floor.'

'It's all she heard for the first nine months of her life. She doesn't sleep when it's too quiet – just ask Magozzi.'

He smiled down at Elizabeth, then gave Charlie a scratch on his neck to let him know he wasn't forgotten or unappreciated. 'When are you going to the lake?'

'Not today, probably not all weekend. Magozzi and Gino pulled a case this morning.'

'Oh. That's too bad.'

'Stop playing coy with the small-talk, Roadrunner. Where the hell have you been?'

He looked at Harley and shifted his shoulders uncomfortably. 'At Hennepin County Medical Center.'

'*What?* What's wrong?'

'It's not me, I'm fine. I was visiting a neighbor. She almost died of hypothermia last night. I found her in that little park by my house.'

'Oh, my.' Annie tapped a metallic nail on her lower lip. 'You've certainly got our attention, now, Roadrunner.'

18

The air in the back room of the club was thick, polluted with smoke, body odor, and the smell of stale liquor. The wooden planks of the floor were tacky and warped from the sloppy spills of drunks that had never been wiped. They were as pickled and twisted as the worthless occupants who inhabited this place. A den of thieves, criminals. Joseph would happily have shot them all where they stood, but they had utility, a place in his world.

The muted percussion of dance music three walls away still thudded a ceaseless, droning beat even though it was day. He'd take care of that as soon as he was finished here. He walked through the reverently parting crowd toward a fat young man wearing a sloppy gray tracksuit and a fake-fur bombardier hat that canted precariously on his head. He was leaning unsteadily against the bar, smoking a cigarette and drinking whiskey from a bottle nearing the end of its life.

As he drew closer, he noticed the florid, angry webs of burst capillaries spreading across the stubby nose and bloated cheeks – a devoted drinker showing the signs far in advance of his age. Not at all what he'd been expecting from someone who supposedly possessed great talent. 'You're Stefan?'

He turned his head and assessed him with droopy,

vacant eyes that reminded Joseph of shiny brown beetles, the kind that skittered for cover when you moved a corpse. 'You must be the man who has a job for me.'

'Possibly.'

He took another swig from the whiskey bottle and offered it guilelessly. 'Want a sip?'

The effrontery! The very suggestion that he might drink from the same bottle this disgusting troll had nursed and drooled on repulsed Joseph. It was more than enough reason to kill him but, regrettably, that wasn't a practical choice at the moment, so he made an effort to hide his revulsion. 'You come highly recommended.'

'I'm good at what I do.'

'Bit Monster?'

His beetle eyes sparked with interest. 'That was genius. Sorry to say it wasn't my work.'

'That's fortunate for you, because I lost quite a bit of money. I'd like very much to know who stole it.'

'You and me both, but that's not going to happen.'

'You're so smart, tell me why,' he said sharply.

'Black Hats operating at that level? They're ciphers. Their lives depend on it.'

'What are Black Hats?'

'Hackers. Ones who don't work for any government or corporation.'

'Hackers like you?'

'I'm not a White Hat, if that's what you're asking.' He dropped his cigarette on the floor and crushed it with a scuffed brown snow boot. 'So what are you in the market for?'

'I want my money back.'

'Tell me who you want to hack and I'll tell you if it's possible.'

'Bit Monster, of course. They owe me a debt and I aim to collect on it.'

Stefan reared his head back and the bombardier finally made the inevitable plunge to the sticky floor, but he didn't seem to notice or care. 'That's crazy, dude. You never hit a target twice. It's too dangerous, thin ice nobody steps on. Besides, word is they've hired outside help to tighten up the ship.'

Joseph knew nothing about computers, but he did know about taking advantage of opportunities. Every successful criminal did. Any organization, legitimate or otherwise, was at their greatest vulnerability when there was any change or upheaval. 'In that case, it seems to me that now would be a perfect time. There will be confusion and dis-array, and that, Stefan, is what we all wait for.'

Stefan's doughy face shifted. It wasn't fear, but it was something close. 'I would normally agree with you.'

'But you don't now?'

'This is different. Bit Monster hired Monkeewrench to handle their security. Do you know them?'

'No.' Joseph assessed Stefan curiously. 'You're afraid of them?'

'Everybody is. They work with the law – all over the world – and nobody's ever been able to breach them. They're wizards.'

'Interesting. Perhaps I'm interviewing the wrong per-son for my job.'

'I told you, they work for the law and they're virgins, pure White Hat. They wouldn't take a job like yours.'

'Oh, I think they might, with the right persuasion.'

'You didn't hear me – they're working for Bit Monster now. They won't help you get your money back. They're just trying to make sure hacks don't happen again.'

'If they're so pure, then they'd want to help me and others who were robbed get our money back, find out who was responsible and bring them to justice. Especially for a finder's fee, wouldn't you say?'

'They probably already know who was behind it, or have a good idea, anyhow. That's the first part of a job like this, figuring out who got in and how. Then you fix the rest. But whatever information they have, it will get passed on to the authorities. Law and order, I'm telling you.' Stefan drained what was left of his whiskey bottle.

'That's interesting.'

His drunk, sloped eyes expanded. 'Oh . . . no, no, no, I won't try to hack them, if that's what you're thinking. If I do, I'll end up in prison.'

'Then you're not so good at your job after all?'

'That's not what I mean . . . Hey, you just want your money back, right? Isn't that the most important thing?'

'It's the first priority, but not the last.'

'I can get money for you, but that's it, okay?'

'Interesting that I haven't even hired you and you're making rules.'

'I'm not . . .'

Joseph held up a hand. 'You have your rule, so I have one, too. The money has to come from Bit Monster. It's a matter of principle. If you can't do that, then we're done. You have five seconds to decide. I'm very busy, so don't waste my time.'

Stefan minced around in place, seeing dollar signs float away before his whiskey-glazed eyes – Joseph had seen the look dozens of times before: greed ripe for exploitation.

'Bit Monster is vulnerable now. You're right about that.'

Joseph waited patiently, but his hands were clenched at his sides. 'Okay, I'll do it.'

'Then consider yourself on retainer.'

Stefan's blubbery lips twisted in a cunning little smile. 'For the right price. I've got a lot of offers on the table right now.'

Joseph laughed genially and put an arm over the man's spongy shoulders while simultaneously jamming a gun into his ribs. 'I'll let you live. Does that seem like the right price?'

19

The Resnick/Feinnes Gallery was the most prestigious in the Twin Cities, the Midwestern outpost of the Resnick/Feinnes galleries located in the places that really mattered in the art world, like New York and London. It was tucked away in the only remaining quiet area of the warehouse district, where there was no hope of foot traffic. But foot traffic was not their clientele.

The gallery occupied a large stone building that had once manufactured men's shirts before it had been repurposed to display important art. There was an enormous banner on the side of the building that read: 'RADO – SYZYGY OF ART AND TECHNOLOGY'.

It looked lonely and devoid of life on this Arctic day, until Gino rounded the block to the front entrance, where a dozen or so protesters were pacing, shouting and brandishing signs, passionate enough to be outside in subzero weather. Now that was commitment to a cause. Or else they were being paid to be there, which was a definite possibility and probably more likely. Even art was hijacked to serve a political agenda now. Or maybe it always had been.

Their signs were varied, but they espoused the same theme: Violence against women is NOT art. Resnick/Feinnes just say NO! STOP SELLING BRUTALITY. SHAME ON YOU. Et cetera.

'This is interesting,' Gino commented. 'You used to be an artist. Do you know anything about this Rado character?'

'I used to paint. I was never an artist. And, no, I don't know anything about him, except he's obviously controversial.'

They got out of the car and were immediately confronted by a protester wearing a ski mask and swathed in multiple layers of clothing, a combination that eliminated any hope of determining gender.

'Violence against women is not art!'

Definitely a woman. Men couldn't scream at that octave.

Gino had been in an epically dark mood earlier, but he seemed strangely unaffected by the aggression. Maybe Cheezy Puffs really were therapeutic. 'What are you protesting, ma'am?' he asked politely.

'Have you seen the vile garbage inside?'

'Not yet. And, according to you, we're not supposed to.'

'Go ahead – go in and look for yourself. Tell me what you think when you're done.' Her eyes were visible in the twin holes of her mask, and they narrowed. 'Are you cops? You don't look like cops, but you act like it.'

'We're detectives.'

'Are you here to arrest us for exercising our right to free speech?'

'No. Stand out here all day long and freeze your tuchuses off, we really don't care.'

'Are you here to arrest them?'

'Them?'

'The people who run the gallery.'

'For what?'

'For displaying exploitative trash.'

'For a minute I thought you were a fan of the First Amendment. Free speech and all that.'

'It needs better guidelines for the modern era.'

'Who's going to set those guidelines?'

'People who understand how destructive art can be.'

'That's very Mao of you. Or maybe Stalin – he came first. Killed anybody who looked at him cross-eyed. Twenty-five million is a conservative estimate.'

'There are slippery slopes everywhere.' Magozzi decided to share Tommy Espinoza's insightful comment.

She let out an indignant huff, a sputter, then resumed marching with renewed vigor and anger. 'Just go in and see what I'm talking about!'

Magozzi and Gino took her advice and walked through heavy glass doors etched with the slick Resnick/Feinnes logo. After a couple of seconds of silent scrutiny, the security guard surprised them by nodding at their concealed weapons. 'Do you two have ID?'

They showed their shields and Gino asked, 'Are you still on the job?'

He seemed grateful for the recognition. 'Retired, St Paul PD. Mike Vierling.'

'Gino Rolseth, my partner Leo Magozzi. How do you like the security gig?'

'Never thought I'd do it in a million years, but it's actually pretty good. The pay isn't half bad and I don't have to worry about getting killed on the job. Makes the wife happy, and a happy wife makes a happy life, right? Plus, I don't have ulcers anymore.'

'Good for you.'

'You're obviously here on business. Can I help you with something?'

'Maybe. Were you working here last night during the show?'

'Sorry, I only do days.'

'Thanks anyhow.' Gino nodded toward the door. 'Protesters been a problem?'

'Nah, they're harmless, saying their piece, keeping their distance. And I get where they're coming from. You will, too, once you go inside.'

20

Even the grim auguries of the protesters and Mike Vierling hadn't prepared them for the horrifying Kelly Ramage déjà vu that awaited them in the gallery – it was nothing short of grievous assault. The main exhibit space was polluted by projections of stuttering, repeating black and white videos of gagged, blindfolded, naked women in bondage, being whipped and smothered by pillows. The films were accompanied by an intermittent soundtrack of human cries. In addition to the stomach-churning live action, there were sketches and still photos that repeated the bondage theme, accompanied by large sculptures planted in black granite bases that looked like wavy, holey ribbons and made no sense at all.

There was definitely a major shock factor, which wasn't unusual in the world of modern art, but there was also a stark inhumanity entirely absent of any underlying message, at least that Magozzi could see. He found it chilling, if not downright diabolical.

'This crap is bound to attract all kinds of freaks and copycats.' Gino's angry voice echoed in the large space full of flat planes and hard surfaces.

A handful of well-dressed people cast scornful looks in his direction, obviously offended that such a cretin was in their midst, ruining their perfectly lovely afternoon of viewing human degradation.

'Inside voice, Gino,' Magozzi whispered. 'Anybody here could be a suspect.'

Inexplicably, Gino obeyed and lowered his voice to the decibel level of a leaf-blower. 'I call the fat guy wearing mom jeans who's glaring at me. He looks like a pervert.'

Gino's beneficent mood had clearly reversed course, so Magozzi turned his back on ensuing confrontation and spotted a tall, emaciated woman standing in a corner, observing the proceedings with annoyed hauteur. She was pretty, but everything about her was severe, from the jutting angles of bone to the funereal black dress she wore. Her dark hair was twisted into a tight bun that seemed to stretch taut the pale skin of her face, and there was a spooky lack of life in her stone-colored eyes.

He grabbed Gino's arm and redirected him. 'Let's move on.'

They approached the woman and got an icy smile. 'May I help you?'

'Minneapolis detectives Leo Magozzi and Gino Rolseth. Do you work here?'

Her eyes widened slightly and the frost melted just a bit. 'Yes. I'm Madeline Montgomery, the gallery curator.'

'Were you here last night?'

'Of course. We had a large event. Rado's opening.' She gave Gino a look of subdued malice as he pushed a blow-up of Kelly Ramage's driver's license photo toward her face. 'Do you recognize this woman?'

Her eyes swept the photograph, but there was no sign of familiarity. 'Not specifically.'

'What does that mean?'

'She's an attractive blond woman. They don't exactly stand out in Minnesota.'

'This attractive blond woman will stand out to you for the rest of your life, Ms Montgomery. We're investigating her death. We believe she was here last night before she was murdered.'

Her cool decayed quite a bit more and her eyes darted around the gallery. 'Please, let's step into my office.'

Madeline Montgomery's office was as minimalist as the rest of the gallery but, thankfully, without the disturbing artwork. She gestured to two chairs that looked like molten resin blobs with wings, then sat down in her own weird, different sort of blob chair behind a pale birch desk. 'What can I do to help you, Detectives?'

'We need to see any surveillance footage you have from last night.'

'Certainly. Would you like to view it here, or shall I have a copy made?'

'A copy would be fine. Thank you.'

Madeline didn't seem the least bit put-out, and spoke softly into a tiny discreet com unit that had been concealed beneath the fluted black fabric of her collar. Magozzi noted that the words 'police' and 'detectives' came up a couple of times.

'Our tech person, Mr Mauer, will have a copy for you shortly, Detectives.'

'Thanks.' Gino looked around the unadorned room. 'So Rado is a pretty controversial figure. Seeing his work, I understand why.'

'He has his detractors, as you surely noticed on your way

into the gallery. But no artist's work is meant to express the literal or obvious, and his intentions certainly aren't to promote violence against women. His work is widely misunderstood.'

'What are his intentions?'

'To highlight the analog between actual physical bondage and violence to that engendered by technology. In his opinion, there is no distinction.'

Gino presented his best 'Gosh, golly, gee, I'm just a hick' impersonation. 'Maybe you can explain that. I'm not really an art guy.'

She smiled back, and not in an entirely patronizing way. 'Aren't we all enslaved by our devices to one degree or another? I certainly am. Rado's point is that willingly relinquishing control is dangerous under any circumstances, and technology is supremely seductive in that way because it seems harmless at first. It's a clever deception. But look at all the acts of violence, all the death that has been caused by the preeminence of technology in our lives, from cyber-bullying to terror recruitment to normalizing violence of all kinds. His art isn't meant to incite. It's meant to illuminate one of the greatest challenges of our time.'

Magozzi noticed that Gino was making an exhaustive effort not to roll his eyes or puke. 'That's a pretty big leap, isn't it?'

'It's conceptual, Rado's interpretation of what he sees in the world.'

Magozzi thought Rado was just a glorified porn peddler and a shock jock, but he kept his opinion to himself. 'So where does the technology come in?'

'For one thing, all of Rado's shows are extensively out-fitted with cameras and microphones so he can see and hear the viewers' reactions. Some of the microphones are ultra-high sensitivity and can pick up heartbeats and breathing patterns.'

Gino grunted. 'That's kind of creepy. What does he do with the data he gathers?'

'Nothing. Rado doesn't attend his shows, so it allows him to be present.'

'Is the whole anonymity thing part of his schtick, too?'

She bristled at Gino's use of 'schtick'. 'Artists can be eccentric.'

Or crazy, Magozzi thought. 'How do the sculptures fit into the whole concept?'

'They represent the isolation, the holes in people's lives when they become immersed in technology to the exclusion of genuine human interaction. They also symbolize archaic computer punch tape.' She assessed their skeptical glances. 'Art is subjective. May I suggest you view the exhibit with a fresh eye while we wait for Mr Mauer to bring the copy of the surveillance footage? Perhaps you'll find a new understanding of it now that you've heard part of Rado's artistic vision.'

'Thanks, but no thanks,' Gino said, settling into his blob chair more firmly. 'Personally, I find his stuff pretty offensive. And in my line of work, that's saying something.'

'The freedom to offend is essential to artistic creation.'

Magozzi realized then that Madeline Montgomery was a true acolyte, a Rado disciple of the highest order. And maybe Kelly Ramage had been one, too. It was going to be really bad PR if Rado's offensive art was a catalyst for murder. 'You said Rado doesn't come to his shows. Have you ever met him?'

'No. No one has that I know.'

'Isn't that strange?'

'It's my understanding that he's quite infirm and unable to attend public functions. In fact, this show may be his last.'

Which would be a benefit to society, Magozzi thought. 'Are his high-sensitivity recordings part of the surveillance you'll be providing?'

'No, of course not. That's proprietary, part of his show, not our security.'

'Do you know how to reach him if we need to?'

'Rado?' she asked incredulously, as if Magozzi had asked her for a meet-and-greet with God Himself.

'Yes. They might pick up something your surveillance doesn't. We're talking about a homicide, ma'am, and anything that can help solve it.'

She nodded crisply, opened a desk drawer, and slid a card across the table. 'You can try his agent, Michael Dorn, but he's not an easy man to reach.'

'People get a little more cooperative when you've got a gun and a shield,' Gino pointed out brusquely.

Madeline Montgomery was disgusted with them, had been from the onset: that much was clear. Her inner dialogue was probably filled with expletives she would never use in her polite, cloistered world, which filled Magozzi with glee. She'd been accommodating out of necessity, but he knew she viewed them as flecks of boorish, unsightly dirt sullying her domain.

There was a soft knock on the door. A young man with

swooshy blond hair and a hipster vibe walked in. He placed a CD on the desk and bobbed his head dutifully. 'The surveillance footage you asked for, Ms Montgomery.'

'Thank you.'

He regarded Magozzi and Gino curiously, then gave them a polite nod.

Gino pulled out Kelly Ramage's photo again and showed it to him. 'Were you working here last night, Mr Mauer?'

'You can call me Wolfie. Yeah, I was working – we had a big opening.'

'Do you recognize this woman?'

He gave it a cursory look, then shook his head, dislodging a carefully coiffed sheaf of hair. 'No, but that doesn't mean much because I'm never on the floor. I'm the tech guy behind the scenes. I make sure everything's working the way it should.'

Gino handed him the photo. 'Are you sure? Take a closer look.'

Wolfie examined it more closely, and his expression shifted. He risked a furtive glance at them and realized he didn't have a great poker face. 'I guess she looks kind of familiar. I might have seen her around. Not here, but some-place else.'

'Where?'

'I don't know, I don't remember.'

Magozzi knew Wolfie was lying from his body language alone. Most people were atrociously bad liars. Only psychopaths could pull it off convincingly. 'She's a real looker. I'd remember if I'd seen her. And where.'

He shook his head and shrugged uneasily. 'Sorry.'

Gino stood up, pocketed the CD, and gave Madeline

Montgomery a gracious nod. 'Thank you for your co-operation, ma'am, we appreciate it. Wolfie, maybe you can show us to the door.'

'It's just out front . . .'

'It's a big place.'

He gave his boss a helpless look.

'Go ahead. Show the detectives to the door. Please.'

Emphasis on 'please'.

21

'You ever have any run-ins with cops before?' Gino asked earnestly, as Wolfie walked them to the door.

'No. No!'

'I didn't think so. Criminals, they'll talk you to Kathmandu and back and make you believe you lived there. On the other hand, law-abiding citizens like yourself have a tendency to get a little tongue-tied when they're in this type of situation, getting questioned out of the blue. We're just looking for information, Wolfie. And I think you have some. That pretty woman in the picture is Kelly Ramage. She was murdered last night and we need to find out who killed her.'

Wolfie stopped in his tracks and gaped at Gino. 'She's dead? I just thought maybe she broke the law or something.'

'Can you help us?'

He nodded miserably. 'I didn't want to say anything in front of Ms Montgomery. I really need this job.'

'That's okay.'

Wolfie looked around, probably assessing the range of the microphones he'd set up for the show, hoping they wouldn't pick up his confession. Apparently, he wasn't willing to take the chance.

'Right about now is when I make a run to Pâtisserie Maude for her. Do you know it?'

Magozzi wasn't certain, but he thought Gino's eyes glazed over with rapture. 'It's just around the block.'

'Can you meet me there in five minutes?'

Definitely rapture. 'No problem. No problem at all.'

'Thanks. I'll walk you to the door, go get her order, then run right over there.'

They walked from the office area into the gallery space, with its sparkling glass façade and view of the street. Magozzi wondered if Madeline had the poor kid washing windows, too.

'I'm surprised the protesters are still out there,' Wolfie mused. 'I was hoping the weather would chase them away.'

'I don't think they're going anywhere.'

'Why are they even here, protesting art? There's a lot worse things going on that they could be shouting about.'

'I'm sure they have their reasons.'

'It doesn't make any sense to me.' Wolfie gave Mike Vierling a cordial smile. 'Everything good, Mike?'

'Just fine, thanks.'

'I'm about to make my run. The usual?'

'Yeah, that would be great. Thanks, Wolfie.'

Magozzi and Gino walked out of the gallery and got smacked by a cold, howling wind that had gathered formidable strength while they'd been at the horror matinée. The protesters were huddled together now, stomping their feet for warmth, but they still bravely held their signs and railed against Rado.

Magozzi was surprised there weren't any media present. Any protest, no matter how small, usually merited at least a couple of cameras and reporters, no matter how bad the weather was. 'I think you bonded with Wolfie.'

'I don't know how he feels, but I definitely bonded with him. Pâtisserie Maude. This is never going to be a good day, but it just got a hell of a lot better. Even Cheezy Puffs pale by comparison.'

'What do you think about Madeline Montgomery?'

'Not much. She sounded like a brain-washed cult member when she was talking about Rado and his "artistic vision." What a steaming crock of shit. I wonder if anybody actually shells out for it.'

'I wonder if Rado's even real. Everything in that gallery was such a disgusting, pretentious, illogical mess, it makes me think he's actually a consortium of asylum inmates.'

Gino actually smiled. 'I like that theory.'

Their angry friend noticed them, peeled away from the group, and approached them, a combative swagger in her step. 'So what did you think, Detectives?'

'I think you were right,' Gino admitted. 'Rado is a sick freak and his work sucks.'

She smiled in vindication. 'I told you.'

'But he still has the right to produce it and show it, as much as you have a right to be out here protesting it. The cost of living in a free society.'

She lowered her eyes and the fury seemed to drain out of her suddenly. 'You're homicide detectives.'

Gino nodded.

'It happened again, didn't it?'

22

Gino and Magozzi held a collective breath for a moment. 'What happened?'

'Rado inspires sick people to do sick things. That's why I'm here. A young art student from Minnesota was killed in California last year. She was bound and gagged, tortured and then suffocated with a pillow, just like in some of the Rado videos. After it happened, the police found people on social media saying that her murder was the greatest piece of art Rado had ever inspired. Can you *fucking* believe that?'

'Sadly, I do. The Internet can be a cesspool and there's a lot of abhorrent stuff out there. A lot of sick people.'

'Was the murder solved?' Magozzi asked.

She shook her head. 'They never found any suspects or evidence that led anywhere. The posts were written by some disgusting Internet trolls obsessed with Rado, but none of them was good for the murder. In my eyes, Rado inspired it, which makes him responsible. An indirect killer, but a killer all the same.'

'You know an awful lot about a murder that happened fifteen hundred miles from here,' Gino observed.

She looked down at her booted feet and scuffed the snow-covered sidewalk. 'That's because the victim was my sister. Her name was Delia Sellman.'

'We're very sorry,' Gino mumbled, through half-frozen lips. 'What's your name?'

'Annabelle Sellman.'

'Where in California did this happen, Annabelle?'

'Los Angeles. Westwood – that's where Delia lived during the school year. You might want to look into it.'

'We absolutely will.'

Her sad eyes tracked to a young couple heading toward the gallery, chattering excitedly. 'I don't understand these people.'

Pâtisserie Maude was filled to near capacity, but Gino had managed to elbow his way to an open table in the back. He was tucking into his second pâté-filled croissant when Wolfie joined them. 'So tell us what you know about Kelly Ramage,' he said, without preamble or pause in his feast.

'I've seen her at a place called Club Provocateur. I DJ there sometimes.'

'The strip club?'

Wolfie nodded. 'I went to Caltech. I've got a ton of student loans, so I take extra work wherever I can get it. But if Ms Montgomery found out, she'd fire me. She's a hard-core feminist.'

Magozzi marveled at the absurdity of an ardent Rado disciple claiming the moral authority to pass judgment on a strip club. Apparently, exotic dancers didn't fall under the aegis of art and were therefore a protected class. 'She won't find out on our account, you have our word.'

'Thanks. And, to be fair, the place isn't really a strip club anymore. That rep is a holdover from back in the two-thousands.'

'What is it now?'

'An alternative dance club.'

'What's that supposed to mean?' Gino asked.

'It's more of a . . . swinger's place. I guess that's what you'd call it. Well, not just swingers . . . like I said, alternative. It's private, members only, so people do what they want. Whatever they're into, and trust me when I tell you some of them are into really weird shit.'

'Bondage? S and M?'

Murder? Magozzi wondered.

'Some of that, yeah, but bondage seems normal compared to some of the fetishes and cosplay. Last weekend, there was a group of people dressed in Godzilla suits grooving on the dance floor with some steampunk folks and a bigger lady dressed like a slutty Snow White. You can't un-see stuff like that.'

'Do you remember if Kelly was with anybody?'

'Not that I noticed. She was just kind of milling around, watching. Maybe that's her thing, or maybe she was getting a feel for the place. I only saw her there twice.'

'You said it was members only.'

'Yeah, but I don't think she was a member. The members are pretty friendly with each other.'

Magozzi wondered what 'friendly' meant, then decided he didn't need to know or want to. 'Then there are exceptions to the members-only rule?'

'One of the bartenders told me that if you're a pretty woman under a certain age, you can get in with just paying a cover charge, no strings attached.'

'Do you know who runs the place?'

'The manager is a guy named Ollie. He's the one who hired me. If you talk to him, can you keep my name out of it? I really need that job, too.'

'We can do that. Anything else you can think of? Troubles at the club or with customers?'

'No, nothing like that.'

Gino brushed crumbs from his hands. 'You said the protesters didn't make any sense to you. Just to put your curiosity to bed, we talked to one of them on the way here and got her story.'

'What is it?'

'She's out there because her sister was murdered last year and the crime scene was modeled after some of Rado's work. Afterwards, there were people talking online, saying Rado had inspired a great work of art.'

Wolfie blanched. 'That's sick.'

'It sure is. She blames Rado. That's why she's protesting.'

'No wonder. I don't blame her.' He looked at the service counter anxiously. 'If that's all, I should get Ms Montgomery's order in before they run out of pains au chocolat.'

'Grounds for firing?'

'Almost anything is.'

'Go ahead. Thanks for speaking with us.' Gino gulped down the rest of his coffee as he watched Wolfie hurry to the counter. 'So, Club Provocateur. It sounds super creepy and just like the kind of place where fantasies can get out of control.'

23

Gino and Magozzi found an empty conference room in City Hall and cued up the CD Wolfie had given them while they waited for a callback from the Westwood detective who had handled Delia Sellman's homicide. It was a Hail Mary, but stranger things had broken cases.

The grainy black-and-white footage of the gallery was from four cameras, their views tiled on the screen. They all showed a lot of pretty people milling around, sipping champagne. The clientele ran the gamut from the traditional suit-and-tie crowd to flamboyant artsy types, with tattoos, piercings, and edgy hairstyles that didn't exist in the human palette. There was even an older man with a bulbous nose wearing a fur coat.

Gino pointed to him. 'I've never seen a dude in a fur coat. That's weird.'

'It's a weird crowd. I half expected to see a dominatrix or two leading some guy in leathers and a ball gag by a leash.'

'I don't think people wear their S and M costumes in public, but what do I know? We should probably educate ourselves a little about this whole bondage thing. There's probably a community or something. There's a community for everything.'

'If what Wolfie told us is true, Kelly Ramage was new at Club Provocateur – maybe she was just testing the waters. And Rado's oeuvre fits in perfectly with the whole scene.

You can call it whatever you want, but it speaks to a certain type of person.'

Madeline Montgomery and her icy smile appeared in frame three and struck up an earnest discussion with a middle-aged couple. Mr Fur Coat joined them. He seemed animated and possibly drunk. People came and people went, drifting in and out of range of the cameras' watchful lenses. Kelly Ramage finally made her entrance at seven forty-five, according to the time stamp. Gino paused the tape.

'She didn't lie about going to the opening,' he said, his eyes fixed on the screen. 'She was supposed to pick up Eleanor at seven, which would have put them at the gallery around seven forty-five, so she kept to the timeline she told her husband about.'

'But she didn't pick up Eleanor, so what happened in those forty-five minutes?'

'Nothing important, because she's still alive at this point. My guess is she went to Eleanor's, made sure everything was up to snuff for her guest, then headed to the gallery as planned.' He restarted the tape. 'She's alone, at least so far.'

Magozzi watched her take a flute of champagne from a roving server before making her way through the exhibit. She downed it, then got another. 'She's not talking to anybody, but she's drinking like a pro. And she keeps checking her phone. She's nervous.'

'Waiting for somebody. There.' Gino jabbed a chubby finger at the screen. 'That guy in the long leather coat and riding boots. He's dressed like an SS officer and he's keeping an eye on her.'

'Every man in the room is keeping an eye on her. She's beautiful. Was beautiful.'

'Yeah, but now he's dogging her.'

They watched as the man followed her, then finally approached and said something. She nodded, responded with what appeared to be a few polite words, then returned her attention to the art. 'She doesn't know him and she's not interested in him. She's interested in whoever she's expecting to contact her.'

Thirty minutes later, Kelly Ramage checked her phone again, then walked out of the frame, a small smile lifting her mouth. The hopeful suitor watched her walk away, then shrugged and started hitting on another woman. Magozzi fast-forwarded the footage, but Kelly Ramage disappeared from the frame and never appeared again. She'd gone to meet her killer.

Gino shook his head morosely. 'She came alone and left alone. There goes an easy lead.'

'The agent, Michael Dorn. Call him. Maybe Rado's surveillance shows another angle of the gallery.'

Gino pulled the card out of his suit pocket. 'It's just an email, no numbers.'

'Send him a note, tell him we want Rado's footage, and if he balks, tell him we'll have a warrant by the end of the day.'

Gino typed a brief missive that sounded suitably official and threatening. A few moments later, his computer pinged and he swore under his breath. 'The email got kicked back with an out-of-office notification.'

'What else does it say?'

'Nothing. Just that he's out of the office and will respond as soon as he's able. Asshole is probably in Tahiti, enjoying his Rado commission.'

Magozzi sighed and started drawing a timeline in his

notebook. 'Kelly left the gallery at eight thirty. Eleanor Dray's house is a twenty-minute drive away, maybe a little longer considering the weather, so if she went directly there, we're talking around a nine o'clock arrival. Royston Wade was keeping an eye on Dray's place while she was out of town and he didn't see anything before he went to bed at ten.'

'So Kelly Ramage didn't go straight there after the gallery. She said she had a dinner date with her friend, but maybe she really had a dinner date with her killer. Or met him at Club Provocateur for a little foreplay, which makes more sense.'

'They don't open for a few hours, so let's pay a visit to Todd Ramage and pick up Kelly's computer.' When Magozzi's phone rang, he jumped on it, hoping it was Westwood or Tommy with some good news about the phone, but it was McLaren.

'Hey, Johnny, miss us already?'

'Yeah, Freedman and I miss you so much, we want you to get your asses over to Blanca Szabo's shop. Anant is here and we just rolled her over. She wasn't an accidental death, she was a homicide. Somebody duct-taped her mouth and nose. Her eyes, too.'

24

Eaton Freedman was McLaren's partner, relatively new to Homicide, but a veteran of the MPD. He was monolithic, cast of solid muscle by the genetic gods and the gym, but like many men of significant stature, he had an easygoing, amiable nature. Unless you pissed him off, Magozzi suspected, but not many would ever be stupid enough to make that mistake.

McLaren was book-ended between him and Anant, looking like a miniature human guarded by two giants of another species. They were all standing back from Blanca's body, making space for Magozzi and Gino to get a closer look. 'From what you told us about Kelly Ramage's scene, nothing synchs except the duct tape. Looks like a tool of opportunity to me – it's sitting right there on the ladder.'

Gino stepped away from the body. 'Yeah. Her head's not encased in it, she's fully clothed, no bondage aspect. This wasn't sexual. If it's the same guy, the motive is totally different.'

Freedman frowned. 'Pretty strange that she came to you with a vision of somebody else's murder yesterday and now she's dead. I guess this is proof positive that psychics don't exist. Otherwise she would have seen this coming.'

'Maybe she did in a way,' Magozzi said. 'Her vision probably germinated with one of her clients. Psychics operate by making connections, prising out enough information and feeding it back in a different form so you think they can see beyond. Her subconscious pulls some bits and pieces together, maybe a client gave her the creeps, and she forms a murder scenario. She was just wrong about the victim.'

'Johnny and I were thinking wack-job customer, too. People like Blanca Szabo probably attract a lot of weirdos, maybe even homicidal ones.'

Gino looked at Anant. 'Anything jumping out at you, Doc?'

'We will have to wait for the autopsy, of course. However, after my initial examination, I made note – with reservation – that there don't appear to be obvious signs of a fall severe enough to break her neck, contusions or other broken bones, for instance. No sign of defensive wounds, either.'

'So maybe the killer broke her neck before she knew what was coming.'

'Then why the tape?' McLaren asked.

Magozzi stripped off his latex gloves and slipped on his leather ones. 'That's for you guys to figure out, because I don't see a definitive connection to Kelly Ramage either. But the tape is enough that we need to keep an open mind. And if there is a connection, you two hotshots will find it.'

25

For the first time in his life, Roadrunner was having trouble focusing on his work. Every time he started to get lost in the beautiful symphony of code he was writing, his mind would veer away from the orderly array of numbers and letters and symbols and summon the disturbing image of Petra's motionless body and blue lips. Equally disturbing were her final words in the hospital.

I wasn't trying to kill myself . . . but if I had died, I wouldn't have minded.

Wasn't wandering outside in hazardous, subzero temperatures and not caring if you died just a passive form of suicide? Was there even a distinction between a passive and an aggressive death wish? It was little wonder he'd chosen almost exclusively to inhabit the digital domain: everything in it made perfect, logical sense, but nothing outside it seemed to, especially people's behavior.

As if to validate that world view, Harley stood, stretched his arms above his head, and announced, 'I just bought five million dollars worth of crypto from Bit Monster.'

That statement animated everyone except Grace.

'Why on God's green earth would you do something so stupid?' Annie sputtered.

'You said I was losing my mind. I just wanted to prove it beyond the shadow of a doubt.'

'Mission accomplished,' Roadrunner said, happy for the distraction.

Harley turned his attention to Grace, who seemed completely unaware that a mild furor was happening beyond her work station. 'Gracie, you haven't chimed in with an opinion on my mental stability.'

She lifted a finger, indicating she was in the middle of something far more important than her partner's irrational behavior, then finally spun around in her chair. 'You didn't spend a dime, you spoofed an account.'

Harley gave her a broad smile. 'Exactly. That's our booby-trap. Whoever pulled off the big heist isn't going to risk a large-scale attack again. But a new account with a substantial balance is too tempting, especially since I made it look super-vulnerable. It's a big, fat online bank account without any security, and the hackers are going to descend on the easy money, like flies on a ripe carcass. I also embedded that nasty little virus I was talking about, and it will lead us right to them. If this was an inside job, they'll see low-hanging fruit and take the bait with the poison pill. If this was an outside job and they're still trolling Bit Monster, five million might just be enough to pull them back in for some extra pocket cash. Either way, we'll figure out how they got in and who they are.'

'That's pretty brilliant, Harley.'

'Thank you. You hear that, Annie? I'm pretty brilliant. Not remotely insane.'

She gave him a sour look. 'It was a fine idea.'

'I'm finished with one security patch for Bit Monster's old platform,' Grace said casually, as if she'd just completed a mundane household chore. 'It's up for a vote. If we put it in place, the trap may not work.'

Harley paced around his desk, his heavy boots making loud, percussive echoes on the maple floor. 'Obviously, my vote is to hold off. It doesn't have to be for long.'

Annie gave a reluctant nod of assent. 'As repugnant as it is to concur with you on anything, Harley, I confess that sounds reasonable.'

Annie and Harley agreeing, the end of the world, Grace thought. 'Roadrunner, what do you say?'

He nodded. 'Yeah, hold off a while. Bit Monster's not expecting things to happen overnight.'

'How is the new code coming along, sugar?'

Roadrunner shrugged. 'It's going okay.'

'You're usually not ambivalent about coding,' Annie observed.

'I'm having trouble focusing today.'

'Little wonder, you've got some unfinished business.'

'What do you mean?'

'I mean, when you save somebody's life, you don't just walk away when you find out they're okay. The shared trauma ties you together, even if you never see them again.'

'That's sort of what Petra said.'

'See? And Good Samaritans always meet up with the person they saved once they're out of the hospital. It's closure for both parties. If you ever watched afternoon talk shows, you'd know this.'

'I can't just show up on her doorstep – she might think I'm a stalker.'

'You said she didn't have anybody to visit her in the

hospital, that she's alone. If that's the case, I think she'd be grateful for the company,' Grace pointed out. 'Has she been discharged?'

Roadrunner nodded sheepishly. 'I checked.'

'I thought you might have.'

Harley folded his arms across his barrel chest. 'For God's sake, go see her and get your closure. Just don't show up empty-handed.'

'I already brought her flowers.'

'Christ, you have no imagination. Bring her some food. She just got out of the hospital, and I can tell you, from unfortunate personal experience, the only thing you want after you get cut loose from that shitty experience is real food somebody else cooked.'

Grace smiled at him. 'I have an idea.'

26

Petra wondered if she'd ever feel warm again. She turned the thermostat up to eighty and clicked on the fireplace remote before settling on the hearth to absorb the heat of the gas flames. The doctor had suggested she stay in the hospital longer for observation, but what was the point? Her core body temperature was back to normal, she was rehydrated after drinking too much vodka, and everything was fine. A little brush with death was nothing new to her. Nothing at all.

She'd been stupid. And she felt guilty. The Level I trauma center she'd visited had more pressing things to worry about than a tranquilized, half-drunk woman, who'd been careless enough to wander out in a dangerously cold night to pass out on a park bench. It wouldn't happen again. When she needed to drink vodka, take lorazepam, and pass out, she would stay home.

She didn't feel any different mentally, and didn't know if she should. Maybe there would be some lingering shock or distress, some incapacitating post-traumatic manifestation that would plague her later. But those feelings were so normal to her, she probably wouldn't be able to determine which trauma was the culprit. The overall emotion she felt now was vacancy: loneliness.

Lonely people checked their phones, so she did. There were no messages, just texts: one from Martin, saying how nice it had been to see her, two from her bank, alerting her that automatic payments had been made to her mortgage and credit card. The third and final one was from early this morning: Blanca, asking her to call back as soon as she could.

Sweet, crazy Blanca. No doubt she'd had some kind of a vision and would exhort her to come in for a Tarot reading or some other ouija board nonsense. But she loved Blanca, loved her cozy, disorganized shop filled with strange objects she swore held magical properties. Aside from Martin, she was the closest thing to a friend Petra had, and that was exactly what she needed right now.

Petra called her, left a message, then sent a text. While she waited for a response, she made tea and wandered around her house, grateful she'd survived to brush dust from neglected surfaces and pick lint from the rugs after her two weeks abroad. She had Roadrunner to thank for that and wondered if she could construct a new friendship with him. Maybe it was something to explore in the future. They were neighbors, after all.

Her suitcase was still sitting at the foot of the stairs. She unzipped the outer pocket and took the file Martin had given her to the sitting room, where she curled up on the sofa in front of the fire. The flames were mesmerizing, rising from a bed of pumice stones, and nearly put her to sleep before she'd even opened the file. But after reading the cover page, she was wide awake. Martin had undersold his work, because there was good information here.

He'd finally tracked Peter Praljik's illegal entry into the United States under false refugee status in 1996, something they hadn't known before. Another thing they hadn't known was his last-known alias, Peter Saveride, and his last-known address, in Forest Lake, Minnesota, where the trail had gone cold in 2008. Now she had a real place to start, and right in her backyard.

Her hands became unpredictable flighty things, trembling like butterfly wings as she punched Martin's number into her phone. She unconsciously resurrected a bad habit and gnawed on her thumbnail while she listened to a robotic female voice telling her to leave a message.

'Damnit, Martin, I just started reading the file and now you're not answering. Call me back as soon as you can.'

Petra returned to the file and immersed herself in it to the exclusion of everything else. She was unaware of time passing, of the sun making its downward trek in the winter sky, filling her house with gloom. Even the knock on her door didn't dispel her focus – whoever it was, they would go away soon, because it was too cold to stand outside anybody's door, begging for a signature on a petition or hawking whatever they were trying to sell.

It suddenly occurred to her that nobody did door-to-door anything in January, yet they kept knocking, more insistently. And that finally shattered her concentration. She stomped irritably toward the door, then saw the yellow daisies on the foyer table, which moderated her mood. She had absolutely no reason to believe or hope it might be Roadrunner, but they had a connection now and she was certain he'd felt it, understood it, so she couldn't eliminate it as a possibility.

It wasn't Roadrunner. It was two men, one a short, slight redhead, the other an imposing African American who dwarfed his companion. They looked ridiculous together, but not dangerous. 'Can I help you?'

They both presented police shields. 'Minneapolis detectives McLaren and Freedman. Are you Petra Juric?'

Police? 'Yes.'

'We'd like to speak with you about Blanca Szabo.'

'Blanca? Is something wrong?'

'May we come in?'

Petra's throat tightened. Something was obviously very wrong. 'Of course.' She ushered them inside and closed the door, shivering with the chill that had followed them in. 'Tell me what's happened.'

The redhead spoke. Was he McLaren or Freedman? 'I'm sorry, ma'am, Blanca Szabo was murdered in her shop sometime early this morning.'

She gasped reflexively, but there didn't seem to be any air in the room. 'I need to sit down.' She retreated to the living room and took her place on the sofa as if nothing had happened, because what the detectives had just told her was impossible. They'd made a mistake. Surely they'd made a mistake.

'We're here because you were listed as her emergency contact on her phone.'

That, more than anything, brought her back to reality and made her eyes sting with tears.

'Are you family?'

'No. Blanca doesn't have any living family, but she is an old friend.'

'She sent you a text late last night, asking you to call her. You hadn't had contact with her for a while before that.'

Petra felt herself withdrawing to the familiar mental sanctuary where nothing could reach her. 'She didn't communicate often. Not with living humans, anyhow. She was a medium and dwelled in a different realm. You obviously have her phone.'

'We do.'

'So you probably know I didn't respond until recently.'

'Is there a reason you didn't respond earlier?'

'I didn't get the text until a few hours ago. I was in the ICU at Hennepin County Medical Center. Hypothermia. Things might be different if I'd gotten to it earlier.' She saw pity in their faces and looked away.

'So you think she might have been calling you for help?'

'She never has before, she's never needed help, but considering she was murdered . . . yes. It's a possibility.'

'Were you aware of any troubles, any concerns she had for her safety?'

'Not at all. Blanca didn't have issues with anyone. Her life was with her spirits – she barely had contact with the outside world. Except for me, she had no friends. And if you don't associate with people, you have no enemies, either. You don't believe it was random?'

'We don't think it was a robbery. She had a box of cash in her office that was untouched, and she was wearing a gold necklace that looked very valuable.'

Her amber necklace. Her great-grandmother's. 'It is very valuable. It's a family heirloom.'

'There wasn't a computer at her shop. That's the only thing that might have been stolen.'

'She didn't own a computer. Her phone was her only concession to modern communication.'

The detectives both raised their brows. 'Did she ever mention any troubles with clients?'

'Never. She had a very loyal clientele. She was loved.'

'She also accepted walk-ins.'

'She did, but I can't imagine you're looking for a walk-in client who was so disenchanted by their psychic reading that they were driven to kill over it. If you believe in that sort of thing, it wouldn't be very good karma, would it?' She pressed her hands against her temples, trying to hold things inside. 'I'm sorry, Detectives, I didn't mean to sound dismissive. I'm just very upset.'

'You have every reason to be.'

Her words were sounding so hollow, so bereft of the sorrow and regret she felt. Two pairs of sympathetic eyes watched her, but they were also gauging her expressions, her moves, assessing everything she did, as if she was a suspect. And, from a cop's point of view, she probably was. 'How was she killed?'

The two detectives shared an uncomfortable look. Then the African-American man spoke softly, in a rumbling, smooth bass that hit a rare frequency in the human range. 'We really can't discuss details at this point, ma'am.'

'I'll find out eventually, along with everybody else. I *have* to know.' She was surprised by the urgency in her voice. 'This may sound strange, but I owe it to her to know what her last moments were.'

Petra felt the resistance, still there but weakening. 'What you say won't surprise me or shock me, Detectives. I'm well-acquainted with human wickedness. Blanca was, too.'

His eyes softened, his expression changed, and so did his partner's. They knew human wickedness, too. It was part of their job to know it, just like it was part of hers.

'The details won't be released until the investigation is complete . . .'

'I certainly won't share them. Even if I had someone to share them with, what would be the point?'

'The cause of death is uncertain right now. Her neck was broken, but she also had duct tape covering her mouth, nose and eyes, so she may have been suffocated. We won't know which came first until the autopsy.'

Petra felt her face cooling as the blood leached out of it. It was such an odd feeling, and she wondered where all that blood had gone. The detectives' sympathetic eyes were now curious, hopeful, maybe even suspicious.

'Does that mean something to you, ma'am?'

'No.'

'Are you sure? It could help us if it does.'

'I'm sure. It's just shocking. Either way, a horrible way for my friend to die.'

They stayed silent, waiting for her to say something more. But there was nothing else to say, so she waited them out.

'Ms Szabo came to City Hall to speak with some detectives yesterday morning. She said she'd had a vision of a homicide. Would you know anything about that?'

Petra shook her head sadly. 'No, but Blanca has . . . had visions all the time. She genuinely believed she had a special gift, but I knew her for a very long time, and the visions were always amalgamations of past experiences or sometimes based on dreams she'd had. Even though they weren't grounded in reality, they seemed very real to her.'

'So she was delusional?'

'Not in the clinical sense, no, I don't believe so. She simply lived in a world of her own creation. She didn't want to be a part of this one.'

'Okay, thanks for speaking with us.' They stood and gave her their cards. 'Please call us if you think of anything that might help.'

She nodded and her head felt heavy, a strange, leaden thing on the stalk of her neck, as she walked them to the door. When they drove away, she retreated to the warmth of the fire and called Martin again. He still wasn't answering, so she left another message with the infuriatingly soulless robot.

'Martin, Blanca was murdered. I think Peter Praljik is still here.'

27

'She was different,' Freedman said, once they were in the car. 'Intense. She's got an investigative mind, too.'

'She turned white as a sheet when you laid out Blanca's scene. She's not giving us something.'

'I don't know about that. We both turned white as a sheet when we walked into that crime scene. Well, you're already so pasty white, who could tell? And you could soak me in a barrel of bleach for two weeks and I'd never turn white, but you know what I'm saying.'

'Petra admitted Blanca might have been calling for help. And she made the call last night, but she was killed this morning. There are some deeper waters here.'

'So, she had suspicions about a client, like Magozzi said. She tries to call her friend to talk about it, next thing she knows the client shows up and kills her. Her appointment book might tell the story. What do you think about the duct tape?'

'It made sense that it was a tool of opportunity until I saw Petra's face. She winced when you brought up the broken neck, but her real reaction was when you mentioned the tape. And the fact that Blanca's eyes were covered bothers me. Whether she died from a broken neck or suffocation, it was superfluous, nothing to do with her death.'

'Maybe he didn't want her to see what was coming.'

'If he'd taped her before he killed her, she would have

fought. Anant didn't see any defensive wounds and neither did we.'

Freedman looked at his partner skeptically. 'You think it's a message?'

'I'm not counting it out.'

'For whom?'

'Maybe it was a message for Petra and she got the picture. I'm telling you, Freedman, her reaction was strange.'

Magozzi and Gino were back at City Hall, but no follow-ups or preliminary reports had come through yet, so they started bundling up for their frozen foray to the Ramage house to get Kelly's computer. They hadn't even escaped their cubicle when Magozzi's phone interrupted them. 'Los Angeles area code, Gino. It's Westwood.' He put it on speaker and they heard the background clamor of a big city cop shop. 'Detective Magozzi.'

'Jared Lerner, LAPD. You called about Delia Sellman?'

'Yes. Thanks for the callback, Detective. We just pulled a case here in Minneapolis that's similar, a bondage scenario. My partner and I are hoping you can help us out.'

'I'll do my best, but you know the Sellman case was never solved, right?'

'We know. We also understand that she was bound and suffocated. Any sexual assault?'

'No. The only thing we got were a couple partial male prints in her bathroom that didn't synch with anybody she knew, and they didn't match anything on any registry. The scene was pretty slick, so we figured this guy had been operating before, but we never found an MO match on any violent-criminal database. We finally had to drop it because of manpower, so I'm glad to hear from you.' He paused, covered his phone, and shouted something unintelligible. 'Sorry about that, we're busy today. Anyway, back to physical evidence. Do you have any?'

'It's early. We're still waiting on results from the lab and the autopsy. We don't think she was sexually assaulted, but there was definitely a sexual component. She was nude and spread-eagled, and we believe it was a consensual encounter, at least at first. She'd been exploring BDSM.'

Jared Lerner paused for a moment. 'Same with Delia Sellman. What you'd call bondage curious, I guess. She'd been in regular contact with someone new a month or so before her murder, so we chased every tail imaginable, but we couldn't track it down. She was using an anonymous chat app. How is the Sellman case on your radar, anyhow? It was a year ago and it didn't get much national coverage.'

'We ran into the victim's sister at a Rado protest this morning.'

'Ah. Annabelle. She took a semester off school to come out here and fight like hell for her sister, but the Rado connection never panned out. He has a bunch of twisted groupies, for sure, but there was nothing. There's a Rado show in Minneapolis now?'

'It opened last night – the night our vic was killed.'

'Delia Sellman was murdered on the night of a Rado opening in West Hollywood. Looks like we've got ourselves a pattern. The timing could be some acolyte's twisted version of a congratulatory gift to his idol, like a cat dropping a dead mouse on the front steps. I hope he made a mistake in Minneapolis.'

Magozzi appreciated the way Lerner's mind worked. He

also appreciated the fact that he hadn't given up on Delia Sellman, even though his current caseload was probably bigger than his and Gino's for an entire year. 'We'll take a look at other cities where there were Rado shows. Did you place Delia Sellman at the gallery?'

'She was there, but she didn't have contact with anyone that we could see from the surveillance.'

'The more you tell us, the more this is sounding like a mirror image of our case. Did your perp use duct tape in any way?'

Lerner coughed into the phone, like he was choking on something. 'Delia Sellman's nose and mouth were covered with it, but that never saw the light of day. The official line is she was suffocated with a pillow, because we found one over her face, but the tape was the murder weapon. We're keeping it off the record as exclusionary evidence.'

'Our vic's head was entirely wrapped in it.'

'Jesus.'

'Did Delia have duct tape over her eyes?'

'No. Why?'

'We have another homicide here, just this morning. Her eyes, nose and mouth were covered with duct tape, but nothing else synchs, no sexual component. We're looking for connections.'

A few urgent background shouts emanated from Magozzi's phone, then Lerner covered his and barked, 'Give me a second! Listen, Detective Magozzi, we definitely need to talk more, but I've gotta run. Call my personal phone later when you have some more info.' He rushed through the numbers, then hung up.

'Son of a bitch,' Gino mumbled. 'Rado is a traveling freak show in more ways than one.'

28

Petra lived in a Victorian at the end of Roadrunner's street. He'd never paid much attention to it before, but in the snowy January landscape, its colorful façade and lacy gable trim seemed whimsical and reminded him of a holiday gingerbread house.

He knocked lightly on the dark green door, and a few moments later, she opened it with a smile, but her eyes were red-rimmed and glassy, as if she'd been crying.

'I was hoping you would visit,' she said, gesturing him in out of the cold.

'I would have called first, but your number is unlisted.'

'A computer genius like you couldn't find an unlisted number? I find that hard to believe.'

He blinked in surprise. 'You looked me up.'

'I wanted to know a little bit more about the Roadrunner who saved my life. There are hundreds of articles on you and your partners in Monkeewrench and your work with law enforcement, so it wasn't a difficult task. You do wonderful work.'

There was that odd lilt in her voice again, there and gone in an instant, the barest indication that her tongue might be familiar with another language. Or perhaps it was the lingering remnants of a speech impairment that had been overcome in childhood. 'So you know I'm not a stalker.'

'I don't know that for certain, but I'll take your word for it.'

Roadrunner shifted his backpack off his shoulder. 'I brought you some homemade soup. Three kinds.'

'How lovely of you. So you're something in the kitchen, too?'

'No, but my colleague Grace is. We thought you might not be in the mood to cook.'

'You're right about that. Thank her for me. Come in and warm up by the fire.'

'I can't stay. I just wanted to drop this off . . .'

'Please. Just for a little while. I could use the company.'

Roadrunner reluctantly followed her into a room done in muted shades of gray and yellow, clean and modern. But there were also brightly painted ceramics, elaborately embroidered pillows and wall hangings, wooden carvings. They seemed out of place, but he liked them.

It was a sitting room, not an office, but paperwork was everywhere: stacked haphazardly on a side table, scattered all over a leather sofa, spilling out of file folders. A laptop computer sat open on a coffee table. 'I'm interrupting work.'

'The work won't go anywhere. Sit down, make yourself comfortable.'

There was nothing comfortable about the situation – it had the same surreal quality as his visit to her hospital room, but Roadrunner tried to shake off his apprehension and took a wing chair by the fire. 'Are you feeling okay?'

'Physically, yes. Mentally, no. I just learned my friend was murdered.'

It was a shocking thing to hear and Roadrunner had trouble finding words – in his mind, they all seemed so trite. He wondered if Magozzi and Gino felt the same way whenever they had to give such a notification and express their condolences. 'I'm so sorry,' he finally said.

'Detective McLaren and Detective Freedman just left a little while ago. You must know them, with all the work you do for the Minneapolis Police.'

'Sure, I know them. They're excellent detectives and even better men. They'll solve your friend's murder.'

'I hope they will.'

The awkward silence that followed heightened tiny insignificant details of the strange, frozen moment. Road-runner was suddenly hyper-aware of the heat of the fire starting to prickle the skin on his neck, the soft ticking of a clock, Petra's sad dark eyes watching him. He focused on the paperwork, which seemed safe and neutral. 'What are you working on? If you don't mind me asking.'

'I'm looking for someone. A very bad person. That's what I do for a living.'

He lifted his brows. 'You're law enforcement?'

'I'm an historian who inadvertently got into law enforcement. I'm sorry, I'm being so rude. Would you like something to drink, Roadrunner? I'm drinking tea. Or would you like something stronger?'

'Nothing – thank you, though. What type of law enforcement?'

'I work for a special investigation unit of Immigration and Customs Enforcement.'

'What do you do for them?'

'I hunt down war criminals from the Balkan conflict. People seem to have forgotten about it, even though it wasn't that long ago.'

'The Yugoslavian War of Independence.'

'I see you haven't forgotten it. But I don't call it that. I call it the most complicated civil war in history. There were so many conflicts, insurgencies, and individual wars of independence. Today's borders tell the story.' She paused and sipped from her mug. 'We estimate that there are still between three and six hundred in the United States, butchers and their henchmen who have evaded justice all this time, living normal lives.'

'I had no idea. What happens when you find them?'

'They're deported to stand trial, either in their home countries or the international court at The Hague.'

'Are they hard to find?'

'Very. There was no access to wartime records when the refugees started coming to the US, so it wasn't possible to know if they'd lied about who they were on their applications. The system was based on people telling the truth, and of course they didn't. The records we do have now are incomplete, because militant groups destroyed many of them before the war was over. Or they were simply lost in the destruction.'

'Where do you start?'

'By looking for puzzle pieces to put together, often thousands of them: military and police records, eye-witness accounts, interviews with concentration-camp survivors, records of crimes written on old scrap paper. We've even found evidence hidden in children's schoolbooks recovered from villages where massacres took place. We search everywhere.'

Roadrunner thought of all the atrocities, the genocide he'd read about as a country was torn to pieces and neighbors became mortal enemies. It was almost impossible to comprehend. 'I hope you find them all eventually.'

'That's what I work on every day.'

'This man you're looking for, do you know much about him?'

'He was one of the worst butchers of all. *Vrag* means devil – that was his sobriquet. I also think he's here in Minnesota. My colleague tracked him to Forest Lake, but he disappeared in 2008. No sign of him since – at least that we've found so far.'

'That was a long time ago. He could be anywhere now.'

She tipped her head and considered. 'He could be, but I have a feeling he didn't go far.'

Roadrunner took a deep breath. 'We might be able to help you.'

'No, absolutely not. You have your own work, and it's equally important.'

'This is part of the work we do.'

'I already have a debt to you I'll never be able to repay. Adding another is bad luck.'

'We don't believe in bad luck.' He gestured to her papers. 'If you give me a copy of what you have on him, we can at least look. It won't take any time at all. We have a giant parallel processor called The Beast that runs special software we developed to do exactly this sort of thing. As a matter of fact, I can't imagine why your agency hasn't requested the software. There's a version that's compatible with standard equipment.'

'Our division has a tight budget.'

'It's free to law enforcement.'

Her eyes shone in the firelight. Roadrunner couldn't tell if it was from tears or just a trick of the light. 'That's very kind of you.' She gathered up some loose papers and put them in

135

a manila file folder. 'His name is Peter Praljik. Last-known alias is Peter Saveride. He's the man we're looking for.'

Roadrunner took the folder and stared at the tab, which read 'THE DEAD CITY' in block letters. The name of the opera Harley listened to all the time. 'What does "the dead city" mean?'

Petra touched the scar on her face, but it wasn't a conscious gesture. 'That's what we called our village when Vrag and his men were finished. It was one of the greatest massacres of the war. Not just men and soldiers, but women, children, babies, the elderly and infirm, all the most helpless souls. Even family pets.' She looked down at her lap. 'The few who survived suffered worse.'

Roadrunner felt a cold chill slither up his spine as he suddenly understood the ephemeral trace of an accent that occasionally colored her speech. 'You were there.'

She nodded.

'You were just a child then.'

'I was eleven when they took me. My friend who was murdered last night – Blanca – she saved me, and later I saved her. We escaped together and came here. So now you see why I have such an intricate and strange rapport with death. Perhaps a fascination with it. The fear of it is always with us, Roadrunner. In different ways, but always there.' Unexpectedly, she grasped his lumpy, misshapen hands in hers and held them tight. 'This happened when you were young. Your bones were never properly set.'

He recoiled from her touch, but her grip was unyielding. She wouldn't let go.

'You're no stranger to cruelty, either. Who did this to you?'

Roadrunner was suddenly swept back in time, ten years

old again, pinned down in a chair at the kitchen table, watching in horror as the hammer came crashing down on his hands over and over again. There was excruciating pain, but the sounds – the crunch of bones and the wails of his mother – those were what he remembered most. 'My stepfather,' he finally said quietly.

'And that's how you came up with your name. You were always running.'

'I found an old bike in the neighbor's trash and fixed it up so I could get away. My mother wasn't that lucky. I don't know why I'm telling you this.'

'Stories are told when they're ready to be told, so it must be time. What happened to your stepfather?'

'He died.'

'Did you kill him?'

Roadrunner didn't respond, couldn't respond, and in that blinding instant, Petra Juric knew he bore the stain of a murderer. She was the only person in the world who did – even Grace and Harley and Annie didn't know – and he couldn't understand how that had happened.

When she drew him into her arms and hugged him tight, he didn't understand how that had happened either, but it felt good, and he hugged her back.

'You and I, we're the same,' she whispered in his ear. 'We refuse to be victims.'

29

Annabelle's throat felt swollen and raw and she couldn't stop shivering, even though she'd been sitting in cozy La Cucaracha for half an hour, drinking hot coffee with sugar and whipped cream. She risked a glance at herself in the mirror behind the bar. There were dark smudges beneath her eyes and her skin was pale, not in a good, porcelain-doll way. She was fighting some nasty bug and her immune system was losing the battle.

She turned away before somebody would notice her staring at herself and mistake it for vanity. Not that anybody would pay much attention to the unremarkable young woman at the bar. She had always felt invisible, isolated, and she'd retreated further into her protective shell since Delia's death.

Sometimes she felt like her zealous mission for justice was the only thing that gave her a sense of purpose. As long as she was fighting, her life had true meaning. And when she was fighting, people noticed her, and she had to admit it was a good feeling. The detectives had listened to her today, had taken her seriously, and that renewed her hope.

She sipped her coffee and thought about Delia. She'd gotten all the good genes: the pretty genes, the gregarious genes, the ones that made her the star of the family and would make her a star anywhere she wanted to go. Annabelle had never resented her for it: she'd just been happy to orbit the dazzling light that was her sister. And then Delia's bright star had become a black hole, just like that, devoured by a darkness from which there was no return. She wouldn't stop until her killer was behind bars.

La Cuc was usually quiet this early, but it was filling fast as a continuous wave of bodies pressed through the doors. The atmosphere was alive, vibrant, and she tried to absorb some of the energy, feed off it, but whatever aura surrounded her seemed to repel it. Still, there was comfort in the noise, the excitement, the promise of something, and better than going back to her lonely apartment to wait for the meeting at Greta's later.

'Are you sure you don't want a little whiskey in your coffee? It's not an Irish coffee without it, you know.'

Was the cute bartender with the mischievous smile flirting with her? She smiled back, hoping it would mitigate her pall of sickness. 'Thanks, but I think I'm fighting a cold, so I'll stick with the non-Irish coffee.'

'Just give me a shout if you change your mind. It's on me,' he called over his shoulder, as he hustled down to the other end of the bar where a new batch of arrivals were clamoring, holding out fistfuls of money in the hope of getting served first. She looked at the single empty barstool next to her. As crowded as the place was, no one had taken it, because they were in groups and they'd rather stand together than be stuck sitting alone next to the sick girl. She laid a twenty on the counter and waited patiently for the bartender to come back and give her change.

'Is this seat taken, Miss?'

She started and looked at the man standing to her right. He was older than she was, with an attractive but weary face. He had on a black knit cap and wore a working man's clothes beneath an open black parka. There was some stubble sprouting on his chin, like he'd just gotten off a long shift and needed a drink. 'No.'

'Then you don't mind?'

'Please. I'm sorry.'

'For what?' he asked, sitting down next to her.

'I didn't mean to be rude. I'm just tired.'

'You weren't rude, and I'm tired, too, so we'll be good company. We can just sit here and be tired together. Can I buy you a drink?'

'I'm good, thanks.'

'That sounded bad, didn't it? Like a pathetic pick-up line.'

Annabelle smiled a little. 'Kind of.'

'I'm not that guy, but from the looks of the crowd, I'll bet there are a lot of them here. Something must be going on at the Target Center.'

'Probably. It's not usually this crowded in the afternoon.'

'So you're a regular?'

'I wouldn't say I'm a regular, but I live nearby and they have excellent Mexican food.'

'Good to know. My name is Lance, by the way.'

'Annabelle.'

'Nice to meet you. I won't bother you anymore, promise.'

Awful as she felt, she wasn't bothered at all. Lance was a

pleasant distraction and turned out to be a congenial bar companion. The small-talk they shared took her out of the dark places in her head and she found herself enjoying the easy camaraderie of two strangers making idle chat in a crowded bar.

Lance ordered a margarita and a basket of jalapeño poppers, which he shared with her. The heat from the chili peppers made her nose run, and she excused herself to go to the restroom and blow it. When she came back, there was a fresh virgin Irish coffee waiting for her. Once she'd slurped off all the whipped cream and drunk part of it, she asked the bartender for a new one, because it was too bitter, like the dregs from an old pot that had been scorched on the hotplate.

They talked some more, about the weather and hockey and who was going to win the Super Bowl. She told him she was a history major at St Thomas and found out he worked for the home-repair division of Xcel Energy and was on overtime, helping to handle the influx of cold-related furnace failures.

When a plate of enchiladas appeared on the bar in front of them, Annabelle started feeling really sick. She shouldn't have eaten all those jalapeño poppers. Lance continued to talk, but she couldn't process what he was saying, because her thoughts were starting to splinter as soon as they formed, and she was having trouble keeping her eyes open. Even her speech seemed slurred and she knew she had to get home and sleep.

'Is something wrong, Annabelle?' Lance's voice seemed very far away, and his face wavered in and out of focus.

'I . . . I don't know. I need to go home.' She watched his lips curl up in a strange smile, not his normal smile, and she thought she heard him chuckle. Why did he think this was funny?

'But we're having such a good time. Besides, home is boring. I have a better idea.'

30

Tommy Espinoza strolled into Homicide with a satisfied grin and placed Kelly Ramage's phone on the neutral border between Magozzi's and Gino's conjoined desks. 'Full access, my friends.'

Gino gave him a fist bump. 'Way to go, Tommy.'

'I took a look to make sure you could get into everything. It's wide open, no lock boxes or any other additional security. She wasn't very judicious about clearing her browsing history either. It goes back months and it's plenty interesting.'

Magozzi started scrolling through the phone. 'How so?'

'She spent a lot of time on a site called BaDSaMmatch. com. BDSM in all caps. It's a hook-up site, like Tindr, except for bondage aficionados. It's the only site like it she visited, and she visited regularly.'

Gino rubbed his hands together. 'She met her killer on the site. What do you bet?'

'It's a good one. She had an account, but it's password-protected, no surprise there. I looked for a password-storage app, but she keeps them someplace else. Does she have a personal computer? A lot of people keep a list there.'

'We've been trying to get out the door for the past half-hour to go get it.'

'Ah. That's why you're sitting at your desks in your coats. I wondered. So things are popping for you?'

'Sluggishly popping. We've got a possible connection to a murder in LA and another one here.'

'How is that sluggish?'

'Because we don't have anybody in cuffs yet. Can you take a look at Kelly Ramage's computer today?'

'I'm all yours until the next big thing comes along.'

Gino scoffed. 'You sound like my junior-high girlfriend.'

'She said that to you?'

'Nah, but it was expressly implied. Anything else, Tommy?'

'Yeah. Kelly Ramage stopped visiting BaDSaM about a month ago when she loaded Signal. It's an anonymous messaging app and it works like any other texting program, but the content is encrypted.'

'So she could chat privately with her match. With her killer.' Magozzi looked at Gino. 'Just like Delia Sellman.'

Tommy frowned. 'Who's Delia Sellman?'

'The LA victim. She was using an anonymous chat app, too. Tell us about Signal.'

'It's awesome, which is a problem. It has a disappearing-message feature, which means the user can let messages self-destruct in as little as five seconds or up to a week. Poof.'

'But there's still a contact log associated with a phone number, right?'

'Yeah, but depending on how smart the user is, there are workarounds, ways to conceal your identity, use a different phone number not associated with your personal information. I'm going to have to dig into it.'

'Signal doesn't sound like the kind of thing an average suburbanite like Kelly Ramage would have on her radar,'

Magozzi pointed out. 'Especially one who isn't security-minded enough to clear her browsing history.'

'Right. I'm guessing it was the killer's idea and she climbed on board thinking she could keep her secret from her husband. It's easy to use once you install it. Go get her computer and I'll keep working it from this end.'

31

Todd Ramage was alone and he looked as desolate and broken as a human being could. He was still wearing his suit, but it looked as abused as he did, like he'd spent the night on a bench in a bus station. He seemed lost in his own house as he led Magozzi and Gino to a sunken seating area with a large stone fireplace. There was no cheery, crackling blaze warming the hearth tonight – it was in mourning along with its owner.

There was a half-drunk glass of red wine on the coffee-table, which seemed so sad to Magozzi, even sadder than the dark fireplace. On any normal Friday evening, there would have been two glasses and two people.

Todd drank the rest of his wine and sagged into a puffy velvet sofa. 'I'm glad you're here, Detectives. I arrived an hour ago and I couldn't even go into the bedroom to change. I can't stand this. Kelly is everywhere, but she's nowhere. She's gone.' He looked up at them with glassy, swollen eyes. 'Please tell me what happened. This may seem twisted, but I'd rather know the worst than not know anything at all.'

'It doesn't seem twisted at all, Mr Ramage. Uncertainty makes it difficult to process the death of a loved one.' Magozzi cringed inwardly, because he sounded like a shrink, and he hated shrinks. There was truth to what he said, but his delivery sucked.

Todd's brows lifted as he ran a hand along the grizzled

stubble on his jaw. 'Yes, that's exactly it. Thank you for understanding.'

'We haven't spoken with the medical examiner yet, but we believe your wife was suffocated. There were no signs of breaking or entering at Eleanor's place, no signs of struggle, and several things about the scene indicated that it had been a planned meeting.'

He dragged his hands down his cheeks. 'She was having an affair, then.'

'We're not sure about that.'

'What do you mean? You said you thought it was planned.'

'This could have been her only encounter.'

'I don't understand.'

'Mr Ramage, do you know anything about a website called BaDSaMmatch?'

He shook his head. 'No. What is it?'

'It's a meet-up site for people who are into bondage and sado-masochism. Your wife had an account.'

Magozzi had expected shocked disbelief, denial, anything but narrowed, angry eyes. This wasn't a surprise to Todd Ramage.

'Bondage,' he said in a flat voice. Not a question, a statement.

'Yes, sir. It was an element in the crime scene.' The antiseptic language sounded cold and impersonal, but it was a hell of a lot better than laying out the ugly details. Todd Ramage was enduring his own torture right now, and it just seemed cruel to elaborate on his wife's.

'Kelly was fascinated by it,' he continued bitterly. 'And by auto-erotic asphyxiation. But I – I couldn't. It was repulsive to me. I loved Kelly, and you don't debase people you love.'

Gino cleared his throat. 'You didn't suspect that she might have been exploring it on her own?'

'God, no. Never. I thought it was a flight of fancy. She was younger, and a little wild, but . . .' He put his head into his hands. 'But she was obviously compelled to find some-body who would . . . do those things. And he killed her.'

'We're sorry, Mr Ramage.'

'I never understood it. But maybe I should have tried harder. She had a difficult childhood, a very cruel, abusive father. He tried to drown her once, in the bathtub. He almost succeeded.'

Magozzi looked at Gino, who gave no indication that he remembered Blanca Szabo talking about the victim in her premonition almost drowning.

A tear tracked down his cheek and he brushed it away absently. 'I wish she'd talked to me. Or that I'd talked to her. Please tell me you're getting close to finding the bas-tard who killed her.'

'We're working multiple leads right now, but we need her computer. There might be something useful there.'

'Of course, anything.' He led them to his wife's study, where there was a closed laptop computer on a neat oak desk. No knick-knacks or clutter, just a notebook with a pair of kittens on the cover and a wedding photo in a heart-shaped silver frame.

'That's Kelly's computer. I didn't touch it, as you asked.' He gestured to the notebook. 'You should take this, too. It has a list of all her passwords and phone numbers. She liked to keep a hard copy in an old-fashioned place in case we were ever robbed.' His breath hitched. 'She said that no robber would ever think of taking a notebook with kittens on the front.'

148

Magozzi had initially wanted to jump and click his heels together when Todd Ramage had offered the notebook of passwords, but the poignant detail that followed crushed the joy. 'Thank you.'

'She loved cats. Especially kittens. Who doesn't love kittens? I'm allergic, but she showed me a website once with cats that are supposed to be hypoallergenic. I should have bought her a pair right then and there.' He shook his head. 'You must hear this all the time, the regrets of surviving family members. I can't seem to remember anything I did right, just the things I didn't do or did wrong.'

Gino, as bullish as he was, had some deft skill in handling the bereaved. 'What happened wasn't your fault, Mr Ramage. It was a tragedy. Don't let it take away your good memories. That's what you have and it's how you'll get through this.'

He nodded woodenly. 'It's good advice. I hope I can follow it.'

'Were you able to spend some time with friends and family today?'

'Mostly on the phone. Eleanor's flight arrives in a few hours, and Kelly's mother is flying in tomorrow morning. My family is on their way down from Duluth. Thank you for asking.'

'Take care of yourself, Mr Ramage. You have our cards, call us anytime.'

He nodded, then left them to box up the computer – Todd Ramage wasn't interested in watching them remove evidence from his wife's office. With her notebook of passwords in hand, the computer wasn't as critical now, but there was always the possibility that she kept some of her secrets there and no place else. Tommy would let them know.

As they left the room a little emptier and sadder than it had been a few minutes ago, Magozzi noticed a shelf stuffed with books on fashion, film and art. One of the larger volumes was titled: *RADO – A Syzygy of Art and Technology*. He pulled it off the shelf and paged through, seeing some of the same disturbing images he and Gino had observed in person today. No secret notes or scribblings in margins, although a book like that would be a good place to hide them – most people would throw it across the room in disgust after the first few pages.

Todd Ramage walked them to the front foyer, a replenished glass of wine in his hand, and a few drops sloshed on the floor. He didn't seem to care about that or how his evening would end, because his world had already ended, at least in the short term, but he was still gracious. 'Thank you for your attention, Detectives. I know you'll find out who killed my wife and that gives me peace.'

'We will, sir.' Magozzi paused at the door while Gino trundled the computer out to the car. 'Mr Ramage, did your wife visit fortune-tellers or mediums?'

Todd Ramage looked at him curiously. 'Not that I know of, but as I found out today, she kept things from me.' He took a hefty gulp of wine. 'That's a strange question. Why do you ask?'

'It's nothing, just an unrelated detail. They come up sometimes in the course of an investigation so we have to ask, just to cover every possible angle.'

'You're being thorough. As an accountant, I appreciate that.'

32

While Gino ran the computer to Tommy, Magozzi stopped in the break room to grab a sludgy cup of coffee he hoped wasn't decaf. There wasn't much left on the snack table, so he took a pass, even though he was starving. He had fleeting thoughts of his conversation with Gino about the Donner party and decided to order pizza, double cheese, sausage and pepperoni. Plenty of fat: no way he was going to die from protein poisoning tonight.

McLaren and Freedman were at their desks when he walked into Homicide. McLaren looked tired or hung-over or both; Freedman was sorting Skittles by color and arranging them on the edge of his desk. Magozzi didn't ask – they all had their foibles and nervous habits when they were deep into a case.

'What's the latest on Blanca?'

Freedman looked very unhappy. 'She was a hermit, by all accounts, and none of her clients are good for the murder – we went through her appointment book and talked to every damn one of them. No notes about any walk-ins and the woman didn't own a computer.'

Magozzi stripped off his coat and gloves and sagged into his chair, rubbing his frozen hands together in the hope he'd get some circulation back. 'Blanca said the woman in her vision almost drowned once. We just found out Kelly Ramage almost drowned when she was younger. There could be a connection there.'

McLaren rolled his bloodshot eyes away from his computer screen. 'Kelly wasn't in her list of clients, and there was no other personal connection that we could find, but where the hell would we find it? She only had one contact on her phone, and it wasn't Kelly.'

Freedman folded his big arms across his bigger chest. 'Minnesota is the Land of Ten Thousand Lakes. I almost drowned once, and so has half the population. Don't tell me you're starting to buy into the psychic stuff.'

'For God's sake, I'm just looking for links. So, no skeletons in Blanca's closet?'

Freedman popped all the carefully aligned yellow Skittles into his mouth. 'No, but something was on her radar. She sent a text to her one contact the night before she was killed, asked for a callback ASAP, but the friend never got the text until this afternoon, and by then Blanca was dead. McLaren thinks something's screwy with the friend, too.'

'How so?'

'I think she was holding something back. Freedman doesn't think so, but I got a weird vibe from her. We told her about the duct tape, which pricked up her ears.'

'Well, that might be something,' Magozzi said, wondering why he was sounding so optimistic. Probably because a pizza was on the way. 'While you're digging deeper, keep an eye out for any connections to a Delia Sellman. She was killed in Los Angeles last year and her crime scene was a dead ringer for Kelly's, right down to the bondage. Just because Blanca's scene didn't have sexual overtones doesn't mean there isn't something in her past that attracted the same killer.'

'Sounds like you've got some footing.'

'We've got some ingredients for pot luck, so let's throw everything into the stew and see what happens.'

While Gino scoured Kelly Ramage's notebook, Magozzi pulled up the BaDSaM website. The opening page had a very slick, professional photo of a model wearing a blindfold, her glossy red lips parted provocatively. Given the tacky appearance of the rest of the page, it was probably unlicensed. BaDSaM was never going to win a Webby.

Magozzi read the accompanying script aloud: '"Find your perfect match, someone who can fulfill your deepest, darkest desires, your every fantasy. There are hundreds of people and possibly a few killers waiting to meet you on our private, discreet site. Enter here."'

Gino jerked his head up, then rolled his eyes. 'You had me for a millisecond.'

'You haven't had enough coffee. What's Kelly's user name?'

'Naughtykitten32.'

Magozzi typed it in and got another prompt. 'Password?'

Gino passed him the notebook. 'It's a jumble, one of those computer-generated passwords you don't have a prayer in hell of remembering.'

Magozzi slowly pecked in the series of letters, numbers and symbols carefully, then hit return. Gino pulled up his chair and they both watched as Naughtykitten32's profile page popped up along with an upper-body shot of Kelly Ramage. Her beautiful face and tawny hair looked angelic, but the leather bustier and studded collar she wore didn't. It was disturbing. 'I don't understand the draw.'

Gino shrugged. 'Naughty cheerleader next door. Or, in this case, the accountant's wife. The corruption of innocence. It appealed to her for whatever reason. She had a shit childhood, and that's where stuff like this starts.'

Below her photo was a personal statement: *Inexperienced sub seeking gentle dom male for encounter. Forty or under, no exceptions. Light bondage only, NO hardcore, fetish, or pain.*

Gino pointed to the user dashboard. 'She has over two hundred messages. Seeing her picture, that's not a surprise.'

Magozzi clicked on the message icon, which pulled up exactly nothing. 'The two hundred messages aren't here.'

'She probably erased them. Hit PRIVATE CHAT.'

PRIVATE CHAT was empty, too. 'Maybe she deleted everything when she went over to Signal.'

'But her photo's still up and she didn't close the account.' Gino tapped his pen on the edge of the desk. 'Check out her contact list.'

Magozzi navigated and clicked on it. There was only one saved contact: JamesBondage007.

'Oh, that's real cute,' Gino seethed. 'Let's track this asshole down.'

33

Tommy looked up abruptly when Gino and Magozzi filled his doorway. 'Jeez, you two look like you're late for your own funerals.'

'We have a user name from the bondage site: James-Bondage007.'

'You're kidding me. Sounds like a bad porn movie.'

'Can you do a little digging, see if you can get his personal information?'

'Not without a warrant, you know that. City Hall is not Harley's mansion. There are eyes and ears everywhere. But you might not need to go the gray area route. I've been poking around in Kelly Ramage's Signal account. The messages are gone, but I pulled a phone number from her log and I'm checking it out now. It's the only one that contacted her through Signal, and the contact was regular, including five messages from yesterday, when she was killed. Last one was around eight thirty last night.'

Magozzi looked at Gino. 'That was the text she read before she left the gallery. Nothing after that, Tommy?'

'Nope.'

'Is it just a number, or is there a name, too? Please tell me there's a name,' Gino beseeched the acoustic tile ceiling, which was as close to God as you could get in City Hall.

'No name, just a handle.' Tommy's affable face went still

for a moment, then the corner of his mouth quirked up. 'His handle is JB007.'

Gino snapped his fingers. 'That's him. How long until you can match the number with a name?'

'About thirty more seconds.' Tommy's fingers clacked on his keyboard. Then he started scrolling with his mouse. 'Phone numbers are easy and completely legal. No gray area here.'

Gino snuffled indignantly. 'We've never done anything illegal in our careers.'

'None of us have. Okay, I've got it.' He tilted his head and stayed silent for a maddening long second. 'Huh. I wasn't expecting this.'

Gino gestured his impatience.

'This number is registered to Pavel's Gym. I figured it would belong to a throwaway cell or a Google Talk number with fake personal info, not a legitimate business.'

'Not everybody is as paranoid as you, Tommy,' Magozzi reminded him. 'I'm guessing the average person takes anonymous messaging at face value and doesn't ever think that somebody could track them down. Or care enough to do it.'

'That's true. Kelly Ramage used her personal phone and associated information for Signal. Most regular people do.'

Magozzi raised a questioning brow at Gino. 'Isn't Pavel's that hardcore lifting place?'

'The same one that got some heat a few months ago when one of the members got nailed for selling performance-enhancing drugs out of his locker. It's as good a place as any to find somebody who's into domination. A little 'roid rage, and suddenly you're killing women. Makes sense to me.'

Magozzi's memory bank woke up from a pizza coma. 'I

remember that. It was Ty Overgaard's case. When I talked to him about the X this morning, he mentioned a snitch who was into synthetics and steroids.'

'Great. Maybe his snitch knows about Kelly Ramage's murder, too.'

While Gino negotiated the short but slippery drive to Pavel's downtown gym, Magozzi put his phone on speaker while Ty talked.

'Pavel isn't just the gym owner, he's my informant, and he's a good family man, straight up. Every snitch I've ever dealt with is low-life street meat, but this guy isn't that. He's just neck-deep into some bad shit and I'm trying to give him a way out. He got pressured into the role with the steroid thing, but he won't give me anything more than bottom-tier dealers. A guy like Pavel, he wouldn't be in this gutter unless somebody with a big hand was pushing his head down. Can't imagine how or why, but that's the scoop on him and why he's a pain in the ass.'

'So Pavel's not good for murder.'

'Pavel's not good for anything, but anybody in his gym might be. Look, murder is at the top of the heap, but don't spook the guy if you can manage it. If I can get him to talk, he's going to give us a big fish and get a lot of product off the street.'

'No reason for us to bring up drugs with him, we're just chasing down a homicide and the X is a minor factor at this point.'

'Thanks, Magozzi. So, what you said about the blow-up doll. I was thinking of getting something from Victoria's Secret to accessorize. What do you think?'

'I think that's a fantastic idea. I don't know how big the doll is, but I'd get a plus-size just to be safe.'

Ty let out a scratchy laugh. 'Will do. We'll see you soon, and be safe.'

Gino ran over a curb as he parked. 'What the hell was that all about?'

34

Pavel's Gym had a rank smell: an amalgamation of cleaning chemicals, sweat, and something murkier – given the history, probably unnaturally high levels of testosterone. The lobby was small, but spacious enough to accommodate a large glass case filled with trophies, medals, and photographs of greased-up muscle men flexing for the camera. Another case held supplements, protein powders, and wearable swag emblazoned very simply with the name of the gym arched over a globe.

There was a leathery, older man with thinning gray hair at the front desk, wearing a lime-green Pavel's muscle tee. Not exactly January-friendly garb, but good advertising – he had an impressive collection of bulging muscles to display, even though they were showing life's inevitable progression of time, along with the flesh that covered them.

You can run, but you can't hide, Magozzi thought, remembering a sweltering Fourth of July party at his grandparents' when he was in junior high. His grandpa had been a cop, and he was the strongest man he'd ever seen. But in his tank top, sweating at the grill, Magozzi had seen how the big muscles had grown flaccid, how the skin around them had withered and wrinkled, how his grandpa's sure and confident step was a little unsteady as he brought half-burned, half-raw hamburgers to the picnic table. It had been one of the worst moments of his young life, because why couldn't Grandpa cook like he used to, and why didn't he look like he used to? It was a few years later that he'd learned about Alzheimer's.

They showed their shields, and bright blue eyes set in a web of wrinkles widened. 'How can I help you?'

'Detectives Magozzi and Rolseth. We'd like to speak with the manager.'

'I am the manager. I'm also Pavel Kosic, the owner. Is something wrong?'

'We just have a few questions.'

A giant entered the lobby from a hallway that led to the locker room, according to the signage. He didn't really have a neck, just a shaved head and thick ropes of muscles that attached it to the solid wedge of his shoulders. Deep scowl lines were etched into his face and his expression resembled the snarling-tiger tattoo on his right arm. As he passed, he gave Pavel a friendly nod, then shot them both a suspicious glance before ducking into a weights room.

Pavel shifted uncomfortably in his chair. 'Perhaps we can go to my office where it's quieter.'

Most people they confronted in public took the first opportunity to stash them behind a closed door, Magozzi mused. It was understandable – guilty or not, having cops hanging around your place of business elicited discomfort in the paying customers. Or, in Tiger Man's case, possibly bloodlust.

The office smelled a lot better than the reception area and was the antithesis of Madeline Montgomery's cold, sterile cell. There was a miniature water garden and a low table with a porcelain teapot and a tray of Japanese-style cups. Joss sticks smoldered in an urn next to a wooden

Buddha. Pavel didn't look remotely Asian, so he was either an avid *feng shui* practitioner, or he'd undergone a religious conversion at some point.

'Please sit, Detectives. Would you care for tea?'

'Thank you, no.'

Pavel poured himself a small cup, then settled into the chair behind his desk. 'Tell me, how can I help you?'

'Do you know a woman named Kelly Ramage?'

'No.'

'Are you sure?'

'I'm positive.'

'Somebody with a phone number listed under Pavel's Gym was in regular contact with her.'

He shook his head. 'That's impossible. The only phone listed under Pavel's Gym is my business mobile. Kelly Ramage was not a client or an associate, and I've never been in contact with anyone by that name.'

'Do any of your employees use your phone?'

Pavel seemed shocked by the question, as though they'd asked if he shared his toothbrush with strangers. 'Never. They have their own phones.'

'Under Pavel's Gym?'

'No, I told you. I'm the only one who handles the business, calls and otherwise.'

'But they have access to your computer.'

'I have two employees, my daughter and my wife, so of course they have access to the computer, although I don't even know why we have one. We are what you call a mom-and-pop shop. We have loyal clientele, serious lifters and body-builders, some of them competitive internationally. They know my gym is open to use from ten to ten. They come and they go between those times and don't expect anything more. I don't even have a website. It's all word of mouth.' He paused and took a sip of tea. 'Detectives, I really don't know what you're looking for, but I tell you again that I don't know Kelly Ramage and have never spoken to her.'

'Do you know somebody who goes by the handle James Bondage or JB double-oh-seven?'

Pavel gave him a blank look and Magozzi felt the doldrums of a dead end slinking into the space where there had once been optimism. 'Do you use an app called Signal?'

'Signal? I've never heard of it. What is it?'

'It's not important,' Gino said. 'So you have your phone on you at all times?'

'Absolutely.'

'Do you mind if we take a look at it?'

Pavel's face hardened and color bloomed on his cheeks. 'I mind very much. What's on my phone isn't your business and you have no right to my private information.'

Gino looked around casually. 'Under normal circumstances, you're absolutely correct, but we're homicide detectives and Kelly Ramage was murdered last night. So your phone *is* our business now.'

His mouth worked uselessly around words that wouldn't form.

'Yeah, you're shocked, I can see that. Problem is, your number showed up on her phone multiple times under some very suspicious circumstances. Now, we can get a warrant, that won't be a problem, but if you don't have anything to hide, we can handle this here and now and nobody gets inconvenienced later.'

'There's a mistake, a terrible mistake. I don't know Kelly Ramage and I'm sorry for her death. But I had nothing to do with it. Ask my wife – I was with her yesterday, all day and all night, like always.'

Magozzi gave him a sympathetic look. 'We believe you, sir. And we don't want to have to get a warrant, but we're trying to find a murderer, so we will if it's necessary.'

He shook his head sadly, projecting disappointment and defeat that Magozzi sensed had deep roots that reached far beyond the current situation. He pulled his phone from his pants pocket and placed it on the desk. 'I don't know how somebody got my number, but it wasn't me who was contacting her. I have nothing to hide. Look for yourselves.'

'Thank you.' Magozzi went through his phone while Gino tried to distract him by asking him neutral questions about his business, the trophies and medals in the case out front. Pavel was miserable and not particularly responsive, but eventually he seemed to come to life a little, explaining the differences between body-building and power-lifting, and shared some memories of his glory days as a world champion power-lifter and Olympic bronze medalist for the former Yugoslavia.

Magozzi finally placed his phone back on the desk. Unless Pavel was a computer genius, which seemed highly unlikely since he wasn't too happy about owning one, or a world-class liar along with a world-class lifter, he was innocent. There was no Signal app on his phone, no calls or texts to or from Kelly Ramage, no web search history of BaD-SaM or any other site that catered to bondage enthusiasts. He had very few photos, and all of them featured him with a round, older woman, presumably his wife, surrounded by gaggles of smiling children at family gatherings.

But they still had to take the phone and bring it to Tommy to make sure nothing had been scrubbed. Just because Pavel seemed innocent, and Ty thought he was, didn't mean it was true. Cop instinct was good, but it only went so far.

'You're disappointed nothing's there,' Pavel said circumspectly.

'I'm glad to confirm what I believed, that you're not our killer. Disappointed that we haven't found him yet. But we still have to take the phone to our tech. With your permission, or else we will get a warrant.'

His broad, strong shoulders slumped in resignation. 'Of course you will. Please remember that's my livelihood you're holding. When can I get it back?'

'We'll make sure you have it by the end of the day.'

'If you find out who hacked my phone and intruded on my privacy, I hope you'll let me know. Your incursion is understandable, theirs is unforgivable. They could ruin my life, and I've worked very hard to earn my place here.'

'Is there someone you suspect might want to harm you? Hack you, set you up?' Gino asked.

'Personally, no. But as homicide detectives, you would know as well as anybody, there are many people in this world who would destroy anything or anybody for their own personal gain without a pang of conscience, because they have none. I have nothing of value to give, except perhaps a phone number to hide behind. I just didn't realize a phone number could possibly be valuable until now.'

*

'Ty was right. No way he's a drug-dealer, no way he killed Kelly,' Gino said, as they forged out into the frigid wilderness of downtown Minneapolis and fell in with the indigenous herd of puffy parkas with legs. 'Still, why was his number on her phone? And why wasn't hers on his? Explain that one.'

'Tommy said there were workarounds. Somebody cloned his number for some reason.'

'What reason? Why not just go buy a burner phone and use that, like Tommy mentioned?'

'When we find the killer, we'll ask him.'

Gino grunted, wholly dissatisfied by the answer. 'Maybe somebody really is trying to set him up.'

'Could have been random. Maybe he was an easy target.'

'The monster with the tiger on his arm looks like a stone killer to me. And he fits Kelly Ramage's under-forty requirement.'

'Maybe I'm being prejudiced, but he doesn't strike me as the tech-savvy type.'

'If the brain was a muscle, he'd be a frigging genius. As long as we're out freezing our asses off, what do you say we do a drive-by of Club Provocateur? Maybe they're open for tea.'

'Let me call Grace first. She said Monkeewrench was available to help and this James Bondage is too greasy for Tommy to handle. He's also a multiple murder suspect and he's here. At least, he was last night.'

35

Grace, who found diversion only in cooking, had always been amused and somewhat fascinated by the distractions Harley employed when he needed to burn off nervous energy, strategize, or work through a dilemma. Sometimes he paced, like he was doing now, sometimes he ate or drank to excess, and when those didn't yield the desired results, he would retreat to one of the places where he stored his collections. The carriage house held his motorcycles, the cellar his wine, a glass-walled room his arid forest of cacti, and the media room his beloved opera. It seemed to her to be the mark of a very complicated mind, although Annie would vehemently disagree with her.

She surreptitiously watched Annie's slow simmer of annoyance creep to boiling point. If you considered her contempt in just the right way, it was charming and a sign of deep affection.

'For God's sake, Harley, if you don't quit pacing, you're going to wear a hole in that beautiful maple floor straight to the other side of the world,' she finally snapped.

'Can't stop, can't stop,' he mumbled.

'Of course you can, you four-sided fool. Even you have free will. You're just too impatient to relax and let things gel.'

'I'm too pissed to let things gel. Nobody's taking my bait, I can't figure out how these ass clowns got into Bit

Monster, and I'm not going to stop pacing until I come up with a new idea.'

Annie stood up and clicked delicately over to the refrigerator on purple velvet heels, which instantly stopped Harley's anxious feet, and probably his heart. She pulled out a beer, opened it, and pushed it into Harley's hands. 'If ever there was a time you needed some alcohol . . .'

'Thanks, Annie. I'm touched. You really do care.'

'No, I really don't. You're just driving me insane. And don't trot out your stupid crack about it being a short drive.'

'It never crossed my mind.' He took a swig and looked at the clock. 'Roadrunner's been gone for a while. Shit, do you think he may actually like this woman?'

'Wouldn't that be a lovely thing?' Annie helped herself to his beer, took a sip, then grimaced. 'Beer is disgusting.'

'Then why did you take a drink?'

'To remind myself that beer is disgusting. Listen to me, Harley, you need to let this go for a while. Forget about the hack and help us with the software patches. We're obviously missing a vulnerability and that's one way to find it. Not to point out the painfully obvious, but it's all connected and there are always multiple paths. You're just being single-minded and mule-headed, and we all know mules aren't known for their common sense.'

'I don't believe you've ever compared me to a farm animal before, Annie.'

'You are so wrong about that. I've called you a pig on several occasions.' She smiled at Grace with a look of satisfaction, having gotten the last word, at least by her estimation. 'What did Magozzi have to say?'

'He asked for some help with their case. They found some similarities to two other murders, one here that McLaren and Freedman are working, and one that happened last year in LA.'

Harley clapped his hands together. 'What a great diversion, just what I need. Let me fire up The Beast.'

'We don't need The Beast for this. It's straightforward, just a hunt for some personal information on a web alias. I can launch a search from one of my rigs.'

They all looked toward the elevator vestibule when they heard the car whirring upward. Roadrunner stepped into the office, set his backpack on his desk, and stripped off his coat. When he noticed three inquisitive pairs of eyes staring at him, he shrugged. 'What? Did I miss something?'

'Nothing at all, sugar, just a discussion about farm animals. We were wondering about you. Did you have a nice visit with Petra?'

He nodded and looked at Harley's beer. 'Are you celebrating or drowning your sorrows?'

'Neither. Don't think you're going to slime out of a debriefing, Roadrunner. You were gone a long time.'

'We talked. When she got home from the hospital, she found out her friend was killed last night. It's not Magozzi's and Gino's case. McLaren and Freedman are the detectives in charge.'

Grace looked up abruptly. 'I just spoke with Magozzi and they think their cases could be connected. What did Petra tell you about it?'

Roadrunner blinked at her, dumbfounded. 'Nothing, just that her friend was murdered. That's all she said.' He sat down and started wringing his mangled hands together nervously. 'I'd like to help her with something. Nothing to do with the murder, and it wouldn't be a distraction from Bit Monster or anything Magozzi and Gino need, it's just a search.'

Grace raised a brow. 'What's the search?'

'She's looking for a war criminal. That's what she does, and she thinks he's here in Minnesota.' He cleared his throat uncomfortably. 'She didn't ask, I offered. Actually, I insisted.'

'She's got a track on him, then.'

Roadrunner nodded and pulled a file folder out of his backpack. 'Everything she has on him is here, and there's a lot to work with. This should be easy.'

Harley smiled. 'Now we can wake up The Beast. She's been lonely.'

'I can do it, Harley. You stay on Bit Monster.'

'You're the one who pointed out that Bit Monster isn't going to happen overnight. Besides, I've been told I need to step away for a little while.' He glanced at Annie, who ignored him. 'What better hiatus than finding a homicidal scumbag? That's exactly the kind of inspiration I need.'

36

Jimmy Grimm called at the very critical moment when Gino was turning onto a snowy, ice-slicked street that sent the sedan sliding toward a row of parked cars. How he avoided smashing into them was the day's only miracle so far. 'Jesus,' Magozzi muttered, answering his phone.

'Funny, you sound just like Magozzi, not the Lord my Savior.'

Magozzi snorted. 'Why are you in such a good mood?'

'I'm not. What's got you so tight?'

'Gino's driving is as shitty as the people he spent all morning complaining about. What's up?'

'Nothing that's going to break your case right now, but I'm hoping it will get you closer. Ready?'

'Fire away. I just put you on speaker.'

'Okay, I found some footprints under the snow at the Ramage scene. Frozen solid, like I was hoping for, so we made some casts. One set matched the high-heeled boots Kelly Ramage was wearing, the other two sets were men's boots, and they didn't match the trampled mess from this morning.'

'Two sets? Are you sure?'

'Positive.'

'Made around the same time?'

'This is imprecise, so there's really no way to tell exactly. One set may have come first, the second a little later. There was overlap on the way out, they screwed up some of their own prints, but they all froze in a similar way, so it's a safe bet to say they were made close to the same time. Last night sometime, not this morning.'

'Then there's a possibility there were two perps.'

'Sure, but she could have had a guest and the killer came after he left. Or she could have ordered a pizza.'

'No signs she did. Anything unique about the prints?'

'One was the standard lug-sole pattern of a million different kinds of snow boots – I just checked the database. But the second set had a unique pattern, something a little fancier, so I'm working on that now. I also found some resin dust in the prints.'

'Resin dust? Where the hell would that have come from?'

'Any place somebody was sanding resin. Construction sites, manufacturing plants – hobbyists use it. It's common, you could pick it up in a lot of places.'

Magozzi thought of Madeline Montgomery's resin blob chairs. 'From furniture?'

'A piece of resin furniture won't give off dust unless you sand it.'

'Did you find anything inside the house?'

'The killer worked clean, very hygienic. No body fluids besides the blood on the pillow, and fingerprints came up empty. All the prints we pulled belonged either to Kelly Ramage or another female, presumably the home owner. Get her in to give us a ten-card for disqualification.'

'Will do. Anything else?'

'Yeah, a couple red fibers on Kelly's neck that didn't match any of her clothing. Silk, like from a scarf.'

'The missing ligature.'

'That was my thought. Find the scarf, you might find your killer.'

'How about the SUV?'

'Only Kelly's prints. We took a very close look at the passenger's seat and surrounding area, but there was no unusual trace, nothing that wasn't present in other places in the vehicle. I don't think she gave anybody a ride.'

'What about Blanca Szabo's scene?'

'Apples and oranges – at least, I thought so at first. Nothing that links the two at all, besides the duct tape, and that's thin. But once I got back to the lab, I found resin dust in some samples from there, too. On the floor and on her clothing. Not much, but it was there. And no source in her shop. I haven't had time to run comparisons yet. No red fibers, though.'

'Great work, Jimmy, thanks.'

'Where are you guys at with things?'

'Trying to find a digital trail, but the killer has good hygiene in that regard, too.'

'Is Monkeewrench on it?'

'Just. Our next stop is a sex club.'

'That's one way to relax. Talk to you guys later.'

Gino let out a blast of air as the annoying voice of the GPS calmly informed them their destination was five hundred yards on the right. 'So we've got some trace that could connect Blanca's and Kelly's murders. A warped artist who might be inspiring other warped freaks to kill women. Pavel's Gym, digital chicanery – what am I missing?'

'Potentially two killers and where Delia Sellman might figure in it. If she does at all.'

172

'Call Jared Lerner in LA. There was duct tape at Delia Sellman's scene. Maybe he has red silk fibers and resin dust, too.'

Jared wasn't answering, so Magozzi left a message while Gino parked awkwardly on an unplowed curb in front of a barber shop that had steel bars on the windows. It was impossible to tell if the place was still a viable business or if it had been shuttered for years. It was that kind of neighborhood.

37

Club Provocateur had definitely downgraded its location since its glory days as a downtown strip club. The reboot was in a warehouse situated in a grungy, crime-infested part of the city that had probably sent the rats fleeing to safer places.

The understated black and white façade around the entry seemed to be aiming for an illicit speak-easy feel, the kind of place that required a password or secret handshake to get in. Neither of those was necessary – the door was open and Gino and Magozzi let themselves in.

The large space was empty and dismal and depressing. There was a long bar, a small raised stage for a DJ setup where Wolfie and his colleagues would spin and scratch, and a scuffed wooden dance floor that consumed most of the first level. A staircase ran up the north side of the building, but it was cordoned off with a red velvet rope, the only thing that looked remotely clubby in this seemingly deserted and derelict venue.

It was exactly the kind of place that opened for raves on a random night and shut the doors indefinitely the morning after. It was also eerily silent. Too early for music, too early to take little green smiley-face pills and boogie the night away in feverish, erotic bliss.

'Hello?' Gino called. The only answer was the echo of his voice. 'This is weird. It looks abandoned.'

Magozzi walked to the bar. Bottles of liquor sat on crude

wooden shelves next to stacks of plastic cups. 'This can't be the right place. Who would pay a membership fee for the privilege of spending time in a dump like this?'

They froze when they heard the unmistakable sound of a bullet being chambered. 'Get out of here. We don't open until eight.' The voice was male, smoky, harsh.

'Minneapolis Police, drop your weapon now!' Gino barked, as they drew their own and scuttled for cover behind the bar.

They heard a heavy clunk as the gun fell to the floor. 'Whoa, whoa, my apologies, my mistake! There was trouble here – just last week one of my employees was assaulted. I'm unarmed now and my hands are up. I'm halfway down the stairs. I'll stay here.'

The harsh voice was now a tremolo, and Magozzi rose slowly, his gun aimed in the direction of the staircase. He finally caught sight of a chubby man, with graying, slicked-back hair, in baggy jeans and an Aran sweater. He looked frightened and completely harmless, but he'd been carrying, so all bets were off. 'Walk down slowly. Keep your hands in the air.'

He obeyed, then stopped when he reached the velvet rope. Gino and Magozzi approached cautiously, but he just stood there motionless, patient, his hands up. 'I'm really sorry, Officers. I'm Ollie Kampa, the manager. I was upstairs in my office and heard intruders. At least, I thought you were intruders.'

'Your door was unlocked.'

'It was?'

'We didn't break in.'

'Of course you didn't. Kirk must have forgotten to lock

it when he left,' he said, an angry edge coloring his voice. 'He's an excellent bouncer but he doesn't possess the wits of an ant.'

Gino frisked him and gestured him down. 'So you've had some trouble here?'

'Some street thugs thought they could attack my bartender and steal the liquor.'

'Did you dissuade them with your gun?'

'I wasn't here. Kirk was in the storage room, heard the commotion, and knocked their heads together. They won't be back, trust me. Kirk is an excellent bouncer,' he reaffirmed.

Gino gestured to the sad, empty space. 'This is supposed to be a private club?'

Ollie raised his brows in amusement. 'It is, but this part of it is all for show. A setpiece. The real club is in back, very posh, but our clientele like the feeling of a little grunge, a little danger when they walk in.'

'More danger than the real ones lurking outside, waiting to assault your bartender for some booze?'

'Thrill-seekers don't ever get enough danger. What can I do for you, Officers?'

'Detectives. We're investigating a homicide. Do you recognize this woman? Her name is Kelly Ramage.'

Ollie took the much-circulated photo and nodded sadly. 'She was murdered?'

'Was she one of your clientele?'

'No. Well, she's been here a few times, but she wasn't a member. We allow some guests in as a courtesy if they pay the cover charge. I checked her in when she came – that's part of my job, vetting non-members.'

'Making sure they pass muster?' Gino asked cynically.

'There are some requirements. I don't make the rules, I just follow them.' He looked down at Kelly Ramage's photo again. 'She seemed like a sweet lady. Shy.'

'Not the sort who'd be interested in a dangerous sex club?'

Ollie looked offended. 'This is a dance club. I don't know where you heard it was a sex club.'

'Rumors float around, you know. We're cops, we hear lots of rumors. We also heard you have an adventurous clientele, on the kinky side.'

'It's a safe place for people to explore their fantasies and meet like-minded people. That's it.'

'Bondage is a big thing here?'

Ollie sighed. 'Not specifically. I see it all, but I'm telling you, it's just a place where people get together, drink, dance. It's a social venue for people outside the main-stream where they can come to have fun in a place where they won't be judged. The only murders that happen around here happen outside the doors and they don't involve our clientele.'

'Back to the photo. Was she here last night?'

He nodded. 'She was, but she didn't stay long. Maybe an hour – could have been longer, though.'

'Did you notice if she socialized with anyone?' Magozzi asked, ending Gino's tenure as chief inquisitor.

'From what I saw, she kept on the fringes. She was shy, like I said. But old Georgie chatted her up, or at least he tried. He's always here and he talks to everybody. He's an ugly bugger who dresses like a drag queen and wears these crazy fur coats, buys drinks for the house all the time. He throws around a lot of cash.'

Mr Fur Coat with the bulbous nose from the gallery tape? 'Do you know who he is?'

'He's an old guy named George Bormann. I think he said he was Austrian, or maybe German. He's kind of pathetic, constantly telling people he has a partial interest in the club, but that's just a line to get people interested in him. He gave me the same spiel, angling for VIP treatment. So I asked him about Vrag Entertainment and I might as well have been asking him his opinion on quantum physics.'

'What's Vrag Entertainment?'

'It's a company out of LA. They own this place and sign my checks. If he doesn't know the name, then he's not an owner.'

'He sounds like a problem.'

'No, not at all. He's wacky but harmless, never ruffles any feathers and people seem to like him. Or, at least, tolerate him. We've never had any complaints. He's just another odd duck in a whole pond full of them.'

'Did you notice if Ms Ramage left with anyone?'

'I saw her walking out alone, so I kept an eye on her until the valet brought her car. You know what a dicey part of town this is – there are predators around every corner.'

'What time did she leave?'

'I don't know . . . Maybe around ten? It could have been later, though. It was a busy night and I wasn't watching the clock.'

A door opened on the far side of the empty dance floor and a big man in a heavy coat slogged in and dropped a duffel bag on the floor. Ollie's cheeks flared red. 'Kirk, you forgot to lock the door. Don't ever leave without locking the door before or after hours. You know what happened last week.'

'Sorry.'

'Don't apologize. Just don't do it again.'

Kirk turned his back on them and shrugged off his coat, exposing inhumanly large muscles that stretched a tight, black T-shirt to its limits and also exposed a tattoo of a snarling tiger. 'I won't,' he mumbled, then thudded across the wooden floor without giving any of them a glance.

'Hey!' Gino called, and Tiger Man looked up, startled. 'Remember us?'

There was a flash of recognition in his reptilian eyes. Then he scowled, deepening the angry lines that were already permanently etched on his face. 'What are you doing here?'

'Not following you, but maybe we should be.'

'Who are you?'

'Homicide detectives.'

His grim face didn't seem capable of much movement, but he did seem slightly nonplussed by the revelation. 'Who got killed?'

'This nice woman, just last night,' Ollie said, walking over the photo. 'Do you remember her?'

'Sure. Came and went. She didn't die here.'

'So you were working last night?' Gino asked.

'Until close.'

Ollie nodded. 'Kirk was here until two a.m.'

'I was here until three, helping clear the place out,' he corrected.

'Then what?' Gino asked, increasingly churlish.

'I did what normal people do after a long day, Detective. I went home, ate, showered, slept. I'm a busy man. I work out at Pavel's, come here, then go to bed and start over the next day. Trust me, I don't have the time or the energy to kill anybody. Not these days.' A poor imitation of a smile jerked his lips upward.

Gino was fuming – Magozzi could feel his anger sucking the oxygen out of the room, making the vast space seem close and airless. 'You're being unpleasant, Kirk. Actually, you're being a smartass, which is really inappropriate under the circumstances. Maybe you'd like to take a vacation from your day-to-day drudgery and kick up your heels at City Hall for the night.'

'It would be a waste of your time. I didn't kill anybody.'

Magozzi saw the ferocious tiger that circled his arm quiver, which seemed dangerous and an analog to the current situation. Gino was poking a stick in the cage, and the tiger was going to break out and eat them all, unless somebody shot it first. It wouldn't happen that way, but there was a dark promise of something bad.

'That's a unique tattoo, Kirk,' Magozzi commented casually. 'Does it mean something?'

'I like tigers.'

'Didn't figure you for an animal lover,' Gino said.

'Are you done? I need to get ready for my shift.'

Gino shooed him out with his hand, glowering at his broad back as he walked away, then turned to Ollie. 'He's a real charmer. In an asshole kind of way.'

'I didn't hire him for his personality, that's for sure. How do you know him?'

'We don't. We just ran into him earlier, chasing down a lead. It's an interesting coincidence, don't you think?'

'I wouldn't know. All I can tell you is Kirk shows up on

time, works hard, and doesn't complain. And he really was here all night.'

'What's his last name?'

'Johnson.'

'Do you do background checks on your employees?'

'Vrag Entertainment does. He made their cut.'

Gino's eyes were busy. 'I don't see any surveillance cameras.'

'We don't have any. Privacy is extremely important to our clients.'

Gino nodded. 'I'm sure it is. I'm wondering about drugs, Ollie. Ecstasy, in particular. Green pills with smiley faces on them. You ever see anything like that here?'

Ollie's face darkened. 'No, absolutely not. This is a legitimate establishment, not a rave club, and we don't deal drugs.'

'I wasn't implying that you did, but our victim had some in her personal effects and it might be extremely helpful if we knew where they came from.'

'We're a hospitality business, and what people do on their own time is beyond our control. Do they sometimes come here high on something? Of course they do, but we don't provide anything except alcohol. The nature of our club puts us under intense scrutiny, Detectives, and our record is pristine. We've never been in violation of anything, which is saying something in a hyper-regulated city like Minneapolis.'

Magozzi didn't doubt that, because it would be easy enough to look up, but he did find it interesting that Ollie had given such a long-winded defense. He was nervous, and nervous people talked – it was human nature. Most of the time it was meaningless, anxiety-ridden blabber to fill

181

an uncomfortable lapse in a conversation taking place under duress, but sometimes they had something to say, or something to hide. Kirk Johnson could have something to do with it, and he made a mental note to mention him and Club Provocateur to Ty.

But, right now, Ollie wasn't much use. George Bormann, on the other hand, might be. A lonely old gadfly would be an observer, and would also be on top of any gossip. And more than happy for some attention, even if it was from the cops.

38

Annabelle woke up to absolute darkness and a screaming headache she was certain would split her skull any moment. She'd never felt such devastating white-hot pain before and it was frightening. Something was very, very wrong, but she didn't know what. Her body ached almost as much as her head, but when she tried to turn over onto her side, she couldn't move. Her limbs were numb, heavy, useless, her thoughts furred and disjointed.

What happened?

Intermittent images flashed through her mind: leaving the protest to thaw out in a coffee shop, or was it a bar? Strangers everywhere, then the thud of someone falling. No, not just someone, *her.* She had been upright, drinking something warm, then suddenly her cheek was pressed against a cold floor with no memories before that. Gasps, voices, a strong hand pulling her up off the floor and a distant, foggy voice . . .

I'm sorry, excuse me, my friend is sick . . .

What friend? She hadn't been with a friend, had she? A name started to form in her mind, and a face to go with it, but the image suddenly fragmented, flared brightly, then went black.

Why can't I move? Why can't I think? Why can't I see?

Minutes, or maybe hours, later, her senses were gaining sharpness, enough to nurture a sickening panic. She tried to call out for help, but her mouth was dry – cottony and foul – and she started retching. When the vomit had nowhere to go, she slowly began to understand her situation with escalating horror. She was gagged. And bound. And blindfolded. That was why she couldn't speak, couldn't move, couldn't see.

A scream built deep inside, but it was trapped, choked by vomit, stifled by the gag. A chill racked her body . . . her naked body. *She was naked.*

And splayed out like a gutted carcass.

Her eyes stung with tears, but she couldn't brush them away as they escaped the blindfold and dribbled down her cheeks. That simple helplessness shriveled her soul as she became aware of her reality: she was dead – maybe not yet, but she would be. How long it would take wasn't clear, but her destiny was fixed. Dead, dead, dead. Just like Delia.

She heard a sound – the creak of a door. A sliver of light bright enough to penetrate her blindfold. Soft footsteps, then gentle hands touching her face while something soft circled her neck like a silky snake.

'Annabelle. You're just as lovely as your sister was. I'm looking forward to getting to know you.'

39

Petra was deep into a stack of paper, but she was frustrated by the scattered, unfocused track of her mind, which kept diverting from work to Roadrunner to Blanca to Martin. Blanca had been murdered: there had been duct tape on her mouth, her nose, her eyes, and instinct told her Peter Praljik was responsible, but why would he kill her?

Roadrunner's generous offer of help was also oddly distracting because she couldn't suppress the nascent hope that Monkeewrench's software would make easy work of finding him. And the fact that Martin hadn't called back was troubling, made more so by his precarious health. Her collective worries were turning to dread, so she left the sitting room and went into the kitchen. Food would help. Feed the brain, feed the body, feed the soul.

Grace MacBride's soup was delicious – she'd chosen a jar at random, and it turned out to be beef with vegetables and barley. But even more tempting than eating a second bowl was the frosty bottle of Stolichnaya in her freezer, beckoning her to partake in just one glass to soothe her nerves. Just one, savored slowly in front of the fire. It wouldn't kill her. It seemed that nothing could.

She settled onto the hearth with her drink, found Martin's home number, and punched it into her phone while she took a deep sip of vodka, savoring the burn in her throat, the spreading heat when it hit her stomach.

'Petra?'

Emmanuelle's French-accented voice greeted her, but it sounded strange. 'Emmanuelle, I'm sorry to bother you . . .'

Petra heard her voice hitch, then a soft, heartbroken weeping. 'Petra, Martin is dead.'

The room, the flickering light of the fire, the papers and folders around her seemed to swirl and blur in a dizzying kaleidoscope of color and light. The grief she felt was instant and overwhelming, but usurping that was the latent fear that had haunted her most of her life. It was always there on the outer perimeter of her subconscious, and it was fiercely opportunistic and craven, always waiting for a weakness in her spirit before it would assert itself, like it had last night.

Logically, it was unreasonable to suspect that there was anything untoward about Martin's death, but the base, primal voice inside growled a warning. He'd been a very sick man, but he hadn't been at death's door yesterday. He *had* been getting closer to an evil sociopath who'd avoided detection for two decades and perhaps that evil sociopath had somehow known about his work. Their work.

Lifelong criminals weren't leopards who changed their spots, and it wasn't a stretch to imagine that Vrag had formed a new Mafia family in the US and would go to great lengths to protect it. Maybe her paranoia about being followed wasn't paranoia after all.

'I'm so sorry, Emmanuelle,' she finally managed to whisper. 'So sorry. What happened?'

'It was a hit-and-run, while he was taking his morning walk. The police are here now.'

More police and another dead friend. Instinct. Warning.

'I'm so sorry,' she repeated, the words sounding so infuriatingly feeble. 'Will you call me back when you're finished with them?'

'Of course I will. I'm so glad you were able to see him yesterday. He said you had a lovely talk and you drank vodka.'

'We did.'

'You were a daughter to him. He loved you like one.'

'I loved him like a father.'

'I know you did. Thank you. I'll call you later.'

Petra listened to the dolorous beep of an ended call; an ended life. It didn't require suspension of disbelief to imagine who might be next.

40

Roadrunner was beginning the search for any digital trail Peter Saveride né Praljik might have left after his abrupt disappearance in 2008. At this point, it seemed he'd been bright enough to do a fairly respectable, clean sweep of his former identity, but not quite bright enough to close every account under the Social Security number he'd been given after he'd entered the US as a refugee in 1996.

But his two credit cards had been inactive for a decade and the address associated with the accounts belonged to the apartment in Forest Lake he'd vacated years ago. According to State Department records, he'd never been issued a US passport. So far, the social number hadn't shown up anywhere else, but the search was just beginning.

He began inputting more information from Petra's files: scans of old photos, names of a former employer and co-workers from a cab company he'd worked for, his known aliases both here and abroad, and the word *vrag*, just for good measure. If there were obscure links to his present location in the data anywhere on the Internet, The Beast would eventually find them.

Unfortunately, people really could create solid new identities to escape the law, and unless Praljik had made a mistake somewhere along the way, he might be one of those clever, lucky people.

As The Beast churned through the information, Road-runner tracked the progress on multiple screens. It wasn't yet pinging on any connections to Praljik in the present, but it was quickly filling out his detailed past. His eyes were fixed on the monitor as atrocities began to scroll in front of him: countless massacres ordered by Vrag and conducted by his paramilitary unit; rape camps and concentration camps he'd built and overseen during his command; his collaboration with other criminals, torturers, and perpetrators of mass murder. Police and Mafia and butchers all at once. Heroes to some, even now. And Petra had lived through it.

But if I had died, I wouldn't have minded. I was having very nice dreams.

No wonder, he thought, heartsick for the eleven-year-old girl she'd been, as well as the haunted woman she was now. With such a history, how could you not be tempted to consider death a release? But she'd survived and she refused to be a victim. Now he understood what she'd meant by that.

He got up from his chair and started pacing the cooled room that countered the heat output of The Beast when it was operating. Through the glass door that separated it from the main office, he saw Grace and Harley focused on their monitors, Annie speaking with someone on the phone – all of them oblivious to the horrors he'd just unearthed. Suddenly, he couldn't stand to be in the close confines of the room anymore and stepped out to let The Beast do its work unsupervised.

Harley looked up at him and frowned. 'You're kind of gray, buddy, what's up?'

He sank into his chair and took a few deep breaths. 'The man Petra is looking for. He's a monster.'

'He's a war criminal, of course he's a monster. Any luck finding him?'

'Not in the present. I'm waiting to see what The Beast digs up. Speaking of monster . . .'

'Bit Monster? It's getting interesting. Grace had a clever idea, didn't you, Gracie?'

She turned in her chair and smiled modestly. Roadrunner hadn't noticed until now that Elizabeth was swaddled in a fleece blanket and snug in the cradle of Grace's arms while Charlie snoozed just as contentedly at her feet. 'It wasn't bad.'

'See, I was focusing on the large-scale hack on Bit Monster, but Grace suggested I take a look at individual accounts and, sure as shit, I found several big unauthorized withdrawals that occurred before the attack. Every account has bitcoin keys associated with it, and these keys were all stolen – it's like getting your PIN for your cash card stolen. If you have the keys or the PIN, you can empty the accounts. The only problem is, it didn't get me any closer to the assault on the Bit Monster infrastructure.'

Roadrunner tapped a finger on his lips. 'Maybe it did. The keys could have been stolen through personal contact. If you get someone to pay for something with crypto, there are ways to jump their accounts, and once you're in, any flaws in Bit Monster's security could be exploited, making them vulnerable to the larger attack.'

Harley raised a brow. 'That feeds into my inside-job theory. The brass at Bit Monster would know who the big account holders were and target them that way. Make a bunch of small-scale attacks on individuals first, sneak in through the back door instead of risking a full-scale one on the whole system.'

'What about your bait?'

'No hits on the account yet. I'm just sitting here pretending I'm fishing on Leo's lake, watching my bobber. It's boring as hell, but it'll be a cheap thrill when a fish finally pulls it down.'

Annie ended her phone call, stood up, and smoothed the front of her purple cashmere dress primly so the fabric settled properly over her curves. 'I haven't eaten a thing all day. Is anybody else starving?'

'You're looking a little flushed, my sweet magnolia. Was that Mr Bulgaria on the phone?'

She let out a long-suffering sigh. 'You are such a child, Harley. That was my former acquaintance, yes, and he hasn't worked for Interpol in five years and doesn't know anything about Bit Monster. He went private.'

'Who does he work for now?'

'How should I know?' She taunted him with a crafty smile. 'We were just reminiscing about our night together in Brussels. Come to think of it, it was two nights, if memory serves.'

'Only two? He must have been boring.'

Any rejoinder on Annie's part was interrupted when The Beast let out the familiar chime that alerted them when a connection had been made. Roadrunner jumped out of his chair and Harley followed him into the chill room, hovering over his shoulder as he tried to make sense of the lists on the monitor.

'Vrag? A Russian metal band? Violence Risk Assessment

Guide? This is a bunch of shit, Roadrunner, what did you input?'

But Roadrunner didn't hear him. He was staring at the final entry at the bottom of the monitor: Vrag Entertainment, a limited liability company, had been formed three years ago in Los Angeles, but there was an office address in north Minneapolis. It had been chartered by Joseph Koppenhöfer, who was using the same Social Security number as Peter Praljik. The monster had made the mistake Roadrunner had been hoping for.

He zoomed the screen on the entry. 'This is him, Harley. It has to be. He kept his social number off the grid for years so it looked like he fell off the face of the earth, then used it again when he needed a totally legit one to pass government scrutiny to form an LLC.'

'Who was he hiding from? Petra?'

'No, this is new information to her. He was either hiding from somebody else or just paranoid, as he has every reason to be. He's a wanted man.' Roadrunner pecked in more queries to give The Beast sharper focus. 'What doesn't make sense is why he would risk forming an LLC in the first place.'

Harley rocked back on the heels of his boots. 'It's obvious. You're talking about a human stain, and he didn't reform once he got here. So he found a clan of other stains and a niche in the underground, made enough cash that he needed a legit front so he could clean it.'

'Money-laundering?'

'Why not? We've been talking about the Balkan Mafia all day. Maybe it's a little over the top, but it gets the juices flowing, doesn't it?' Harley clapped him on the back.

'You'd better give Petra a call and get her people on it. Shit, dude, you saved her life, then found her war criminal, all in one day? I hope you like her because she's yours forever. If you'd done all that for me, I'd marry you ... What's wrong?'

'What you just said about the Balkan Mafia.'

'Yeah?'

'What's the newest way to clean money now?'

'There are a million ways to clean money ...' Harley's jaw suddenly snapped shut.

'Yeah, you've got it. Cryptos. Virtually untraceable. You can exchange cash for bitcoin in a ton of different places – there are even ATM machines that do it. And you can siphon it into exchanges like Bit Monster, no questions asked. It's totally unregulated.'

Harley pressed the heels of his hands in his eyes. 'Jesus, you think this could all be connected?'

'I think we should merge our searches and find out.'

41

Joseph was enjoying Stefan's discomfort. He was a grotesque toadstool, rubbing his fat thumbs together nervously as his corpse-beetle eyes darted around the office. But he served a purpose, and wasn't it God's irony that this most contemptible dreck could be useful? 'How do you find the equipment, Stefan? Is it to your satisfaction?'

He scowled petulantly, Joseph thought. 'It's dope, yeah, top-notch. I couldn't have designed a better set-up myself. But the thing is, I can't work properly off-site. I need my own gear, my place, my den. That's where the magic happens.'

'I didn't realize there was magic involved.'

'Hacking is an art, man. Art is magic.'

'Hacking isn't art. *That*'s art.' He gestured proudly to his display of priceless paintings, his collection of important twenty-first-century sculptures.

Stefan's doughy face twisted in befuddlement as he focused on the tallest sculpture in the room. 'That's art? It looks like old computer punch tape to me.'

'Proving my point that you have no understanding of real art. And as for magic, I have no time for it. I'm sorry to hear there isn't any here for you. Is that why you haven't had any luck with Bit Monster yet?'

'Please. I've only been working for a day. Hacking takes time – a lot of it. If you try to rush things, you get sloppy, and since I'm on your equipment, it would come right back to you if I get nailed.'

'If I didn't know better, I'd say that was a threat.'

'It's not a threat, it's the truth. I'm the one committing the crime here. If I get caught, I go to federal prison, but you'd be able to slime out of it with a decent lawyer. But I'm guessing you don't want your outfit to see any sunlight. I don't know who you are, and I don't want to. But I know what you are. Otherwise, you wouldn't have found me or hired me.'

'So my criminal friend has more rules for me. That's becoming an annoying habit with you.'

'No, just a simple request. Let me go home and work on this. I'll give you daily progress reports and I'll get the job done. I'm telling you, I can't work in captivity in some warehouse with house music shaking the paint off the walls all night. And I know I'm not worth anything to you dead. I just want to do my job.'

Joseph took a lazy sip from his lowball of vodka and lime. Stefan wasn't really worth anything to him dead or alive if he couldn't produce results. 'How can I be certain you would devote your time to my job if I'm not supervising you?'

'You ever hear of capitalism? Money, my friend. Nice, green money. The retainer was a good start, but we haven't talked about further compensation.'

Of course it was about the money. Stefan's greed was immense. 'I've already given you twenty thousand up front, and I offer two percent of whatever monies you recoup.'

'Ten percent.'

'You're very funny. Two percent is more than fair if

you're skilled enough to reclaim what I've lost. It would be substantial.'

'Five percent.'

Joseph sighed and decided to make a concession – what did it matter? He was going to kill him anyway. 'I'll agree to three percent. For now. But if I don't see progress soon, this verbal contract of ours is up for renegotiation. On my terms.'

'So I can go home with the twenty?'

'No. You're not leaving this building until you finish the job.' He gestured to the expressionless behemoth standing in the doorway. 'I think you'll find this gentleman pleasant company. He won't interfere with your work.'

Stefan's eyes roved to the large gun on his hip, the tattoo of a roaring tiger quivering on his monstrous biceps, and swallowed hard. 'You're holding me prisoner?' His voice was whiny, panicky.

'Think of it as a secure work environment. One free of distractions. I don't think I have to remind you that outside contact is absolutely forbidden. Not that you have anyone to contact to save you, considering you're a criminal yourself, but know you're being watched. And not just by my friend. I can see everything you do on that computer from another room, so don't think you're going to send an SOS to anybody. If you do, I'll know about it, and things won't end well for you.'

'I . . . I won't.'

'Stefan, the sooner you do your job, the sooner you'll be a free man. And a rich one. Sacrifice is necessary for great reward.'

42

Gino parked the sedan in front of a large, mushroom-shaped house that squatted in a wooded lot in a northern Minneapolis suburb. Moonlight glanced off the snow-covered triangular facets of the structure, which created strange shadows and the impression of something broken that had been hastily put back together.

'This is . . . unique.'

'It's a geodesic dome,' Gino recited, from his endless mental compendium of trivia knowledge. 'They were trendy back in the sixties and seventies, popularized by Buckminster Fuller.'

'I've heard of them, just never seen one in person.' Magozzi turned up the heater fan, which was pathetically anemic, barely dribbling out enough warmth to keep his toes from freezing solid.

'Now you have. Sounds like George Bormann is pretty eccentric, so the house matches.'

Magozzi's phone rang and the glowing screen displayed Jared Lerner's number. 'It's Westwood. Don't turn off the car yet, or we'll freeze to death. Detective Lerner, thanks for calling.'

'Sorry it took me so long to get back to you, but I had to pull Delia Sellman's file to refresh my memory.'

'No worries. What do you know?'

'No resin dust at Delia's scene. There were red silk

fibers on her neck and light ligature bruises, but we never found anything that matched. I'm looking at the ME's report right now. Strangulation didn't kill her, suffocation from the duct tape did.'

'Bingo.'

'That's what I'm thinking.'

'We've got something else to throw at you. After we spoke earlier, we found out our victim was also using an anonymous chat app to contact her killer. One called Signal.'

There was a brief pause on the other end of the line, the sound of papers shuffling. 'Yep, here it is. Delia Sellman was using Signal. Damn. I'm going to try to get clearance to put this back on active status. There's definitely something here.'

'We haven't had time to check into other cities where Rado may have had openings . . .'

'I already did that. Besides West Hollywood and Minneapolis, he only had one other in the States, in New York last March, and there were no murders that night that match. A couple women went missing around that time, but they never found the bodies.'

'No digital trail?'

'None. The women were on the fringe, one was on-and-off homeless, the other was an addict. Maybe one of them was a test run for him, but until a body turns up, we'll never know. As it stands now, Westwood was the first organized murder, Minneapolis the second. Seems to me this guy is relatively new to the murder racket, but he works like a pro.'

A good cop, devoted to his job and his victims. Magozzi was impressed. 'You beat us to it, thanks for that. Do you think you could send us a scan of your case files? We'd especially like to take a look at what your cyber division dug up and run it by ours, see if something dovetails there.'

'Sure thing. It should be in the system, so I'll batch that out tonight before I find an empty stool and a full beer.'

'If you're looking at that, you must have had a good day.'

'We got lucky with a brain-dead perp, who left a trail wider than the Grand Canyon. He was still carrying the murder weapon when we caught up with him and he confessed the second after we read him his rights. The buzz won't last long, not in this town, but you have to celebrate every victory like it's your last, because it might be.'

Lerner had a good, healthy sense of fatalism and the twisted *joie de vivre* that every good homicide cop needed to survive until retirement, assuming you lived long enough to collect your pension. 'Amen, Detective. Enjoy the short ride, and we'll be in touch.'

'Thanks, same here. Hey, is Minnesota in January as bad as it looks? Your weather is on the news, even down here, and I saw a couple YouTube videos of people throwing water into the air and it froze on contact.'

'It's not as bad as you think. It's way worse,' Magozzi said, wriggling his numb toes to regain circulation before they became necrotic.

'You ever notice that when it's this cold, snow doesn't crunch, it squeaks?' Gino observed, as they crossed the street.

'The sound of suffering.'

They paused when they reached the front walk of George Bormann's dome home. It had been cleared and sanded, and landscape lights illuminated the way to the front door. It was a weird place, but well-kept.

Gino rang the bell, and the bulbous-nosed man from the Resnick/Feinnes surveillance footage pulled open the door with tremendous enthusiasm, as if he'd been expecting them. He wasn't wearing his fur tonight, just a nice navy suit with an oversized harlequin bow-tie and matching socks. The flesh of his face was shiny and stretched taut, certainly the unfortunate result of either bad plastic surgery or just too much of it. Magozzi wondered uncharitably why he hadn't gotten a nose job while he was under the knife.

His close-set pop-eyes bulged when he realized they weren't the guests he'd been anticipating, and the overall impression was bizarre, like gazing on a living comic-strip character. He was surprised, but the fact that they were complete strangers didn't seem to hamper his exuberance in the least, which seemed even more outlandish than the man's appearance.

'Coq au vin is on the menu tonight,' he proclaimed happily, in a slurred Germanic voice. 'It's almost ready, and I have several excellent wines decanting. Please come in, come in.'

Definitely drunk. 'Are you George Bormann?'

'Yes, of course. That's why you're here. I'm famous for my dinner parties.'

'We're Minneapolis police detectives,' Magozzi informed him.

'Oh? Well, all the better!' he crowed, clapping his hands jubilantly. 'I've never met any police. I think you're horribly underpaid for the work you do, so I'm happy to offer my hospitality. Welcome to my home!'

Magozzi felt like he'd just stepped into a weird parallel universe. George Bormann wasn't just eccentric, he was nuts or senile or both. And alcohol wasn't the only thing he'd been abusing – his pupils were huge. He mentally ran through the list of drugs that dilated pupils. Given his demented euphoria, Ecstasy seemed like a reasonable choice. 'We'd just like to ask you a few questions.'

'Well, it won't do to stand in the doorway. Come to the kitchen with me while I finish my final meal preparations. I'll get you a drink and we can chat there. Coq au vin is largely a low-maintenance peasant dish, but care must be taken at the end to ensure the proper finish, caramelizing the condiments before adding and so forth. As tempting as the convenience of frozen pearl onions is, you mustn't ever use them – they won't glaze properly, remember that. And once the mushrooms go into a hot pan, don't touch them until they're perfectly bronzed. But I'm rambling. Come in out of this dreadful weather and follow me.'

They did, into the vast, open house that was as sedate as its owner was flamboyant. The décor was modern, with slate floors, low-slung furniture, and dramatic lighting. The aroma of George's coq au vin filled the space and it smelled pretty damn good.

He stumbled but caught himself as he walked up to a gleaming quartz kitchen island where four crystal decanters held red wines of subtly different hues. There were several goblets lined up, waiting to be filled.

'You're expecting a lot of guests?' Gino asked.

'Oh, I'm always expecting guests. My friends have an open invitation to dinner every night, but they don't always come. People are so busy nowadays. It's tragic. What could be more important than sitting around a dinner table, enjoying good food, excellent wine and conviviality?' His observation subdued him as he expertly filled three glasses. 'We'll start with the Côte de Nuits.'

'No wine for us, thanks.'

George looked crestfallen. 'Well, I don't trust anybody who doesn't drink wine, but I suppose you're on the job. It's such a shame, though, this is quite a miraculous elixir, and the selection gets even better as the evening progresses. Wine is one of my passions.' He took a sip, rolled his tongue around his mouth blissfully, then grabbed the decanter and glass and shambled toward the living area in his harlequin-patterned socks. 'Let's sit while we chat.'

The living room was a surprise in that three large Rado sculptures dominated it.

'You're an art collector, too?' Gino asked nonchalantly.

'Oh, yes, I've got rooms full, but this artist is my most recent discovery and one I'm pleased to show most prominently. His name is Rado. Do you know his work?' He didn't wait for an answer before he continued: 'His sculptures are inspired, simply inspired! He has tremendous vision – his message is so appropriate for the times. He touches me deeply. He is as disturbed by the stupefying effects of technology as I am, and that's what these sculptures are, a message and a warning. I've tried multiple times to contact him. I think he would appreciate my dinner parties and my shared point of view, but I've heard he's quite decrepit, ill with some rare blood disease. But don't artists always have tragedy and hardship in their lives? I believe it's what drives exceptional work.'

Magozzi thought the sculptures didn't look too obscene without the accompanying pornographic videos and photos, but he still hated them. He was also starting to suspect that guests never came to George's dinner parties because he was such a kook. Why else would two homicide cops get invited in to eat a meal and drink great wine? 'So you must have been at the opening last night.'

'Oh, yes, of course I was. It was the fête of the year!'

Magozzi showed him the photo of Kelly Ramage. 'This woman was also there last night, do you remember her?'

His face glowed with warmth and fondness. 'This is a face you won't forget. Dear, sweet Kelly. Such a lovely woman, and a stunning beauty. Unfortunately, I didn't have the opportunity to speak with her at the opening last night, she wasn't there long, but I have made her acquaintance twice at a club I frequent.'

'Club Provocateur?'

'Yes! You know it?'

Gino nodded. 'Kelly was murdered last night.'

His mouth sagged open and his eyes jittered strangely in their shadowed sockets. 'Oh, that's unthinkable! Heartbreaking! How could someone kill such a beautiful young woman, so filled with promise? This is just awful news.'

'It is awful. Can you think of anybody at the club who may have been an acquaintance of hers? A friend?'

'You mean like a murder suspect? I wish I could tell you that, but she wasn't social with anybody at the club. I only managed to have brief conversations with her because I'm quite gregarious.'

'We noticed,' Gino said, under his breath.

'This is just awful news,' George murmured again, letting out a miserable sigh.

'What did you talk about?'

'Nothing, really. My attempts to engage her were unsuccessful. I always like to make the unicorns feel welcome . . .'

'Unicorns?'

'A single person. Usually a woman, hoping to discover a new facet of her identity. If you know the club, then you know that it's the sort of place to find relief from the ordinary banalities of day-to-day life, to explore curiosity and embrace freedom. But she was at the beginning of her journey, and told me she preferred to be alone. She was polite about it, though, which I appreciated. So many young people are lacking in basic manners nowadays.'

'We talked to Ollie earlier. We asked him about drugs. Ecstasy, in particular.'

George let out a merry laugh. 'Ollie must have been upset by the question.'

'As a matter of fact, he was.'

'He's quite paranoid, and perhaps there's a reason, considering the libertine spirit of the club. But I'm sure you know drugs are everywhere.'

'Where do you get yours?'

He gave them a guiltless shrug. 'I don't buy drugs, so I couldn't tell you where they come from. People are generous, particularly with Ecstasy. They pass it out like candy. Complete strangers come up to you and offer it. It's a social drug, not something to do alone.'

'But you're alone now and you're just starting to fly.'

'I'm certainly not alone. You're here, and there will be more guests soon. Perhaps not a full table, but it is a Friday night, and I find people are more anxious to celebrate after a long work week, much more so than on Saturday. And after dinner we'll visit the club.'

Classical music suddenly filled the room, and Bormann clapped his hands in a manic staccato. 'Bravo! My handyman has finally managed to fix the sound system. I was getting concerned – the most carefully planned dinner party is doomed to failure without the appropriate soundtrack to set the mood.'

'Is the volume all right, Mr Bormann?' a male voice called from a balcony overlooking the living room.

'It's absolutely perfect.'

Gino stood. 'Thanks for speaking with us, Mr Bormann. We'll let you finish getting ready for your party.'

He jumped from his perch on a sculpted wooden chair. 'Are you sure you won't stay?'

'Sorry, but we can't. We're on the job, remember?'

He looked crestfallen. 'And an important job it is. I hope you find out who killed Kelly.'

'We will.' Magozzi heard the soft pad of footsteps coming down the staircase. He was as stunned to see Wolfie as he was to see them.

'Detectives?'

'You know each other?' George asked.

Gino nodded. 'We met today at the gallery.'

'Well, how delightful!' George cast a beaming smile Wolfie's way. 'This fine young man is an incredibly hard worker – I couldn't do without him. He DJs at the club and one night I saw him fixing the equipment. Right then and there, I knew he was just the lad I needed. I keep telling him he should quit his other jobs and become my full-time caretaker, but I suppose that's no career for someone of such intelligence and ambition, and a waste of an expensive engineering degree.'

Wolfie shrugged modestly. 'I really appreciate all the work you give me, Mr Bormann. Is there anything else tonight?'

'That will be all, Wolfie. Will you stay for dinner?'

'I'm sorry, sir, but it's getting late and I have to be at the gallery early tomorrow.'

George sighed despondently. 'Of course. I'll call you a cab.'

'We can give you a lift,' Gino offered. 'Where do you live?'

'Northeast neighborhood, just off Broadway.'

'It's on our way.'

George pulled a roll of cash out of his pocket and gave Wolfie several hundred-dollar bills. 'What I owe you, plus a little extra for staying so late.'

'Thank you, sir, that's really kind.'

43

'I appreciate the ride, Detectives.'

Gino was watching Wolfie in the rearview mirror as he looked around the sedan curiously, checking out the on-board computer and radio. 'No problem. Like I said, it's on our way.'

'You've got some cool gear in here. What do you have under the hood?'

'A lawnmower engine. Zero to sixty in eight hours.'

Wolfie laughed. 'That's funny. I never thought of police being funny.'

Gino shrugged. 'When you spend a lot of time around dead bodies, you have to find some balance.'

Wolfie sobered. 'Yeah, that makes sense. You must see a lot of stuff you wish you could forget. Do you ever? Forget, I mean.'

'Never. But you learn to live with it.'

'I have a lot of respect for both of you. I couldn't do your job. Did Mr Bormann help you with your case?'

Magozzi turned in his seat. 'No, but he was very cooperative. He's quite a character. What's it like working for him?'

'It's the best job I have. The work is easy and the pay is great. He's way out there, for sure, but generous. I won't lie, I have thought about working for him full-time, at least until I get on my feet, but I don't think I could stand it. Don't get me wrong, I'm not ripping on him, he's just . . . intense.'

'I can see how he'd be a little hard to take in anything but small doses.'

'Yeah. I feel kind of bad for him, though. Sometimes I think he breaks his own stuff so he has to call me. Like he's paying me for my company.'

'He probably is, but it seems like a mutually beneficial arrangement for now. These dinner parties he has, does anybody ever show up?'

'I wouldn't know, but I hope so. He goes to a lot of trouble.'

'So you have an engineering degree from Caltech. That's impressive.'

'I wish some prospective employers thought so. Everywhere I've interviewed, I'm up against people with graduate degrees. I thought about going back to school, but I can't afford it right now. That's what I'm working toward, though.'

'Keep after it,' Gino said, taking a turn off Broadway onto a side street. 'Something will come along. Are we close?'

Wolfie pointed to a corner brick building at the end of the block. 'That's me.'

Gino eased up to the curb where a path was carved between crusty piles of snow. 'Wolfie, you ever hear anything about drugs at Club Provocateur?'

'Not personally, but they're around. A lot of people there seem high.'

'Kelly Ramage had X on her. We'd like to know where she got it.'

Wolfie lifted his brows. 'Do you think the person who gave her X could have killed her?'

'Once you do crime, it's easy to move up to the next level. Maybe it's the same person Mr Bormann gets it from.'

Wolfie grimaced. 'He was pretty wack tonight. I've never seen him like that all the times I've worked for him, usually only at the club. But I have no idea where he buys it. I suppose it makes sense he gets it there.'

'Just what we were thinking. Maybe you can keep an eye out for us next time you DJ.'

'I'll do that. In fact, spending some time with you guys, I think I'll be watching people in a different way for the rest of my life.'

'It might come in handy someday.'

44

Petra's breath made fluffy white clouds in the cold car that fogged the windows with an opaque film. It would become frost if she didn't keep wiping it away. The eyepieces of her binoculars were like super-chilled circular branding irons that seared numb coronas around her eyes. If she wasn't careful, they'd leave permanent marks.

Her impromptu stake-out of a north Minneapolis warehouse had turned up a very strange surprise: a place called Club Provocateur. Its incongruous presence was the only indication that the neglected building hadn't been totally abandoned, and it certainly wasn't like anything she'd ever seen. Party-goers came and went, some choosing to go coatless on such a night to show off their bizarre costumes, as if it was Halloween night. What sort of place was this?

A valet huddled beneath a small striped awning, smoking cigarettes between arrivals and departures and spells inside to warm up. At the edges of the building, furtive figures slunk around in the shadows, avoiding the spill of the few functioning streetlights. They were certainly opportunistic thieves, waiting for a vulnerable person to meander near their dark alleyway lairs. Shouldn't there be police patrolling the streets here?

No, probably not, she decided. There were certain parts of every city that were deemed beyond salvation, and they were largely left alone in the hope they would self-immolate.

Not that they ever did – they just festered and metastasized to become somebody else's problem. It was in places like these that Vrag and his ilk found sanctuary.

She let out a dispirited sigh. Roadrunner had given her only the name Joseph Koppenhöfer and the address of the warehouse, and here she was sitting in front of a deranged nightclub, flirting once again with hypothermia in the foolish hope that her impulsive decision would produce some kind of victory. Had she really been expecting Peter Praljik to waltz out of the front door wearing his uniform and beret, still bathed in the blood of his homeland?

He might not even be there – he might never have been there, because there wasn't any evidence that he and Joseph Koppenhöfer were the same person. Not even Roadrunner's special computer could determine that with absolute certainty – she was the only one who could, by positively identifying him. There was no sense in organizing an operation without that assurance. And she couldn't identify him if she couldn't get close to him, so there was also no sense in shivering in a dark car, hoping a ghost would materialize before her eyes.

'You're an idiot,' she snapped to herself, tossing the binoculars onto the passenger seat and rubbing at the tender, cold-singed skin around her eyes. She was a researcher, not a commando, and there was a cleverer way to do this.

You're willful and impulsive sometimes, beloved daughter. What should I do with you?

Love me as you love yourself, Tata, because you're willful and impulsive sometimes, too. I get it from you.

But she wasn't just here because of her nature. She was here for her parents, for Mirna, for thousands of others, and especially for Blanca and Martin, possibly new casualties of an old war.

She started the engine, waited for the heat to thaw her windows, then crawled past the club and turned on the first cross street so she could make a circuit around the warehouse. The valet didn't seem to notice her trolling car as he cupped a glowing cigarette to shield it from the cold wind.

Aside from the club, the building seemed abandoned. There were no other lights in any of the windows, many of which were broken or missing altogether. Metal doors sagged from their lintels and jagged piles of construction debris dotted the circumference, like snow-covered haystacks stuck with pitchforks.

At the back of the building, there was a loading dock and delivery lot enclosed by a rusty chain-link fence. There was also a car and a van and four men in a huddle, conferring about something. She killed the lights and pulled up, so she was partially concealed behind a dented Dumpster.

She couldn't see much from her vantage point, just bulky men stomping their feet, vapors from their breath rising toward the stars, like smoke signals. Their faces were turned down and away, so the binoculars were useless.

A sharp rap on her window sent her vaulting up in her seat. Her heart was pounding so hard in her chest, she was almost panting as she turned to face a round, pock-marked face glowering at her from the other side of the glass. Not a cop.

She lowered the window and shouted, 'You scared the hell out of me! What's wrong with you?'

'This is private property. You're trespassing.'

'Then I'll gladly leave.' She reached for the gear shift to

jam the car out of park, then felt a tight grip on her shoulder. Why had she opened the window so far? 'Get your hands off me!'

'Maybe I can help you find something? A woman alone shouldn't be lost in a neighborhood like this.'

Petra weighed her options. She wanted to shoot the man in the head for scaring her so badly, for putting his hands on her, but causing a scene by killing someone didn't seem like a sensible solution. Further verbal assaults were out, too — there was a very good chance she was face-to-face with one of Praljik's thugs, and further confrontation would aggravate this caveman and draw unwanted attention. She risked a quick glance at the four men in the lot. They were all looking in her direction. Too late.

'I'm looking for my friend's music studio,' she improvised, reciting the warehouse address incorrectly. 'Six-forty-six Grand Avenue South.'

He released her shoulder. 'You're on the wrong side of town. This is the north side.'

'It is?'

'Try Google maps,' he sneered.

How could such an ugly man become infinitely uglier with a single expression? 'I will, thanks. Have a good night.' She stomped on the accelerator and felt the rear end of the car fishtail, felt cold wind pouring in through her partially open window. A violent shiver racked her body when she looked in her rearview mirror and saw the ugly, moon-faced man staring after her.

45

When Magozzi and Gino arrived at Harley's, they found Annie in the kitchen, tossing Charlie bits of chicken from a mostly stripped carcass. When the dog sensed their presence, he spun around comically, deserted his buffet, and came bounding over clumsily, his claws slipping and sliding on the polished parquet floor. He finally gave up, sat down on his haunches, and slid the last few feet, bumping into Gino's leg.

He dropped to his knees, hugged the wiggling mass of fur, and presented his face for a few lashings from Charlie's pink tongue. 'Hey buddy, good to see you, too, but no French kissing.' He looked up at Magozzi. 'I should really get a dog.'

Annie clicked over to the foyer entryway. 'Well, hello, you two. I just brewed a fresh pot of coffee. Are you interested?'

'Heck, yeah,' Gino said, uprighting himself in an attempt to restore his dignity. 'You're looking stunning as usual, Annie. I don't think I've ever seen you in purple.'

'I've recently discovered it's a flattering color for me,' she said demurely. 'At least, that's what all the boys tell me.'

Magozzi grinned. 'How are you, Annie?'

'Oh, you know, the same, all work and no play, even though I'm wearing my party dress. Come on in.'

They followed her into the kitchen, gratefully accepted two mugs of coffee, and took stools at the granite island.

'How's your case going?'

'Same as you, all work and no play.' Magozzi picked a shred of chicken off the bones.

'Oh, don't eat off that old thing, sugar, it's for Charlie. Let me put some of Grace's soup on – it won't be a minute.'

Magozzi thought he would wait a decade for some of Grace's soup. 'Thanks, Annie. Any luck with Bit Monster?'

'Baby steps, you know how it is. Grace is still working on your James Bondage, too.' Her face scrunched up in disgust. 'She told us all about it.'

'It wasn't a great way to start the day.'

'Well, I think that when you find him, you ought to do the same to him. It must be tempting.'

Gino slurped his coffee. 'That's the sum total of a homicide cop's fantasy life – dreaming up what you'd do to a perp if you didn't have to cuff him and give him a fair trial.'

'Frontier justice. I'm all for it, as long as I'm the sheriff in town.' She put a saucepan on the stove, then sat on the stool next to Gino. 'While you're waiting on your snack, I have a little news to share. Roadrunner's got himself into a relationship with a very interesting woman.'

Gino coughed, or maybe choked in surprise, and set his mug down abruptly. 'A relationship? Roadrunner?'

'Maybe relationship isn't the proper word. Let's just say he made a connection.'

The day's sadness and exhaustion sloughed off the minute Magozzi saw his ladies sitting on the sofa in the office. They were communicating in their way, Grace leaning over her, speaking softly, Elizabeth tugging at her hair and making noises that reminded him of an aquarium bubbler. He kissed Grace, scooped his daughter into his arms, then he and

Gino engaged in a battle of giddy, ridiculous facial expressions in an attempt to win the fair maiden's favor. It was a draw, in Magozzi's opinion, which made him jealous.

Grace's smooth forehead puckered the tiniest bit as she scrutinized them both with a newly maternal sensibility. She couldn't decide if she was more concerned about their physical condition or their state of mind. Both needed attention. 'You two look exhausted. Did Annie feed you?'

'And gave us coffee. We're almost human again.' Magozzi looked through the glass wall that kept The Beast separate from lesser electronic entities. Harley and Roadrunner were hunched over a monitor, but they broke off for a moment to wave at them. 'They look pretty focused. Are they on to something?'

'They think so. It's early stages, though.'

'Peter Praljik?'

Grace nodded. 'Annie brought you up to speed, then.'

'I don't know if she brought us totally up to speed, but she told us Roadrunner saved a woman's life and now you're helping her hunt down a war criminal. Any luck on James Bondage?'

'Come on over to my station. I'll tell you what I know about him so far. Fair warning, it isn't much.'

Elizabeth let out a happy squeal and her flailing fists connected with Magozzi's jaw. 'Assaulting a police officer, munchkin,' he chided her. 'That's a serious offense.'

Annie walked in with a baby bottle and a pink crocheted blanket. 'Nanny at your service, Grace. I'll take Elizabeth into her room and rock her to sleep. Otherwise these two besotted fools aren't going to be able to focus on a single word you say. Besides, it's way past her bedtime.'

Magozzi reluctantly passed Elizabeth over and pulled up a chair next to Grace; Gino stayed standing.

'JB007 isn't active anywhere else on the web that I've been able to find, so I think it's his specific handle for a specific purpose. He also hasn't been active on the BaDSaM site since his last contact with Kelly Ramage and I can't retrieve any messages from there. I got into Signal through their computer app, but I can't retrieve any of those messages, either. They're all gone. He scrubbed everything and didn't leave a trace.'

'What about the old saw that whatever goes out on the web stays there?'

'Normally it does, it's difficult to erase anything, but James Bondage did, and went to a lot of trouble to do it. He's smart and very tech savvy.'

'That's high-level stuff,' Gino commented.

Grace nodded. 'Yes, it is.'

'What about personal information associated with the account?'

'There isn't any. He was using a burner phone, just made it look like he was using Pavel's. He also used the gym name to set up the gmail account he was using to access BaDSaM.'

Gino frowned at Magozzi. 'Maybe he really does have a beef with Pavel.'

'We'll give him a prod when we return his phone. Thanks, Grace.'

'I'm sorry I couldn't be more helpful.'

'It's not your fault this guy crossed his Ts and dotted his Is. Unfortunately, it's his strong suit. He was as meticulous with the crime scene as he was with the digital stuff.'

'I'll keep working on it. If you get any new information, pass it along.'

'We should have something soon. The LA detective who worked Delia Sellman's case is sending us his report, along with the cyber division's. She was using Signal, too.'

'That could be helpful.'

Roadrunner and Harley finally emerged from the crypt-like chill room; Harley gave his customary, boisterous welcome, Roadrunner his equally warm but more subdued greeting.

'Crazy days, huh, Pops?' Harley said, clapping Magozzi on the shoulder. 'Did Grace and Annie tell you about our new side project?'

'Annie told us a little. Way to go, Roadrunner. There aren't many people who can say they saved a life.'

'Yeah,' Gino said, 'we're always too late.'

Roadrunner's eyes crinkled with his smile. 'So you know about Petra?'

'We just know she's some kind of a special ICE agent who's looking for a war criminal and you're helping her. How's it going?'

'We might be getting somewhere. The Beast turned up something and she's looking into it. Grace told me you thought your case might be connected to McLaren and Freedman's.'

'We're leaning in that direction. Jimmy Grimm found similar traces at both scenes, but the MOs are different. Why?'

'That's Petra's friend's case.'

Magozzi tripped backward mentally. 'Blanca Szabo was her friend?'

'Yeah. Annie didn't tell you about that part?'

'She didn't get that far.'

'Oh. McLaren and Freedman went to talk to Petra about it today.'

So she was the friend McLaren thought was screwy and holding something back. 'Did she say anything to you about it, give you some details?'

'No, just that her friend was murdered.'

Harley sank into his chair and propped his feet on his desk. 'Can I interest you two in a glass of the stunning Côte de Nuits I have decanting in the kitchen?'

Gino raised his brows. 'Man, Leo, what are the odds we'd get offered Côte de Nuits twice in one day?'

Harley blinked. 'No way. Where have you guys been hanging out?'

'An art gallery that's showing some creepy artist named Rado, an even more creepy S and M sex club, and some wine-collecting wackadoodle's geodesic dome, just to name a few of the day's highlights.'

Roadrunner looked astonished. 'There's an S and M sex club in Minneapolis?'

'They say it's not, but I have my doubts. It seems like a pretty shady operation, a joint called Club Provocateur on the north side.'

'A good place to look for James Bondage,' Grace commented.

'We thought so. It's also the last place Kelly Ramage was seen alive, but she left alone. James Bondage knows how to cover his tracks.'

46

Annabelle was doing the breast stroke in her mind, struggling to emerge from the mental bog where syrupy, undulating waves seethed all around her. But her numb, cold limbs wouldn't move. Her fingers and toes didn't seem to respond when she tried to wiggle them. And then she remembered.

You're just as lovely as your sister was.

She would have panicked, but she was incapable because her brain was misfiring, veering off in strange and crazy places, ugly places. And she couldn't remember anything about how she'd gotten here. Maybe she was dead already and this was Hell, a place she'd never believed in until now.

But then she felt the very real, searing pain in her wrists and ankles where the manacles bit into her flesh, where she'd rubbed it raw struggling; became aware of the agonizing thud of a demon's kettledrum between her temples; tasted the foulness of a parched mouth. She was very much alive.

But how long will that last?

She tried to bring her thoughts into focus. They wavered in and out, but somewhere deep in the back of her foggy mind, there was a tiny dim beacon, a miniature lighthouse flashing a signal, and that signal told her to get her bearings, assess the situation, and find a way to GET OUT.

But *how*? She was bound and gagged, blindfolded and

helpless. She'd been drugged, kidnapped, and taken prisoner by the same sick monster who'd tortured her sister before he'd suffocated her. And she was next. Keep it in the family.

She thought of all the tired, inspirational maxims, like 'If at first you don't succeed, try, try again,' and 'Where there's a will, there's a way.' Whatever mindless optimists had come up with those saccharine slogans had obviously never been confined to a torture chamber.

Focus. Keep yourself alive.

She had to pay attention to the lighthouse beacon. It was all she had.

She tried to open up her senses and create a mental image of her surroundings. The first thing she noticed was that the room was very quiet, so quiet that even her breathing and whimpers sounded flat, muffled. It was a soundproofed room, she realized, and felt something go hollow inside.

It was warm and smelled like sandalwood. Or maybe the scent was earth and this was her crypt. It was dark enough to be one – even blindfolded, she registered the absence of light. She was lying on something soft and her head was slightly elevated – a bed?

Because she couldn't move, couldn't use her hands or feet to explore, couldn't even shout to gauge the size of the room, her mental imaging was halted, and most of her hope along with it. All she could do now was stop struggling, save her strength, and wait for an opportunity. Or try to create one when he came back. And he *would* be back, that much she knew.

47

Even in the frigid embrace of January, downtown Minneapolis was a pretty, vibrant city at night. On a subzero Friday, it was busy with diners, theater-goers and bar-hoppers. Get a few cocktails on board, and you were impervious to anything, at least temporarily.

'So, what's your take on everything so far?' Magozzi asked.

Gino snuffled. 'Everything? Give me a couple glasses of Chianti and something might make sense.'

'How about Roadrunner's friend, Petra? McLaren thought she was holding something back when they interviewed her.'

'Like the fact that she's an ICE agent working a local case?'

'That's not an excuse for obstructing a homicide investigation.'

'No proof she is obstructing. Send McLaren a text and let them know who she is. They can run with it.'

They walked up to the entrance of Pavel's Gym, but the closed sign was turned over and it was dark inside, except for a few security lights. 'Looks like Pavel turned in early.'

'Slow night.' Magozzi peered inside and caught a glimpse of movement. 'Somebody's still in there.' He rapped on the door. A few moments later, Pavel appeared under a security light and shouted, 'We're closed.'

'Mr Kosic, it's Detectives Magozzi and Rolseth. We have a couple more questions. We also want to return your phone.'

He stood in place for a long time, then walked to the door and unlocked it. 'Detectives, I'm not well. Can you make this quick?'

Pavel did look like hell. His face was a ghastly shade of white and sweat was running down his face, making dark splatters on his neon green shirt.

'Very quick, then we won't bother you again.' Magozzi handed over his phone. 'Sorry for the inconvenience.'

He stepped away from the door to let them in. Magozzi looked over his shoulder at a disarrayed stack of boxes sitting on the front desk. Pavel followed his gaze, but didn't say anything.

'We wanted to ask you again if you can think of anybody who might want to do you harm. Set you up for Kelly Ramage's murder.'

'I told you before, no.'

'We're asking again, because the person who killed her didn't just steal your phone number. They used your name to set up a gmail account to communicate with her.'

If he hadn't seen it with his own eyes, Magozzi wouldn't have believed Pavel's face could get any whiter. He backed up a few steps and slumped into a chair in the waiting area. 'I don't know,' he said in defeat, then took a few panting breaths. 'I'm being victimized.'

'Are you all right, sir? Can we get you some water or something?'

He looked down and lifted a hand and Magozzi was afraid he was going to lose his dinner right then and there.

'No. Please. I have to go home.' He might have been sick, but it didn't stop him vaulting out of his chair when a loud crash shattered the stillness.

Gino and Magozzi stiffened, instantly on high alert, both hands hovering near their weapons.

'Is there a problem here?' Gino asked warily. 'Do you want us to check it out?'

Pavel started wringing his hands together. 'No, no, it just startled me. It's the janitor. Please don't shoot him.'

'So you do have employees.'

'I have a homeless man I pay cash to clean the place at night. He's a hard worker who fell on hard times. I suppose that's illegal.'

'That's your accountant's problem, not ours.' Gino lifted a brow at him. 'We ran into Kirk again tonight.'

He frowned and shook his head.

'Kirk Johnson, the guy with the tiger tattoo. He bounces at a place called Club Provocateur.'

'Oh? Well, I wouldn't know. Some clients talk, some don't. Kirk is one who doesn't.' He started rocking back and forth on his feet. 'Is that all?'

'Yes. Can we give you a lift home? You really aren't looking so hot.'

'I live upstairs.'

'Sorry to disturb you, Mr Kosic. Feel better.'

'He was either sick or spooked.'

'He was both. Something screwy with Petra, something screwy with Pavel.'

'Something screwy with just about everything. We're in

a maze, Kelly Ramage is in the middle, and we just can't get to her,' Gino complained. 'On the bright side, even mealworms can find their way through mazes.'

'It's kind of late for you to be optimistic.'

'I'm never optimistic *unless* it's late. Did Lerner send his files yet?'

'No. Maybe he got drunk and forgot. I would if I was him.'

'Rado's agent never got back to us, either. Asshole.'

'I guarantee Madeline Montgomery has Michael Dorn's number. We'll hit the gallery again tomorrow morning and pry it out of her. And ask about the guy in the Nazi leather coat that was dogging Kelly at the opening. He's a B-list lead, but we have to turn over all the rocks at this point.' Magozzi's phone chimed. 'Hey, at least McLaren loves us. He just texted.'

'How are they doing?'

'They're about to look at some CCTV footage from the street where Blanca's shop is. He said Anant is hoping to have autopsy results on Kelly and Blanca by tomorrow morning.'

Gino stopped at a red light. 'City Hall or home?'

'Home. It's late, we're out of people to harass, and we need to grab a few hours.'

'I won't argue with you.'

'Mealworms?' Magozzi hesitated, but couldn't help asking.

'Yeah, didn't you have to do that for science class when you were a kid?'

'Hell, no.'

'I'm still not sure what we were supposed to learn from it, but you build a maze, put bran flakes in the middle, then drop your mealworms on the starting line . . .'

Magozzi closed his eyes and let Gino's exposition on the problem-solving capacity of arthropods send him to sleep.

48

His girls were sound sleep when Magozzi got to Grace's, his new home in the city ever since he'd sold his house to McLaren. House and home. Those two words summed it all up: Grace's was home; his old place had just been a house.

He smiled a little, remembering a time when he hadn't always been so welcome there; in fact there had been a couple occasions when he thought she might actually shoot him. But that was when she'd been a person of interest in a serial killing – he and Gino had been lead detectives on the case. People could get so snippy about things like that.

He'd been hoping Grace was still awake so they could share a nightcap while he wound down, but looking in at her peaceful face was almost as satisfying. Elizabeth was asleep in her crib, her eyelids twitching slightly as she dreamed. What did babies dream about? Food? Mom and Dad? The animals hanging from the mobile? Probably everything they saw during the day, he finally decided, wondering if she'd dreamed about snow last weekend after she'd seen it for the first time.

He poured himself a Scotch he knew he'd never finish and wandered the small house. The security system was more suited to a top-secret government installation and had been the ultra-paranoid Grace's impregnable fortress against the evils of the world. It still was – he wasn't so stupid as to think that her old scars had been miraculously healed by childbirth and cohabitation. But she was getting better. There might even come a day when she didn't carry two guns.

He noticed a silver-framed photograph on a credenza he could have sworn hadn't been there yesterday. It was sitting next to the only other framed photo Grace had, one of the three of them at the lake on Thanksgiving weekend.

Magozzi picked up the new addition and smiled. It was from her college days in Atlanta, with Annie, Roadrunner and Harley. He knew it had always been in her desk drawer, but he'd never understood why she kept it secreted, and had never asked. He had his theories, of course, the most likely being that the photo represented a truly happy, innocent time for all of them, before things had gotten very dark and chaotic in their lives. That made it precious, a thing of such value she kept it hidden, like a beautiful piece of priceless jewelry locked away in a safe, never to be worn. It made him inexpressibly happy that it was finally out where it belonged. It was her family photo display, he suddenly realized, modest by normal standards but far more meaningful. She *was* getting better.

He carefully replaced the picture and sank into the sofa to work on his Scotch, but moments after he set down his glass, his eyelids started to droop. Within a few seconds, he fell into a deep sleep and dreamed that Grace was standing over him, shaking his shoulder . . .

'Magozzi, come to bed.'

He opened his eyes and saw two hazy Graces hovering over him. 'You're either awake or I'm dreaming.'

'I've been awake since you shut the car door. Do you really think I'd sleep through someone coming into the house?'

'No. I didn't think that at all.'

Gino walked into his house and smiled at the lingering remnants of Christmas: a ceramic snowman here, a bowl of pine-cone potpourri there. According to Helen, with the full faith and backing of her mother, those items could stay out because they were *seasonal*. It was fine by him: it was one less box to haul down to the basement, where decades' worth of holiday accumulation would languish for another eleven months. Besides, he knew better than to question the decorating decisions of the two women in his life.

The house was quiet, but Helen was still up, sitting cross-legged on the living-room floor with college brochures spread all around her. She looked up and gave him her sweet, crooked smile. 'Hi, Daddy.'

The voice and the smile of his little girl, trapped inside the body of a beautiful young woman. It hadn't happened fast, but it sure seemed like it. It was the same with his thinning hair and expanding belly. One day, you look in the mirror or at your daughter, get the shock of a lifetime, and wish you'd been paying more attention as the years had slipped by slowly and without fanfare.

He leaned over and gave her a peck on the cheek. Her hair smelled like sunshine and flowers. 'Hi, Pumpkin. Where is everybody?'

She thought that was amusing. 'In bed, it's late.'

'So why aren't you in bed?'

'Because I wanted to find out if you and Uncle Leo solved your case.'

'Not yet.'

'You will,' she reassured him.

He sat down next to her and started looking through the glossy brochures featuring smiling coeds and ivy-clad buildings. 'Have you narrowed it down yet?'

'A little bit.' She passed him a brochure from a Florida university. The smiling coeds on the cover were standing in front of palm trees. 'What do you think?'

Gino felt his heart squeeze. 'I think Florida is really far away.'

'It is, but I hate winter.'

'You are definitely your father's daughter.' Gino wondered if all his bitter complaining about winter over the years had poisoned her.

She gave him a sympathetic look. 'Don't worry, I probably won't end up there. But it's nice to think about.' In true teenage fashion, she changed subjects faster than the speed of light. It didn't matter how smart they were, they had the attention span of a gnat, always buzzing around but never landing. 'Brandon and I are going to prom together.'

Another heartbreak. 'You're too young to go to prom.'

She gave him a playful slug on the arm.

'Isn't Brandon in juvenile detention?'

'He'll be out in time for prom.' Helen tried to suppress a giggle. 'You *know* he's not.'

'Huh. I must have done a background check on the wrong kid.'

'He got early acceptance to MIT.'

Florida was sounding better and better. It was at least twelve hundred miles from Massachusetts. 'Prom is going to cost me a fortune, isn't it?'

She gave him a coy smile, like she'd been practicing. She probably had been, or maybe it was a genetic skill passed down through the maternal lineage. 'I'll try to keep the expenses down.'

'Maybe you should get a job.'

'I already have a job at the mall.' Her voice was exasperated, but fondly so, Gino thought.

'You probably have time to pick up a second job. I hear they're hiring at the jail.'

This time she couldn't hold in her laughter. 'You're punchy. You should eat something and go to bed.'

'I think you're right. Is there anything to eat besides algae?'

'*Big* eyeroll, Daddy. It's seaweed, not algae, and it's really good for you.'

'If God wanted me to eat seaweed, I'd be an amphibian. Come on, give it up, I smell garlic.'

'Mom made rigatoni.'

'Now we're talking. Is there any wine left or did she drink it all?'

She thought that was even funnier than the line about getting a second job, which made Gino unreasonably happy.

'There's a bottle of Chianti open. She said to tell you to drink the rest, otherwise it'll go bad.'

Gino's mouth watered. The rigatoni was terrific, but the wine was better. 'Your mother is a saint.'

49

Snow had started falling again, sprinkling down, like icing sugar on a tart. It was a beautiful sight, but Petra couldn't appreciate it because her mind was occupied by the scowling, moon-faced man and his hand gripping her shoulder. She could still feel it, the violation of it.

At the time, she'd been so shocked, adrenalin had overridden any rational thought and her instinct to flee had been all-consuming. But in retrospect she saw it for what it was: wildly inappropriate, feral in aggression, and spine-chilling. What kind of man grabbed a woman so he could offer her directions?

You know what kind of man. A thug. A razbojnika. *Vrag had resurrected his band of criminals here.*

She didn't know that for certain, but no predator ever changed its behavior: it was innate, a fundamental part of the DNA. You could relocate a tiger from the jungle, but it would still be a man-eater wherever it lived. Likewise, you could take the devil out of Hell, but he'd still be the devil and bring Hell with him.

Her eyes filled, thinking of Martin, the only person in the world she could have called. But he was gone and she was alone. She had been desperate to speak with Emmanuelle, but she'd left a cryptic text earlier: *Late, I'll call tomorrow. Suspicious death, police investigating further.*

Did the tentacles really reach that far? It seemed unlikely, but you never bet against someone like Praljik. It was difficult to admit, but she was far out of her realm. The sensible thing would be to bring in support, backup. That was what Martin would have told her to do. But it wasn't time for backup, not yet.

She needed a solid strategy to get to him. She couldn't expose herself, especially after being confronted tonight, so asking for him by name was out of the question. And she obviously couldn't watch the warehouse with a bunch of *razbojnike* guarding it. She knew what happened to people who poked around where they shouldn't.

Petra was suddenly overwhelmed by a maddening sense of helplessness and frustration, and beneath that, hatred and a long-simmering rage. All these years it had been gnawing at her soul, and it was a wonder she had one left. *If* she had one left.

Vodka and tranquilizers. It was tempting, so tempting, but not tonight. A good rest, an early rise, and she would start over tomorrow. Peter Praljik wasn't going anywhere and neither was she.

Calmed by a fierce sense of purpose, she locked up the house and settled in bed, relishing the feel of the heavy down comforter settling over her, like a protective shield. She switched off the bedside lamp and watched the snow fall outside her window, dancing and sparkling in the ambient glow from her porch light. She closed her eyes, imagining it was diamond dust falling from the sky.

She didn't know what stirred her from a sound sleep, but she woke in a nebulous panic, her heart skipping in her chest. She lay perfectly still, held her breath and listened, but the house was silent. Then she noticed a faint wash of light on the wall – a stark white, not the golden glow from her porch lamp.

She slid out of bed, staying low, and carefully withdrew her gun from the bedside-table drawer. Inch by inch, she crab-walked to the window and rose just high enough to peer between the gap in the sheer curtains. There was a car parked across the street. The headlights suddenly switched off, but the engine was still running, she could see the steam coming from the tail pipe. It was an undistinguished sedan, one of thousands just like it in the city. An ordinary car on an ordinary street on an ordinary night. But something told her it didn't belong there. Moon Face, idling outside her house, watching her?

She crawled back to the bed and flicked on the overhead light she never used because it was too bright. By the time she made her way to the window again, the car was gone.

50

Harley was deep into the guts of Bit Monster, continuing the tedious analysis of their system and checking for more individual accounts that had been hacked before the heist. Grace's instincts had been right: this was a way for the bad guys to get into the system, and possibly the set-up for the master attack.

So far, the shark still hadn't taken his five-million-dollar chum, but that was secondary and he wasn't paying much attention to it. If it happened, it would be a nice bonus, but even if it did, it wouldn't necessarily expose the big player behind the mega-hack, or solve the deeper security issues he was starting to uncover. Bit Monster was ultimately going to be about good old-fashioned digital legwork, the same sort of thing Leo and Gino did on the job. And he was finding enough foibles in the security framework to keep him busy for weeks.

He pushed away from the computer to rest his eyes, waiting for the numbers and symbols emblazoned on his retinas to fade. Across the room, Roadrunner was checking on The Beast again, which was totally unnecessary – The Beast let you know when she had something and, besides, he'd passed on enough information for Petra and her crew to run with, something they might never have found without some fierce computing power. Yeah, they'd merged their search of Bit Monster with Petra's search for Peter

Praljik, looking for a possible criminal connection, but Harley knew Roadrunner's obsessive visitations to the chill room had less to do with work and more to do with being a hero.

The poor bastard had it bad for this woman, which was so antithetical to Roadrunner's nature that Harley was having trouble wrapping his mind around it. He'd always been monkish and utterly androgynous, without the slightest hint of sexual predilection either way. There was obviously something very special about Petra, and he wondered what it was.

He rolled his chair back to his computer and refocused on work, happily unaware of time passing. At some point, Roadrunner made an abrupt entrance into the office.

'Harley, The Beast just made another connection. Joseph Koppenhöfer has an account with Bit Monster, opened with Praljik's Social Security number, just like the Vrag LLC.'

'Son of a bitch.' Harley toggled between screens and started typing. 'I'm into the Bit Monster accounts right now, I'm looking him up.'

It took Harley some time to root him out, but when he did, they both stared at the monitor with slack jaws. 'Christ on a crutch,' he mumbled, hardly believing what he was seeing. 'He got shanked for almost twenty million dollars. Am I reading that right?'

Roadrunner nodded. 'Joseph Koppenhöfer doesn't have any other digital footprints besides the Vrag LLC and his Bit Monster account, so he's dirty, he's got to be. That's where the money came from. Question is, where did it go?'

'If he made any transactions with crypto, maybe we can find out. Like you said, it's easier to hack somebody's account if you get a legitimate payment out of them first, and if you're smart, that can open a portal.'

A half-hour later, Harley rubbed his eyes and pointed at the monitor. 'In the five years that Koppenhöfer had his Bit Monster account, he made deposits – shitloads of them – but only one bitcoin purchase, last year, for three hundred K. The vendor's handle is Rado. Hey, isn't that the name of the creepy artist Magozzi mentioned earlier?'

'Yeah. That's a little weird. We should give them a heads-up.'

'On it.' Harley fired off a quick text while Roadrunner examined the monitor.

'Do you think Rado's ripping off his customers?'

'An artist as a hacker?'

'Why not? Check Rado's account, see if he's the one who fleeced Koppenhöfer for twenty mil. If he pulled that off, he could be behind the Bit Monster attack.'

'Can't. He doesn't have an account with them. If he stole the money, he moved it to another exchange. That's the beauty of cryptos, you can be as anonymous as you want.'

'Did any of the other e-wallets that got hacked make transactions with Rado?'

'A couple I've seen so far, but the list of accounts is long. It's going to take a while to go through everything, and the sun's damn near up. We need to get some sleep.'

Roadrunner bobbed his head in agreement. 'At least we're making progress.'

'This might be all the progress we make. Most normal people don't use cryptos, so you can't count on predictable behavior.'

Roadrunner's brows lifted. Then he jumped on his keyboard.

'What?'

'You said normal. So I'm thinking like a normal person.'

Harley scoffed. 'Yeah, right, like that's ever happened.'

'I'm serious. We need to get into Rado's account, and the best way to do that is set him up.' Roadrunner began typing, toggled through a few screens, then stabbed a crooked finger at the page he'd pulled up. 'Look here. Rado: Syzygy of Art and Technology. You can only buy his art with crypto.'

Harley squinted and read further. 'Okay, but what are we supposed to do with that?'

'We're going to buy one of his sculptures with your fake Bit Monster account. If he's hacking his customers' accounts, he'll see five mil in yours and try to hack you, too. Then we can get into his stuff that way. Who knows? He could be the big kahuna, Harley. And he's got a show in Minneapolis right now.'

Harley leaned back in his chair and folded his arms across his broad chest. 'Syzygy of Art and Technology. It's worth a shot.'

'The gallery isn't open at this hour, so let's do our research on this Rado character before we go spend your fake money.'

51

Annabelle started screaming the minute the gag came off. She screamed and screamed and screamed and didn't stop until her throat was burning and she couldn't eke out another sound. But he hadn't done anything to stop her: he'd just waited. Which meant he wasn't worried about anyone hearing her – a very bad sign that didn't bode well for her future. She'd never thought about dying of anything other than natural causes, but now she could think of nothing else.

'Let me go, *please*,' she whispered, wincing in pain. She felt his weight on the edge of the bed and started shivering. 'What do you want?'

She felt cool plastic against her lips.

'I want you to drink.'

She was still blindfolded, still manacled, so she had to take the water as he gave it to her, like a baby animal being bottle-fed, another humiliation on top of so many, and more to come, she knew. But she greedily sucked down the water, not caring if it was drugged or poisoned, almost hoping it was. She started to cry when she heard the crackle of the empty bottle as he crushed it. She had to buy time, had to get better bearings, had to find a way out. She'd come in somehow, and she'd get out the same way. Yes, she would.

Her tears came harder when she thought about Delia,

knowing she'd been through this very same hell and thinking the exact same things up until the minute she'd been suffocated. There was no judgment in her thoughts about what Delia had or hadn't done, just the single crystalline hope that things would be different this time.

She briefly indulged the fantasy that she'd catch her sister's murderer and justice would finally be served. Maybe she'd even kill him if she had a chance. But nothing was going to happen if she just lay here whimpering and crying. She had to make opportunities.

'I need to use the bathroom.'

'I thought you might.'

She started writhing in panic when she felt her buttocks being lifted – 'What are you doing?' – and then she felt cold plastic against her bare skin. A bed pan. 'Oh, my God, no, please, please, LET ME GO!' In her mind, it was a scream, but in reality, it was a weak, raspy whisper.

In a room full of horrors, his chuckle was the worst. She now realized what he wanted: to see her struggle, see her terrified, see her humiliated. Above all, he wanted to witness her suffering.

'I'll give you some privacy,' he finally said.

'No . . . no, don't go.'

She heard him grunt, heard him – no, *felt* him – get closer. His face close to hers. Breath that smelled like mint. She gathered all the saliva she could manage and gobbed it at him. 'YOU SICK FUCK! YOU KILLED MY SISTER! YOU'RE GOING TO ROT IN HELL!'

She felt his weight lift off the bed abruptly. She'd surprised him, pissed him off. It was a small victory, but a victory all the same. It was something to cling to.

'You really shouldn't have done that,' he said, in an infuriatingly calm voice.

'You're a sick, pathetic, fucking bastard.' The rage poured out of her, white hot and dizzying. 'You can't get a woman any other way? You have to drug them and tie them up? Doesn't your dick work? Is that your problem?'

He chuckled again. 'It seems to me you're the only one with the problem. But I appreciate your passion. We're going to have so much fun together after I get to know you better. I knew Delia very well.'

Keep him talking, she thought. Maybe he'll say something important, something that could be useful later. If she survived. 'How did you know Delia?'

'We had a long-distance relationship. You and I are going to have a more traditional one, since you're here. I think I like this better. Are you hungry?'

'No.'

'You need your strength.'

Annabelle rolled her head to the side, away from him. 'Why? You're just going to kill me, like you killed Delia, like you killed that other woman.'

'Not right away, that would be boring. Pointless. No, we're going to spend some quality time together. As long as it takes.'

'As long as it takes for what?'

'It's important to form a bond. A spiritual connection. Without it, death is meaningless, and no death should be meaningless. Do you believe in the spirit world, Annabelle?'

She refused to answer.

'I do, because I can feel the dead souls all around us. And if they have made no true spiritual connection in this plane at the time of their death, they are doomed. They will never find peace, not for all eternity. You don't want that to happen to you, do you?'

'You're insane.'

'No, just a hopeless romantic. I'm sure you're tired, so I'll let you rest. Think about what I said.'

Annabelle went limp when the gag went back in her mouth, but she refused to struggle, refused to fight, even though her body was buzzing with rage. Let's see how much he likes to play with dead things, she thought bitterly.

A few minutes later, she didn't have to force herself to play dead because her mind was suddenly fuzzy again and the small, dark world behind her blindfold began to fold and warp.

52

McLaren and Freedman were already at their desks when Gino and Magozzi got to the office. They were rumpled and haggard and generally looked like shit, but Magozzi reserved comment because he and Gino weren't going to win any beauty contests either.

'Hey, you guys look like shit,' McLaren said cheerfully.

Gino threw his briefcase onto his desk. 'Do you have a mirror in your house, McLaren?'

'Yep, and it told me I looked sharp as hell.'

'So it's a funhouse mirror. That's okay, buddy, live the lie.'

'No lying. Gloria complimented me on my new suit.' He brushed the lapels of a nubby woolen jacket that emitted the distinctive odor of mothballs.

'I did no such thing,' Gloria sniped from the hallway, giving her colorfully beaded corn-rowed hair a haughty toss over her shoulder. 'I said the stench of mothballs was a far sight better than your usual aftershave, and if you think that was a flattering remark, then you're even more pathetic than I thought you were.'

McLaren waggled his brows at Gino. 'What did I tell you? Total compliment.'

She sashayed into the office, her capacious hips moving in perfect synchronicity with the swing of her braids. The withering look she gave McLaren only broadened his smile, so she redirected her ire toward Magozzi and Gino. 'And you two. I don't know what kind of bad juju you got your-selves into, but another lunatic has you in their sights. He left an urgent message this morning, saying you have a per-manent spot on his dinner-guest list, except for Sundays.'

Magozzi sighed and looked at Gino. 'George.'

'Call him back or not, I don't care, but here's his num-ber.' She slapped a pink note slip in front of Magozzi and departed in the same way she'd come in, on a flamboyant rampage he strongly suspected was meant to drive McLaren crazy. From the infatuated look on his face, the strategy was effective. Gloria was a real vixen, and totally out of McLaren's league, which was why it would probably work out between them someday.

Freedman stood up and stretched, his big arms nearly reaching the ceiling. 'George, huh?'

'Yeah, a real mess of a guy, total sad sack.' Gino looked at McLaren, who was gazing at the empty space where Gloria had been. 'Lonely. Attention-seeking. Pathetic.'

Freedman gave him a conspiratorial smile. 'I know the type. So, we've got resin dust and duct tape at both scenes, but no connections between Blanca and anything to do with Kelly Ramage. Definitely nothing to do with Rado or Club Provocateur or bondage, and not Delia Sellman, either. You got any theories?'

'The resin dust checks a new box, even though the MOs are totally different, so let's say we're looking for the same killer, James Bondage. Kelly was cultivated. He was playing her, just like he played Delia Sellman. Blanca was unplanned.'

'That's not a theory, Rolseth, it's a statement of fact.'

'So what does it mean? You're the one who's been dig-ging into Blanca's life.'

'She didn't have one,' McLaren said. 'We tore her phone and her life apart and there was nothing there. The woman didn't have a computer, she was a complete hermit, and none of her clients are good for it. We doubled back and interviewed every one of them again.'

'How about the camera footage?'

'It's worthless. It doesn't show the shop entrance, plus everybody is so damn bundled up for the weather, you can't even tell if you're looking at a man or a woman. Hard to pick out suspicious-looking parkas.'

'Petra Juric sounds like the only person who knew her. Did you talk to her again?' Magozzi asked.

'She's on top of the honey-do list for today. What's the deal about her being a fed?'

Magozzi and Gino told them what they knew about her, which wasn't much.

'She told us she almost died of hypothermia,' McLaren said. 'So Roadrunner saved her?'

'Yeah.'

'That's something else. But it doesn't help us any, except maybe explain why she seemed cagey yesterday. Is she an undercover type?'

'No, just a researcher – at least, from what we know.'

Freedman sat back down and slurped coffee from one of the chipped communal Homicide coffee mugs that identi-fied him as the world's greatest grandma, a runaway favorite if you got to the office early enough. 'I know you think she was acting weird, Johnny, but I'm telling you, the woman was just flat-out shocked when we told her about Blanca and for sure tweaked after a near-death experience. Who wouldn't be?'

'Yeah, maybe.' McLaren checked his computer when it pinged. 'Email from Anant. He says he'll send his reports over by noon.'

'Any hints?'

McLaren ran his finger down the screen, scanning for pertinent details. 'Kelly Ramage was strangled, but it didn't kill her. The head wound didn't contribute . . . green residue found in stomach. No sign of contusions, strangulation, or defensive wounds on Blanca. He doesn't think her neck was broken in a fall.' He paused. 'Jesus, civilians just don't get their necks snapped manually. That's some hardcore shit.'

'It sure as hell is,' Gino said. 'Did you see the name Kirk Johnson in her appointment book or in any of her personal effects?'

'No, who's he?'

'A gigantic goon who works at Club Provocateur. A 'roid head, for sure. He's got the strength and, from what we saw, he's got plenty of anger-management issues.'

'We'll look into it, ask Petra about him. What's up with the green residue in Kelly's stomach?'

'Ecstasy. We've been trying to track that angle down, but no joy.'

'Did you talk to Ty in Narc?'

'Of course we did, but he hasn't seen any around in a while. He pushed a snitch about it, but the snitch hasn't seen any, either.'

'So what's next on your agenda?'

'We're going back to the gallery to follow on a couple things as soon as it opens. You guys?'

'Petra. Then who the hell knows what?'

53

As Stefan tried to work with a mutant breathing down his neck and muffled music throbbing, like an infected wound, somewhere in the building, it occurred to him that they were probably going to kill him either way. If he failed, they'd kill him out of spite, and if he succeeded, they'd kill him so they wouldn't have to share the proceeds. No three percent, no twenty K retainer. Gone, just like that. He wouldn't need it where he was going. That was why they were keeping him here. He couldn't hold information hostage while they wired money to his account when he was sitting in their prison.

Son of a bitch. He'd worked for plenty of criminals, but this was a whole different level of bad and he was suddenly scared shitless. If he had a future, which was very much in doubt at this point, he was going to have to seriously reconsider his choice of clientele.

The room was cool, but sweat started running down his brow and dripping on his hands. He mopped it with his Metallica bandana and turned to the mutant. 'I need to talk to your boss.'

'He's busy.'

'It's important. Really important.'

He blinked at him as docilely as a cow, then exited the room.

Stefan flinched when he heard the thunk of the door

lock, reminding him of his dire situation. He had to think of a more compelling way to frame his argument to leave. The trouble was, he didn't have anything to negotiate with. Except money. It was the only thing people like this understood.

He jumped in his chair when the door slammed open against the wall, and Joseph stormed in. His face was red, his eyes were buggy, and a snarl was frozen on his face. This was who he *really* was, and Stefan realized he'd just made a huge mistake.

'You'd better have good news.'

'I – I have some good news.'

The snarling face relaxed. 'Tell me.'

What the fuck was his good news??

'I think I have some solid ideas about how to do this,' he lied. 'It's going to take time, but ideas always come first, right? But, like I said, it's going to take time, and if I have to work from here, it's going to take even more time because the environment is distracting. No offense! It's just not what I'm used to.'

The snarl started to redevelop and Stefan felt his heart ricocheting in his chest. 'So – so I'd like you to reconsider letting me go home . . . without the retainer. We can settle up after. I can do the work faster there, which means you'll get your money faster.' Stefan held his breath, closed his eyes, and waited for an explosion. When it didn't come, he lifted his lids slowly. Joseph's face had gone still. Scary still, scary calm, which was far worse.

He shook his head in disappointment and swept his arm across the nicely appointed room. 'All these fine things at your disposal? A stocked refrigerator, a stocked

248

bar, cartons of cigarettes, whatever brand you prefer. Comfortable furniture, the best equipment. A digital sound system that will play any song ever recorded just for you. Yet you can't work here.'

'No, no, it's all great.' Stefan rushed and stumbled through the words. 'It's just not ideal, is what I'm saying. I want to be able to perform at my best for you.'

'You're full of shit, Stefan. Do you think I'm an idiot?'

'No, no –'

'I think you do. I know that if I let you go, you'll disappear. I would have no problem finding you, but I don't want to waste the manpower or the energy.' He let out a derisive snort. 'And I'm extremely angry that you called me out of a very important meeting to listen to you simper because you're homesick.'

Stefan instinctively recoiled when he walked over and sat down next to him, his feral face inches from his.

'Have you ever heard the saying that every man owes God a death?'

He shook his head and was too terrified to feel humiliated by the tears running down his cheeks, unaware that his body was trembling so hard, his teeth were chattering.

'God loans you life, but you have to return it on the day of His choosing. It's the same with the devil. When you make a pact, you owe him your soul.' He smacked the computer monitor and sent it teetering, catching it just before it tipped over. 'Your soul is in here, Stefan, and it's mine. How long it takes you to deliver is your decision, but I'll tell you I'm not a patient man. And don't ever ask for me again until you're finished.'

The concussive slap across his face spun his head

sharply to the right and he cowered and covered his head against more blows that never came. When he finally looked up, Joseph was gone and the mutant was watching him pensively. 'He really is the devil.'

Stefan sniffled and bobbed his head. He knew that now.

54

Gino shook his head wearily as he gazed up at the Resnick/ Feinnes façade. The sun had been up for a while, but it was a cold white ball, distant and uninterested in warming this part of the world. God, he hated winter, and when he got home tonight, he'd tell Helen to go for Florida so he had a legitimate reason to flee the state whenever he wanted to.

Weekends in Boca Raton. Vitamin D that didn't come from a bottle. Brandon a thousand miles away. And, most importantly, spending time with his baby girl and giving all the hormonally deranged frat boys notice that Helen Rolseth was off-limits: touch her and you're dead. So dead. It was a good future he was envisioning. 'Why did Harley text you at five a.m., and why are you just getting it now?'

Magozzi was squinting at his phone's screen. 'Because it's so damn cold, my battery is fried.'

'Then read fast.'

'Huh. He says Rado might be connected to the Bit Monster hack. He and Roadrunner are checking it out.'

'You're kidding me.'

'That's what it says. They'll get back to us when they know more.'

'Well, shit, I don't even know where to go with that.'

Magozzi didn't either. Rado was a player in the murders, but the possibility that he was one in Bit Monster too made his brain hurt. He looked out of the windshield at the frosty group of protesters, already at it. 'They're not giving up.'

'No, they're not. Good for them. Come on, let's go.'

They got out of the sedan, braced themselves against the cold wind that didn't seem like it would let up until spring, and made their way to the gallery entrance. The protesters predictably merged and descended on them as a single organism, shouting grievances that got carried away in a subzero gust.

Gino walked up to the phalanx and Magozzi followed. 'You don't have to shout at me, I'm right there with you.' He scanned the cold-reddened faces. Nobody was wearing a balaclava today. 'Where's Annabelle?'

A diminutive young woman broke away from the pack. 'You're the detectives who talked to Annabelle yesterday.'

'Yeah.'

'Can you help us?'

'With what?' Magozzi asked.

She frowned and chewed her lower lip. 'Annabelle. We can't reach her and we're worried. We were all supposed to get together at my place last night, but she never showed up. She's not answering her phone and she's not at her apartment. I checked this morning.'

'Maybe she had other plans –'

'No,' she interrupted. 'That's not like Annabelle. She wouldn't just disappear and not tell me.'

'Does she have a boyfriend she may be with?'

'No.'

'Parents?'

'I called them. They haven't heard from her.'

'So you can't think of anywhere she might be?'

'No, that's why I tried to file a Missing Persons report this morning, but they blew me off. She's an adult, not a danger to herself or others, no signs of foul play.' She angrily recapitulated the standard requirements for making an official MP report. 'But there's something wrong, I'm telling you. This isn't like her – it's not like her at all.'

Magozzi thought about Delia Sellman, about the red fibers LA had found at her scene. The way it stood now, at least in his mind, her killer was Kelly Ramage's killer, and he was here. A warped Rado disciple. And it wasn't much of a stretch to think that Delia's sister Annabelle was on the killer's radar. 'When was the last time you saw her?'

'We left here at two thirty yesterday when our relief crew showed up. She said she was going to grab a bite somewhere on the way home, then take a nap before we all got together again to make plans and more signs for today. At first we thought she maybe just went to bed – it's freezing out here and she wasn't feeling that great, like she was catching a cold. But I really started to worry when she wasn't picking up her calls this morning. I went to her apartment, and when she didn't answer her door, I called 911.' Her eyes filled with tears. 'I thought maybe she'd be here. I keep expecting her to show up.'

'What's your name?' Gino asked.

'Greta Collier.' She sniffled.

'Greta, come warm up in our car and tell us everything, all the details you can think of.'

'Okay.'

'We're going to have Missing Persons open a case, and while we wait for them to arrive, we'll check her apartment.'

'Thank you,' she said, in a wobbly voice. 'Thank you.'

55

'Oh, my God,' Harley said under his breath. 'Rado is a frigging psychopath. This is repulsive.'

Roadrunner was paler than usual, gaping at the bondage videos with a horrified expression. 'No wonder there are people protesting. I don't want anything to do with this, but we still have to buy a sculpture.'

Harley looked around the gallery at the clusters of people engaged in animated discussions as they viewed the freak show. Whatever they were so excited about, it was coming from a very dark, ugly place and he felt like beating the whole lot of them until they recovered their moral compasses, if they'd ever had any to begin with. 'Christ, I know, and it makes me sick.' He wandered further into the exhibit. 'So which one do we buy? They all look exactly the same.'

'But they're not. Each sculpture represents old computer tape, but each one has a different arrangement of punch holes.' Roadrunner tipped his head, looking at one more closely. 'Those holes represent letters – at least, they do if he based them on the Baudot Murray code. There might be hidden messages in them.'

'From what I'm seeing here, if there are any messages, I don't want to know what they say.'

Roadrunner took out his phone and began taking surreptitious shots of the sculptures. Behind him was clear signage that said: NO PHOTOGRAPHY.

'Excuse me, sir.'

A gaunt woman in black with a stern, ghostly white face approached them. 'Photography is strictly forbidden in the gallery.'

'Sorry about that, my friend gets carried away sometimes. He's mad for Rado.'

Roadrunner pocketed his phone and narrowed his eyes at Harley.

'So who do I talk to about buying one of these?' Harley spoke the magic words and watched her face soften, just like that.

'I can help you. Madeline Montgomery.' She offered her hand. 'Mr . . . ?'

'Erich. Korngold.'

'Which piece were you thinking of, Mr Korngold?'

'Well, I'm partial to that one.' He pointed at random to a sculpture in the corner.

'I'm so sorry, but that's already been sold. Perhaps you'd like to consider another.'

'The show must be going well, huh?'

'We've sold several pieces, yes.'

Amazing. People were truly warped and insane. 'Well, my second choice would be this one.' He nodded to the sculpture he was standing next to out of convenience.

'This is an excellent choice, Mr Korngold. It's one of Rado's most meditative pieces, in my opinion.'

'That's exactly how I would describe it.'

Roadrunner was pretending to examine it closely. 'He showed this at the Venice Biennale last year, didn't he?'

Madeline Montgomery couldn't contain her excitement. 'Yes, yes, he did. You were there?'

'We never miss it,' Harley said, draping his arm across Roadrunner's shoulders and getting a dirty look for his effort.

She gave them an expansive smile. 'Well, I'll give you two some more time to view the exhibit before you make a decision.'

'That won't be necessary. This is the one. Let's draw up a deal and make the arrangements.'

'Very good,' she said brightly. 'Come to my office.'

Harley and Roadrunner took uncomfortable chairs while she cleared some paperwork from her desk and settled behind it.

'We always offer champagne to our clients, but if it's too early, I can offer you another beverage.'

'It's never too early for champagne.'

'Wonderful.' She spoke into a discreet mic nestled in the neckline of her dress, and within minutes, an underfed young woman with blue hair and multiple facial piercings carried in an ice bucket of champagne. Tattinger, non-vintage, which disappointed Harley. He'd been expecting a little more for shelling out six figures.

As she poured champagne, she asked typical small-talk questions and chattered effusively about Rado's art, which he let Roadrunner handle, since he'd obviously paid more attention to his research.

Harley accepted his glass with a gracious nod. 'So you probably get asked about this all the time, but Rado seems to be pretty elusive.'

'He certainly is. I've never met him. Nobody has, as far as I know.'

'No kidding? Well, it's not unusual for great artists to be antisocial.'

Madeline Montgomery nodded. 'You're absolutely right about that, Mr Korngold.'

'Still, it's pretty intriguing. There are lots of rumors floating around. Some people say he lives on a remote island in the South Pacific.' Harley had just made that up, but he liked the sound of it.

'I haven't heard that one.' She smiled politely.

'A guy in Venice last year told me he was Swiss, some big private-equity guy who gave it all up to follow his passion.'

'That sounds vaguely familiar, but I really can't say. I'd almost hate to ruin the mystique, to tell you the truth. It's very much a part of his artistic credo.' She gave them a confidential look. 'Some people say he's really at all of his openings.'

'Wow! That would be something, rubbing elbows with the man himself and not even realize it.'

She got a wistful look on her face. 'It would be, but it's not possible. You must know that he's gravely ill.'

'What a tragedy.'

'It certainly is.'

Roadrunner declined champagne, and after Harley and Madeline had clinked glasses, business commenced as she opened a leather portfolio. 'As I'm sure you're aware, Rado only accepts cryptocurrency as payment.'

'We know.'

'The price of the sculpture is three hundred thousand.'

'Seems like such a small price to pay for something so meditative.'

'It will be an important addition to your collection, Mr Korngold. I think you'll be very pleased with your choice.

Rado is relatively new to the art world, but his star is rising quickly, and I absolutely see him in the pantheon of great twenty-first-century artists. You're clearly passionate about his work, but it's also an excellent investment.'

'I couldn't agree more. So how does the payment work?'

'The transaction will be routed directly through Rado, so expect an invoice from him in your email. You'll enter the appropriate information and, once the funds clear, the sculpture is yours. We'll contact you immediately to arrange shipping.'

'Great.'

'Are you local?'

'Yes.'

'Excellent. If I can just get some personal information from you, I'll start the process and, hopefully, you'll have your sculpture in a day or two.'

Harley winked at Roadrunner. 'We can't wait. Happy birthday, honey.'

'You really shouldn't have,' Roadrunner mumbled.

'For Christ's sake, Harley, did you have to?'

'Come on, we make a great-looking gay couple, don't you think? Madeline ate it up. Besides, I had to have some fun to get my mind off the fact that I was buying a sculpture off some perverted misogynist. Even if it's not real money, it still pisses me off. Hey, how'd you like the way I slid in the Swiss thing?'

'That was pretty good. Interesting she thought she may have heard that before.'

'You never know. See, this is what Leo and Gino do. Computers can't ask questions or read people. It's kind of fun.'

'What's going to be more fun is getting that invoice. What do you bet there's a link you click that directs you to a site where you enter your payment information and, bingo, that's the trap. Simplest thing in the world. Who would think they'd get phished paying six figures for important art? Important in quotes.'

'It could be as simple as that. Or it could be nothing. Rado might just be an artist who only accepts cryptos, end of story. We'll see.'

'What's the deal with Erich Korngold?'

'That's the name on my Bit Monster account. You didn't think I'd use my real one to open up a fraudulent account, did you?'

On the way to Harley's Hummer, Roadrunner noticed a familiar sedan parked across the street. There was a dark-haired man in the passenger's seat. 'Harley, look – that's Leo and Gino.'

Harley squinted. 'By God, I think you're right.' He veered off the sidewalk and crossed the street.

Magozzi opened his window. 'Hey, guys, we just got your text. What's with Rado being part of the Bit Monster thing?'

'Might be, we're working on that now. We just bought one of his sculptures.'

Gino leaned across the front seat. 'Why the hell did you buy a sculpture? It's pure shit.'

'No kidding. And it cost me three hundred grand for that pure shit, can you believe it?' Harley grinned. 'But it's not real money. More on that later, it's a long story, but buying the sculpture is the only way we might be able to nail him. It could be our ticket in. So what's your link to Rado?'

'We think our killer might be some twisted acolyte,

copying his work for real. We were here to follow up on a couple leads, but before we got in there, we found out there might be another missing woman. The sister of the LA victim.'

Harley scuffed his feet in the snow. 'God, I'm sorry. Listen, coincidences are starting to pile up. You and Gino need to come over so we can all put our heads together.'

'Agreed, one hundred percent. We'll stop by later, as soon as we can.'

'Good luck.'

'To you guys, too.'

56

Leonard Foley keyed open Annabelle's door with shaking hands. He was the live-in owner of the building, well into his seventies, and he'd been absolutely devastated when Magozzi had explained why he and Gino were there. His TV had been tuned to the Investigative Discovery channel, so he'd probably watched plenty of cop shows where there weren't happy endings after the detectives asked to enter the home of a missing person.

'Annabelle is the sweetest girl I've ever met. Never any trouble from her. She studies a lot – she's a junior at St Thomas, a history major, I think – and she never has anyone over. She's not a party girl, that's for sure. Oh, and she doesn't have a boyfriend.'

Definitely a cop-show junkie, which made him a great witness. 'Thanks for being so helpful, Mr Foley.'

'Sure thing. Figured you'd have to ask anyhow, so thought I'd save you some breath.' He pushed open the door. 'I pray to God she's okay.'

'So do we.'

He stepped aside stiffly, wincing at his aches and pains. 'I'll just stay in the hall.'

'Thank you.'

Her apartment was small, but neatly kept and decorated nicely on a student's budget. There were throw rugs, curtains, IKEA furniture, little knick-knacks and pictures that made it seem homey. There was also a photo collage hanging in the living room, Annabelle and another young woman who bore a strong resemblance to her. Delia. It seemed sacrilegious to remove a photo from the shrine, but they needed one.

The kitchen was as clean as the rest of the apartment. No spent grounds in the filter basket of her Cuisinart coffee-maker, no dregs of morning java in the carafe, and the hotplate wasn't warm to the touch. Her bed was made, without a single wrinkle on the navy blue comforter.

'She didn't come home last night,' Gino said.

'Doesn't look like it.'

'I didn't hear her come in,' Leonard called from the hall. 'It's a small building, only four units besides mine, so I usually hear when people come and go.'

'Thanks for letting us know,' Magozzi said, looking for a landline, but of course there wasn't one. Hardly anyone had landlines anymore, but especially not millennials. They probably didn't even believe they existed outside the Smithsonian.

He and Gino walked back out into the hall. 'We think Annabelle stopped to get something to eat on the way home, Mr Foley. Can you think of a place she might have gone?'

He rubbed his grizzled jaw. 'There are a few cafés and coffee shops around. I know she liked the Mexican place at the end of the block, La Cucaracha. I'll never understand why someone would name a restaurant after a cockroach, but the food is good. Whenever she got take-out, she always stopped by to ask me if I wanted something. That's Annabelle, always thinking of others.'

'Mr Foley, we've turned this over to Missing Persons,

so there are going to be more officers coming to canvass the area and they'll want to speak with you again and talk to your other tenants.'

'No problem. I'll be here. I don't go out in this weather, not with my arthritis.'

'Thanks for your help, sir.'

'Wish I could do more. Find her, will you? She's a real angel.'

Let's hope she's not an angel, Magozzi thought. 'We're going to do our best.'

The uniforms arrived five minutes after Gino had made the call-out. When they'd briefed the patrol sergeant and he'd given out assignments, they walked down the block to La Cucaracha. Neither of them questioned the shift in focus, or that foul play was involved. They were too late to save Kelly Ramage, but they had a chance with Annabelle Sellman.

The restaurant wasn't open, but some staff were inside, prepping for lunch. Their shields got them in, and the dark-haired, dark-eyed hostess seemed politely freaked out when they showed her Annabelle's photo.

'I recognize her. She comes in sometimes, usually for take-out.'

'How about yesterday afternoon? Were you working here around three?'

'Yes, but I don't remember seeing her. That doesn't mean much, though. There was an early concert at the Target Center, so we were slammed. It was wall-to-wall people and I was running. I didn't seat her in the dining area, and I normally handle all the take-out orders, so she wasn't here for that.'

Magozzi gestured to the adjacent bar area where colorful piñatas hung from the ceiling. 'Maybe she stopped in for a drink.'

Her brows lifted. 'Could be. You can ask Dave. He was bartending yesterday afternoon.' She tangled her fingers together worriedly. 'Did something happen to her?'

'She's missing. We're trying to retrace her steps.'

'Oh, God. Let me get Dave.'

Dave rubbed his sparse goatee and nodded when he looked at Annabelle's picture. 'She was in last night, sat at the bar. She ordered an Irish coffee without the booze, which is something a bartender doesn't hear that often, but she said she was getting a cold.'

'Did you speak to her besides taking her order?'

'Nah, too busy. Plus, she was talking to a guy.'

Magozzi felt his pulse speed up. 'Tell us about him.'

Dave shrugged. 'He was just some guy, came in after she'd been here a while and took the seat next to her. Never saw him before.'

'Did it seem like she knew him?'

'No, they seemed like two strangers who picked up a conversation – it was in the body language. I've been bartending for a while so I can read a situation pretty well.'

'Can you describe him?'

'There wasn't anything special about him. Honestly, I wouldn't recognize him if he walked in right now.'

'Big? Small?'

'Medium, I guess. He was wearing a heavy coat, so it was hard to tell.'

'What kind of coat?'

'A regular parka. Black. Like I said, nothing that stood out.'

'Was he old? Young?'

'I put him at about thirty, maybe a little older.'

'Hair color?'

'I don't know, he had on a black knit cap. He could have been bald under it for all I know.'

'How did he pay?'

'Cash.' Dave cocked a brow. 'Wow, lots of questions. Is this guy trouble?'

'He could be. This woman is missing, so keep an eye out for him and call us if you see him again. Do you know if they left together?'

'They left the bar area together for sure. She seemed pretty sick all of a sudden and he was helping her.'

'What do you mean by sick?'

'You know how your eyes get all glassy when you're catching a cold? She was pretty spacey too, like she took an antihistamine and it was just starting to kick in.'

'Or a roofie,' Gino said, looking at Magozzi.

Dave's mouth sagged open. 'Do you think . . . ?'

'You tell us.'

He blinked fast a few times. 'Shit. I just remembered, she drank half her coffee, then asked for a new one because it was too bitter. But it came from a fresh batch – I'd just brewed it. I was drinking some myself, and it seemed fine to me.'

'Are there cameras in here?'

'All for show, they haven't worked in a while. This place is a printing press for money, but the owner doesn't like to part with it.'

'We're going to send in a sketch artist, Dave. In the meantime, I want you to think real hard about this guy, every single detail you can remember: eye color, clothing, glasses or not, distinguishing features, like moles or facial hair. There's a woman's life on the line and what you remember could make a big difference for her.'

He swallowed and nodded.

57

Stefan's hands wouldn't stop shaking and the toxic bolus that had formed in his gut kept creeping up his esophagus – his body's reaction to sheer terror, the kind of terror he'd only experienced during the worst of his nightmares as a child.

But he wouldn't be waking up from this nightmare. It didn't matter what he did now, the outcome would be the same. The only unknowns were how long he would live, how Joseph would ultimately kill him, and where he would dump his body.

Would his family ever know what had happened to him? Probably not. He would rot away in a swamp or a shallow grave somewhere, and in fifty years, somebody might find a shard of bone or a tooth, if there was even that much left of him.

He looked at his dour watchdog standing woodenly by the door. He'd found out his name was Kirk, and Kirk was the last person who would offer him solace or sympathy because he didn't have a brain or a heart. The bar, on the other hand, was lined with polished bottles that promised oblivion. If he was going to die, he was damn well going to anesthetize himself first.

A few shots into the bottle, he sat back down in front of the computer. The lines of code on his screen glowed at him, mocking him. He wondered if the Monkeewrench people were staring at the same lines right now. It was ironic to think about, and it probably wasn't far from the truth. They would be monitoring Bit Monster, watching every single movement and transaction that happened on the platform, waiting to catch their quarry.

They would be monitoring Bit Monster, watching everything.

And, just like that, an idea formed, an idea so pure and simple he almost laughed out loud. The code was the only thing that could save him. All he had to do was get into Bit Monster far enough for Monkeewrench to see him, to trace him. And they would: he'd make it easy for them. Being the good White Hats they were, they'd call the feds, who would come storming in and bust this operation wide open.

The people he'd feared most until Joseph were now the people who might be his saviors. For the first time since he'd been imprisoned, his fingers started flying across the keyboard.

58

Petra was sipping tea and eating a tasteless breakfast bar at her computer while studying the Club Provocateur website. From what she'd seen last night, it was a very peculiar, disturbing place and if she was going to enter the heart of the beast to look for Vrag, she needed to know exactly what to expect. Preparation had never been more crucial. Her life depended on it, and she had vowed not to be so reckless with it.

It was billed as an alternative nightclub for adventurous adults looking to explore their fantasies, and unless you were talking about science fiction, fantasies meant sex in modern parlance, adventurous meant kinky. It was exactly the kind of place Vrag would operate, a debauched sex den couched in socially appropriate terms and weighty subtext. He probably ran vice out of there as well, drugs and prostitutes, maybe a numbers racket – he'd done all those things successfully before the war. The club would serve two purposes: a front for his illegal activities, and a place where he could feed his depraved hungers. It would explain the overzealous security and the activity by the loading dock. It might also explain the car in front of her house last night. Moon Face had watched her drive away and he'd probably made note of her plate number.

She reflexively looked out of her window, something she'd been doing every few minutes since five this morning.

She hadn't seen anything suspicious since, and the entire incident seemed cloudy and unreal now, as if it had been part of a bad dream that kept creeping into her consciousness. She used to sleep-walk: maybe it had just been an adult manifestation of a childhood affliction.

And maybe Club Provocateur was a legitimate business. Right.

When her phone rang, she snatched it, hoping it was Emmanuelle. Even better, it was Roadrunner. 'Good morning.'

'Hi, Petra. I wanted to see if you'd looked into Joseph Koppenhöfer.'

'I'm working on it, but I haven't been able to confirm he's Praljik yet. In fact, I might need more help, but nothing to do with computers.'

'Of course, what do you need?'

'I'm thinking of doing some field research tonight. It wouldn't be for long, but an escort might be in order.'

'An escort? That's intriguing. Where are we going?'

'To the address for Vrag Entertainment you gave me. I drove by last night, expecting a storefront or office building, but it's a very strange nightclub called Club Provocateur.'

Roadrunner was silent for what seemed like a very long time. 'Club Provocateur?'

'Yes, does that mean something?'

'We're helping Leo and Gino on a murder investigation – Detectives Magozzi and Rolseth,' he clarified, 'and they were there yesterday, chasing down leads. It was the last place their victim was seen alive. They think Blanca's murder might be connected, too. Wow. If Praljik is there, he might be their killer.'

Petra closed her eyes as past and present collided. 'He might be. Once a murderer, always a murderer. He's an evil man, and I think he has his own little *Mafiya* here, too.'

'So do we.'

'What? Why do you say that?'

'Joseph Koppenhöfer, who, for argument's sake, is Peter Praljik's new identity, lost almost twenty million dollars in a hack on a cryptocurrency exchange we're working for, a company called Bit Monster. That money wasn't legal – no way it could be. He doesn't have a presence anywhere else, so he's as dirty as the night is long. That says *Mafiya* to me.' Roadrunner tried to emulate her accent and did a poor job of it. 'Leo and Gino are coming over today to hash through things. Can you come, too? I think we all have a piece of the puzzle and we need to put it together.'

'Of course. I'll be there.'

'I'll call you when they're on their way over.'

'All right. I'll see you later. Goodbye, Roadrunner.'

Petra signed off and punched in Emmanuelle's number. She answered on the first ring.

'I'm so sorry, Petra, I meant to call you last night, but it got so late.'

'I'm the one who's sorry. I shouldn't even be bothering you.'

'I'm happy to hear your voice. This is all so unbelievable. It doesn't seem real. I woke up this morning thinking it couldn't be, it was just a terrible nightmare, but then . . .' her voice hitched ' . . . I reached for Martin and he wasn't there.'

Petra winced at her sobs. They were quiet, contained,

271

elegant, just like the woman. 'It's awful, Emmanuelle. What did the police say?'

She took a moment to compose herself. 'They found a witness who said the car that hit him sped up when he was in the crosswalk. It was intentional. Who on earth would want to kill Martin? What a dreadful world.' She sniffled. 'They have a description of the vehicle, but it's nothing that stands out, and the witness didn't get a license plate. The police are investigating thoroughly, of course, but I don't know what they'll be able to do with so little information.'

'They'll find out who it was, Emmanuelle. Hit-and-runs almost always get solved.'

'That's what the detectives told me. I pray it's true.'

'Me, too, Emmanuelle. I wish I could be there. I wish I could do something to help.'

'Petra, do you think this could have something to do with his work? Your work together?'

'I'm going to find out.'

'Be careful, dear. Be very careful. You know better than anyone what those people are capable of.'

59

'We've got to find him, Leo.'

'We will.'

Gino sighed and draped his arms over the steering wheel as he gazed at the sleek, probably architecturally significant façade of Resnick/Feinnes. 'I'm thinking of Kelly Ramage's timeline. Less than twelve hours after she left her house, she was dead. If the killer is keeping the same one for Annabelle, we're already too late.'

'Kelly was cultivated over time. Annabelle was a grab. That might change his game, extend his timeline.'

'Or shorten it. Annabelle has been out there from the second her sister died, raising holy hell. You know damn well she's been on his radar. He's in Minneapolis for the Rado show and Kelly, but Annabelle's out there, waving her sign and shouting negative things about his idol, and he wants to shut her up. And taking out two sisters in the same family might be an irresistible prize for him. Double the fun.'

Magozzi checked his chirping phone. 'Lerner finally sent his file.' He scrolled through the email and read Lerner's note out loud. '"Sorry for the delay. Cyber's report wasn't integrated into the murder book. Case on my end now active. Keep me posted."'

'So he's not a drunken bum after all.'

'Whatever he is on his downtime, he never forgot Delia.'

'And we'll never forget Annabelle if we don't figure this shit out soon.'

'I'm forwarding to Grace right now. If he made a mistake contacting Delia, she'll find it, and we'll find him. Meantime, let's see if anybody here saw something that can help us with Annabelle.'

As they crossed the street, Roadrunner called and Magozzi ducked between buildings so the voice on speaker wouldn't get carried away by the wind. 'What's up, Roadrunner?'

'I tracked Praljik's Social Security number to a local address for Vrag Entertainment.'

'That's the company that runs Club Provocateur.'

'Yeah, I just talked to Petra and put that together. We think Praljik's using the name Joseph Koppenhöfer now. And we know he bought a Rado sculpture. You said you thought your killer might be a Rado acolyte.'

Magozzi looked at Gino. 'Yeah, and we still do.'

'We also think he's involved in organized crime, and something Petra said really made me think.'

'What's that?'

'Once a murderer, always a murderer.'

'She has a point. We'll head over there again and check it out. By the way, I just forwarded Grace LA's Cyber Division report.'

'We'll get on it. See you later.' Magozzi looked at Gino, who was clapping his hands together, trying to warm them. 'What do you think?'

'If Praljik's at Club P, it could fit. No question he's a sociopath – killing is in his blood. Not much of a stretch to see him torturing and killing women on his new home turf. He's probably been doing it most of his life. Ollie said

Vrag Entertainment was based in LA. That could put him there for Delia's murder.'

'He doesn't fit for Annabelle, and that's who I'm really worried about now. Praljik would be at least fifty by now, probably older than that. The guy in the bar was thirty-ish. Maybe somebody here saw him – he could have followed her to La Cuc.'

Gino raised his brows. 'The guy in the leather coat from the surveillance footage is thirty-ish. Two sets of footprints at Dray's, maybe he's the sidekick, if there really is one.'

'Exactly. Call McLaren and fill him in. I'll call Ollie.'

Ollie's phone rang and rang, but he finally answered in a sleep-thick voice, even though it was almost noon. The nightclub set lived by a different schedule.

Joseph Koppenhöfer would be at the club by two.

60

Mike Vierling was back at his post in the gallery vestibule and gave Magozzi and Gino a warm greeting before getting serious. 'No luck yet, huh?'

'Getting closer, but you know the old saying.'

He nodded. 'Close only counts in horseshoes and hand grenades. My dad used to say that all the time. I'm sorry to hear it, but you'll get there.'

'Thanks. Listen, Mike, one of the protesters is missing, a young woman. Did you see any monkey business when you were working yesterday? Maybe somebody confronting them, engaging them? Watching them, maybe following one?'

'No, everybody avoided them, the usual, like you'd expect.' He shook his head sadly. 'A missing girl, huh?'

'Yeah.'

'That's really terrible. So this is a pretty nasty case you're working.'

'It doesn't get much nastier.'

'I'll keep my eyes open.'

Madeline Montgomery was in a much better mood today, probably because Harley had just lined her pocket with a plump commission, even if it was fake money. She didn't bother to whisk them away and out of sight.

'Good morning, Detectives. What can I do for you today?'

'A couple things. We were hoping you could identify this man,' Gino handed her a printed screen capture of the man in the leather coat, who'd been dogging Kelly. 'He had contact with our victim last night, here at the gallery.'

Her expression soured. 'I remember him, only because he seemed more interested in the women than in the art. But I've never seen him before last night, and I hope he was sufficiently deterred by all the rebuffs he experienced that he won't be back.'

'So you were paying attention to him.'

'Very much so. He seemed to be treating the show like a singles mixer, and one of my functions is making certain none of the guests are uncomfortable. We have a very wealthy clientele, and there are some opportunistic individuals – both men and women – who come to shows for the sole purpose of meeting them in the hope of making a connection. Most are more delicate about it than he was.'

'So he seemed like a real sleaze.'

'He was unpleasant. Obvious.'

Gino looked around the gallery. 'He didn't buy anything, leave a calling card, sign a guest book, something like that?'

'No, his intentions were quite clear, and it had nothing to do with art. Not to presume I know anything about solving a homicide, but he would be far down on my list of suspects. He's a common gold-digger, and killing your intended target would be extremely counterproductive.'

'Do you know a Joseph Koppenhöfer? A client, maybe?'

'No, and I would definitely remember that name.' She let out an anxious sigh as she looked at her watch. 'Is that all, Detectives? I have appointments arriving soon.'

'I'm sure they'll be happy to wait while you get us Michael Dorn's phone number.'

Her gray eyes narrowed. 'I gave you his card.'

'The card only had an email address and he's not answering my pleasant notes, which is really annoying. Especially since he's impeding a homicide investigation. Which happens to be a crime.'

Madeline folded her thin lips together, consulted her phone, then passed it to Gino. 'That's the only number I have for him.'

'Thanks for being so cooperative.'

While Gino stepped aside and punched the number into his phone, Magozzi took over the conversation. 'Ms Montgomery, one of the protesters is missing – she has been since yesterday. Her name is Annabelle Sellman, and we're very concerned for her life. Maybe you noticed something?'

Her hand went to her mouth. 'Oh, no. I'm very sorry to hear that. But I didn't notice anything unusual yesterday.'

'Have you had any complaints about them?'

'Comments, but no complaints. Controversy isn't unusual in the art world. In fact, it's often beneficial. I can't make a direct correlation, but sales are going extremely well.' She pointed to a piece that was positioned as a focal point near the front of the space. 'In fact, that was just purchased by a very nice couple, and it's one of the last available. It was a birthday gift.'

Magozzi had to work hard to conceal his disbelief. He'd just told her a woman was missing and in danger, and she was yammering on about sales, apparently not very sorry at all.

'Wow,' Gino said, trying to keep the anger out of his voice. 'Nice gift. My wife would kill me if I brought home a giant piece of metal for her birthday, no matter how profound it was. How much does one of these things weigh, anyhow?'

'Not that much, you'd be surprised. It's not metal, it's *trompe l'oeil*, trick of the eye,' she translated, in case Gino was as dim-witted as she assumed he was. 'All of Rado's sculptures are resin, but painted and finished with multiple layers of a special sealant, giving the impression of metal.'

'Resin, huh? That's clever.'

'Very. There are many layers to his work and every aspect speaks to the broader message of deception.'

61

'Resin,' Gino muttered into the buffeting, Arctic wind as they hurried to the car. As long as their hearts were still beating and servicing blood to major organs, Magozzi figured they had a good chance of surviving the block-long trip.

'It didn't come from the gallery – the sculptures are sealed.'

'Right. So maybe it came from Rado's workshop. He's circling the drain, so he's got an apprentice helping him. His sycophant would be the natural choice. We know Joseph Koppenhöfer's a Rado fan and he may even be Praljik, who is a mass murderer.'

'One way to look at it. Or maybe Rado isn't circling the drain at all. Maybe he's a hacker *and* a killer and he's here.'

'A hacker and a killer. And an artist. Pretty diversified for a lowlife, isn't it?'

'Just putting it out there.'

'Huh. I guess it's not the worst theory you've ever come up with. But it sounds like the only person who knows who Rado is is his agent, Dorn, and the bastard's not answering his phone, either.'

'Detectives, what a nice surprise!' a familiar voice crowed.

'Oh, shit,' Gino muttered, turning around to see their new best friend hurrying toward them as fast as his cautious, mincing steps could take him.

George Bormann had a joyful expression on his weird,

waxy face. He was fully decked out in animal skins this morning – fur coat, fur boots, fur hat – the purest manifestation of a lurid eccentric, a tarted-up Tussaud's figure. 'Detectives, I left a message for you, I hope you got it. I just wanted you to know that you've been added to my permanent dinner-guest list. You have an open invitation.'

Gino forced a pained smile. 'We got the message, and that's really generous of you, Mr Bormann.'

'Georgie, please! This may sound strange, but I feel like we've known each other for a long time. Providence brought you to my house last night for a reason, and that reason is for us to become friends!' He lifted his furry arms in a theatrical flourish as if conjuring Wagnerian lightning bolts from the grim gray sky. 'Yes, friends! I wish you'd stayed for the meal. The coq au vin was extraordinary, possibly my finest effort to date for that particular entrée. Tell me, have you made progress tracking down your fiend?'

'Some,' Magozzi said noncommittally.

'That's excellent. I assume you're not out for a stroll.'

'Nope. You?'

'I'm paying a visit to the Resnick/Feinnes Gallery. I've decided to purchase another Rado sculpture to add to my collection. Discussing his work with you last night gave me a renewed appreciation of its magnitude, for which I'm eternally grateful. And with Rado's ill-health, I would be a fool not to take the opportunity to expand my investment in his vision. With the added bonus of its aesthetic contribution to my home, of course. Art is about passion and money in equal measure.'

'Two very powerful forces in life,' Gino said dryly. 'And two of the most common motives for murder.'

George seemed extremely pleased by the observation, and chuckled his approval in an odd, guttural way. 'So this must be the way you're approaching our dear Kelly's homicide. Fascinating, I'd never really thought of that, but yes, you're absolutely right, Detective. There isn't much human behavior that couldn't be attributed to either of those two things. I suppose revenge would be another common motive for murder, wouldn't you say?'

'Passion, money, and revenge are the Holy Trifecta in the world of homicide.' Gino gestured toward the gallery. 'If you're looking to get your hands on another sculpture, I'd hurry. Stock is running out, according to Madeline Montgomery.'

'You were in the gallery again? Ooh, how intriguing. Something has obviously garnered your attention there.' He raised a brow inquisitively, then shrugged when that didn't elicit a response. 'Madeline is such an icy flower, isn't she? But quite devout in her commitment to Rado. That's the only reason we get along. I'd love to hear all about your thought process once you've solved your case. And you will, you must. Kelly deserves justice.'

And Annabelle deserves her life, Magozzi thought grimly. 'We agree. There's another missing woman, too. One of the protesters. Annabelle Sellman. We think it may be connected.'

His manic-happy expression went dark and dour. 'No! That's so horrible, so sad. There is just no accounting for the senseless cruelty and barbarism in our world.'

'There really isn't. Maybe you know Joseph Koppenhöfer, too. We understand he owns Club Provocateur.'

He shook his head. 'I don't know him. Ollie tells me the

club is owned by a company in Los Angeles, Vrag Entertainment.'

'We heard that, too. Thanks, Mr Bormann.'

'Georgie, please! And carry on. I don't want to detain you further from your important job. I hope to see you at my table soon, when you can regale me with the stories of your success in finding Kelly's murderer. *Ciao*, Detectives. I have a sculpture to buy.'

He waved a backward hand, and Gino and Magozzi watched him toddle across the street, avoiding patches of ice and snow.

Gino shook his head. 'That guy is so far gone, he was never here. Part of me actually wants to go to his house for dinner one night just to hear his story. Or at least look in his medicine cabinet.'

'You're on your own with that one.' Magozzi answered his buzzing phone. 'Hey, Jimmy. Yeah, we're in the neighborhood, see you in a few.'

Gino lifted a brow. 'We're getting invited to the inner sanctum?'

'He said he has some stuff for us.'

62

Harley was watching Roadrunner consult photos on his phone while pecking on his keyboard and scrawling notes on a sheet of paper with pictures of Rado sculptures. It was curious, because he never wrote longhand; in fact, Harley was surprised he even remembered how to use a pen. 'What are you doing?'

'Seeing if there are messages in the Rado sculptures. Assuming he used the Baudot Murray code.'

'You really want there to be messages, don't you?'

'It would be kind of cool, wouldn't it? How many people would think of it? They just see a series of holes, but I see a potential cipher.'

'And you think Rado would have thought of it?'

'If he's the mind behind the Bit Monster heist, yeah. And maybe it'll help us find him, because from everything we've looked at so far, this guy doesn't even exist. What about other crypto transactions that got disbursed to Rado?'

'I found six more, but the accounts weren't compromised. We could be barking up the wrong tree and Rado might just be an artist, not a scam artist.'

'I guess when he sends his invoice, we'll find out.'

Harley couldn't resist – he walked over to Roadrunner's station and looked at his work. 'These are a bunch of random letters.'

Roadrunner conceded with a nod. 'It's not making any sense now, but maybe it will.' He started jotting more letters that corresponded with the punch holes. Then his bony shoulders sagged. 'B-R-C-K. So far that's what the sculpture you bought says.'

The office elevator started to hum as it ascended, announcing a new arrival. The doors slid open and Grace walked in, carrying Elizabeth, who was bundled up in her pink snowsuit, looking cherubic. Charlie was pretty cute, too, for a lanky, wire-haired mutt with a chewed-off tail, proudly and perfectly at heel, guardian of his own little universe.

'Come here, you.' Harley took Elizabeth and lifted her high into the air. He was rewarded by a shrill laugh, a big, gummy smile, and a tug on his beard. 'She's a perfect child, always in a good mood. Does she ever cry?'

Grace gave him a bemused look, the type reserved for charming fools. 'Oh, she cries, but only to explicate your shortcomings in fulfilling her needs. For instance, if you put her down now, she'd start to cry because she seems to be infatuated with tugging on your beard and she has little tolerance for argument.'

'She can tug all she wants. You and Magozzi are there to say no. Uncle Harley is there to say yes.' He sat down and patiently endured Elizabeth's aggressive exploration of his facial hair. 'I think it's about time for her to get exposed to opera. Nothing heavy at first. Puccini is probably a good start.'

'Why not? Magozzi's already working on Shakespeare, thanks to you.' She settled in at her desk and woke up her computer. 'The LA detective sent the reports from their cyber-crime division, so I'm going to take a look at that.'

'We know – we talked to Magozzi a little while ago.'

'What's happening?'

'It's been a wild morning.' Harley chuckled as he gently disentangled Elizabeth's pudgy fingers from his beard. 'We've got an artist who might be a hacker, a war criminal who might be Kelly Ramage's killer, possibly a secret code, and a client who's been severely compromised by some-body really smart. And they might all be connected.'

Grace's face remained still and serene, a porcelain Madonna without her child. 'Is that all?'

Magozzi and Gino rarely visited Jimmy Grimm in his native habitat, which was a pristine, state-of-the-art lab in St Paul. The Bureau of Criminal Apprehension was regarded as one of the premier forensics institutions in the country; it was consequently well funded and zealously maintained to the highest standard.

Jimmy greeted them and rolled his stool away from the computer. 'I got LA's report, thanks for sending. I can't definitively match their red fibers to ours without the actual fibers here for comparison, but I can tell you it looks pretty good for a match. None of the samples were smooth, like they would be if they came from the actual weave. They were distressed, had a whorl to them.'

'Meaning?'

'Meaning they probably came from ornamentation, like tassels. Same textile, but they fuzz them out – you know what I'm talking about. But here's the bonus. When I was comparing the resin samples from Szabo's and Ramage's scenes, I turned up the same type of fiber on the floor at the fortune-teller's shop. And the resin samples are a

286

match. I'd say you have three murders for the price of one killer.'

'Or for the price of two, from the extra footprints at Dray's. Did you get a make on the fancy tread?' Gino asked, as he examined a tray of empty test tubes.

'Yeah, Prada. Very pricey. So do you have a person of interest in mind?'

'There's a couple possibles. We're on our way to go look at a guy who might be a Balkan war criminal with connections to organized crime.'

'You're kidding, right?'

'Actually, we're not.'

Jimmy shook his head. 'Christ, you two get weird cases. My advice, take partial pensions, enjoy your families, and get the hell out of this business. You're both looking at me like I'm not serious and you're talking about a war criminal and Mafia? Think about what I said, because I don't want to be cleaning up your dead bodies one morning.'

Gino smiled. 'Damn, you really do care.'

'Fuck off, you two. You're pains in my ass.'

'Love you back.'

63

Petra was staring at her closet, wondering how to dress for a possible encounter with her tormenter. Something night-clubbish, so she'd blend in with the crowd, but definitely nothing provocative or reminiscent of any fetishes or fantasies. She also needed something bulky enough to conceal her gun, a necessary safety measure in case things went south. She hoped Club Provocateur didn't wand people at the door – that could be a problem.

She pulled out a black shearling jacket with deep pockets and laid it on her bed for consideration. It was a possibility. It was also a possibility that her plan was a truly horrible idea. If she thought about it too hard, she would wisely back out, so she didn't think. Not at all.

After mining a few other viable options from her scant, boringly black closet, she heard a knock on her door. She recognized the cadence and the restrained intensity of it from yesterday. If you paid attention, knocks could tell you many things about the person on the other side. But the most frightening was when there wasn't a knock at all, just the sound of hinges squeaking and the slice of light that somehow managed to penetrate a blindfold, or even duct tape.

She gestured Detectives McLaren and Freedman into the house, and they introduced themselves again. McLaren was the skinny red-haired Irishman and Freedman was the imposing African-American detective. She offered them something to drink, which they declined, but they did accept her offer to sit down at her kitchen table. 'I'm surprised to see you so soon. You must be making some progress on Blanca's case.'

'Some, but, to be honest, it's slow going, ma'am,' Freedman said, in an easy voice. 'Like you told us, she didn't have any personal relationships besides the one with you. That makes identifying possible suspects pretty difficult.'

Petra stared down at the sheen of film floating on her cooling tea.

'You had mentioned walk-in clients yesterday, which I dismissed, but in retrospect, is that a possibility?'

'There were no notes in her appointment book to that effect, just scheduled meetings with her regulars. We spoke with every one of them twice.'

She lifted her hands in a helpless gesture. 'I wish I could help you. I want to find her killer as much as you do. Maybe even more.'

McLaren nodded sympathetically. 'We know you do. Yesterday you seemed very distressed when we mentioned the duct tape at the crime scene. Maybe it rang some bells for you.'

Petra focused on keeping her posture loose, her breathing even, her face emotionless. 'I'm sorry, no.'

'Oh. That's too bad. We were hoping maybe it did.'

Petra was used to being in the position of interrogator, so she knew the dance and said nothing, waiting them out again, just as she had yesterday.

'Did Blanca ever mention someone named Kirk Johnson to you?'

She didn't have to fake her ignorance with this question. 'I don't recognize the name. Is he a person of interest?'

'Possibly. The medical examiner determined that Blanca's neck was broken manually. That requires a lot of strength, and it's considered an act of rage or desperation or both, which usually means it's personal. His name came up in the course of the investigation.'

'Who is he?'

'He works at a place called Club Provocateur. Do you know it?'

Petra's mouth went dry and the carefully aligned game pieces in her mind scattered. 'I know of it.'

McLaren folded his hands together on the table and leaned forward, reminding her of a psychiatrist. It was meant to be soothing, but it served only to telegraph a difficult question or change of subject.

'Ms Juric, we know you're an ICE agent who looks for war criminals living in this country, and you're investigating a man named Peter Praljik, who may have ties to the club. Do you believe he killed Blanca?'

Petra waited to reply until her heart settled. They knew, of course they did, either through Roadrunner, their own investigation, or through Detectives Magozzi and Rolseth, it didn't really matter. Collectively, the police were closer on his trail than she'd imagined. It was a good thing, of course it was, but, like Blanca's broken neck, this was personal. 'I believe he could kill anyone, Detective, but not specifically Blanca, no. I wouldn't have withheld that information if I'd thought he was responsible. I want him to receive the full force of the law.'

'We want to help you do that.'

'I'm grateful.'

'But we can only help if you're forthcoming with information.'

'You know as much as I do, Detectives. In fact, you may know more.'

Detective Freedman cast a sidelong glance at his partner and they both stood. 'We hope you find him. He shouldn't be on the streets.'

'I agree with you.'

'Thank you for your time.'

She showed them to the door and the short journey seemed to take hours. When they finally drove away, she went to the freezer for the Stolichnaya and took a bracing shot straight from the bottle. Her timeline had just gotten a lot shorter if she was going to find Praljik first. It was time to adjust her plans and call in a favor from her friend Candace Emmer in FBI Cyber Crimes. She wouldn't be thrilled about loaning her identity, but she would understand the necessity.

64

Petra rapped harder on the front door of Club Provocateur, but there was no answer. It was nearly two in the afternoon and she'd assumed somebody would be there by now. Then again, places like this shunned daylight and didn't open until much later. Even evil night creatures had to sleep.

After five or so minutes of knocking, waiting and pacing, she returned to her car to warm up and watched the door, hoping somebody would peek out to investigate. She didn't have much of a story, but she did have a federal badge.

She waited patiently and was finally rewarded when a pudgy man in a sweater and corduroy pants stuck his head out of the door, looked around, then closed it again. She jumped out of her car, jogged across the street, and knocked again. Firm, urgent, but not manic, a law-enforcement knock. Finally, the same man opened the door warily and gave her a quizzical look.

'Was that you, trying to get in?'

Petra waved her shield, hoping it wouldn't garner too much scrutiny, considering it was an ICE shield. Theoretically, she wasn't impersonating a federal officer because she was one, just misrepresenting herself. 'I'm Candace Emmer with the FBI Cyber Crimes Division, investigating some recent credit-card fraud in the area. I'm checking with local businesses to see if they've had any incidents. You are?'

'Oliver Kampa. I'm the manager here and we haven't had any fraud, not to my knowledge.'

'Cyber criminals are very clever nowadays. Often businesses aren't aware that their customers have been victimized.'

He blinked at her, then smiled. 'I'm sorry, you must be freezing. Come in.'

She walked into the dark, barren space and looked around. Not one thing about it said nightclub but, fortunately, it was empty and Moon Face wasn't hanging around. 'Thank you. It's important I speak with the owner, also. Joseph Koppenhöfer, I believe.'

Oliver nodded. 'That's right.'

'Is he available?'

'He's very busy.'

'I'm certain he's not too busy for a federal agent, and if the owner is available, it's required that I speak with him or her. There have been instances where the establishment and sometimes the owner's personal accounts have been compromised as well. This is a syndicate that has evaded justice for some time, and damages have been significant in some cases.'

Oliver was convinced – in fact, he seemed energized. He knew at least something about the Bit Monster hack. 'In that case, Mr Koppenhöfer would definitely want to speak with you. Please wait here and I'll get him for you.'

As soon as Oliver was out of view, dashing up a stairwell as fast as his chubby, corduroy-clad legs could carry him, she took out her phone and punched in an alarm to ring in five minutes in case she needed it. It would be an urgent call from the field office, she'd explain, people were waiting for her and she had to leave immediately, thank you for your time, I'll be in touch . . .

Her heart started hammering and her hands were greasy with sweat. Back in her bedroom, the idea of confronting Peter Praljik had all seemed so distant, almost romantic, but now, as she heard footsteps coming down the stairs, she felt like she might explode.

The ever-insistent presence of her gun against her hip should have made her feel better, but it was only a dark reminder of her existential moral quandary. Was she capable of taking a human life, even his? And if she was, how would God see it? The Ten Commandments were very clear about this, and so was the law of man, but in a just universe, wouldn't the moral turpitude of a mass murderer outweigh a single act of righteousness? Was murder ever righteous?

The pointless, frantic, questioning babble in her mind suddenly ceased when Joseph Koppenhöfer came into view. He was well-dressed in a navy three-piece suit and impeccably groomed right down to the manicured nails. But he had a hard, cruel face, and the vacuous eyes of an amoral, unrepentant killer. She knew without question that she was looking at a very bad man.

But he wasn't Peter Praljik.

65

Harley and Roadrunner's attempts at finding messages in the Rado sculptures were interrupted by a warning alarm on the system that was monitoring Bit Monster. They scrambled to the station and watched the monitor, rapt, as they witnessed Bit Monster's security being breached in front of their eyes. That was the way it went – everything was fine until it wasn't, and after that, things happened in the blink of an eye, because you had to get in and out as quickly as possible, hopefully without leaving a trace. This wasn't an attempted hack in progress, they were already in the system. But now they were just idling there.

'This is too good to be true,' Roadrunner mumbled under his breath, toggling through multiple screens, trying to capture the source.

Harley rubbed his hands together, relishing the moment. 'No, it's not, it's fantastic. We sucked them in, and now it'll be easy to shut them down before they do any damage.'

'This is something different, Harley. It's way too obvious – they're not even trying to hide their tracks. And it's not stupidity, because they got this far. It's like they want to be found.'

Harley ran his fingers through his beard with a puzzled frown, as if the gesture would elicit some thought previously unattainable. 'Are they going for my account?'

'No, they're just dieseling in the system with a big red

flag on their back. It doesn't make any sense. If the original Bit Monster hacker had been this sloppy, we would have found him days ago.'

'So you think this is some kind of a message, too, just like with the sculptures?'

'It seems like a trap.'

'A trap for what? We're the good guys here. There's nothing they can do to us – they're the ones putting their asses on the line. As of now, they're already federal felons looking at a prison sentence. So find them – they're making it easy for you.'

Roadrunner scowled. 'What do you think I'm doing? Shopping on Amazon?'

'That really never crossed my mind.' Harley's inbox chimed an alert, and he frowned when he saw an email from Rado. 'Rado just sent us an invoice. I suppose there's not much of a chance he's sending invoices at the same time he's hacking Bit Monster?'

Roadrunner scratched his jaw. 'I put all the data we have on him from the Koppenhöfer transaction into the algorithm. We should have gotten an alert if Rado was the one hacking right now. What does the invoice say?'

Harley clicked it open and scanned it. 'Well, son of a bitch, our artist is going phishing after all. The most bullshit elementary scam in the world.'

Roadrunner rolled his chair over and saw the highlighted link at the bottom of the page. 'Click the link to complete your transaction,' he read aloud.

Harley smiled, his finger poised over his mouse. 'That's just what I'm going to do.'

*

Grace pushed herself away from her desk and looked across the room at Harley and Roadrunner, who were hunched together like two warlocks brewing a secret potion. They were animated, buzzing with the energy of an imminent discovery, obviously having better luck than she was with James Bondage.

The LA Cyber Division had done meticulous work, but it didn't change the fact that the handle contacting Delia Sellman through Signal was ROUGH-AND-READY, not JB007. Or that ROUGH-AND-READY's phone number belonged to a coffee shop on Wilshire Boulevard and had for ten years, just like the number contacting Kelly Ramage belonged to a gym.

But it wasn't just about solving a murder now: it was about trying to save a young woman who might still be alive. They couldn't fail Annabelle Sellman and they were all feeling the pressure as keenly as Magozzi and Gino were.

She glanced at Elizabeth, asleep in her cradle, and for the first time since her birth, her mind tracked back to her own childhood and the dark knowledge that this world could truly be a horrible place. It was a shocking and unexpected intrusion, pushing up painfully like a forgotten splinter. It was resistant to the giddy joy of new motherhood, and it mortified her.

Annie walked into the office with a plate of fragrant warm cookies – her stress-induced displacement behavior always revolved around food – but Harley and Roadrunner didn't even lift their heads at her presence or the aroma of hot baking, an indication of just how engrossed they were in their quest.

'You need a pick-me-up, sugar. You're looking awfully depressed.'

Grace took a cookie mindlessly and bit into it, but it tasted like dust, and not just because it was the slice-and-bake type that came from a refrigerated plastic tube – the kind Harley stockpiled in quantity enough to get him through Armageddon. 'I am depressed. I hit a wall with James Bondage. A dead end.'

'Then we move on,' Annie said, dropping the cookie plate on her desk. 'Information and connections are starting to pile up and we need to get it all sorted. Call Gino and Magozzi and tell them to come in, and I'll have Roadrunner call Petra. Did you hear that, Roadrunner? Call Petra and have her come in.'

He turned in his chair and looked at each of his partners in turn, clearly bewildered. 'You know the weird hack we were telling you about, the one where they're hanging out inside Bit Monster? I just traced the location. It's not coming from Rado, it's coming from Club Provocateur.'

'I thought Club Provocateur was the one getting hacked. At least the owner,' Grace said.

'You're right. Something's really hinky here, two simultaneous hacks on Bit Monster.'

'Magozzi and Gino are on their way to the club. Should I tell them to hold off?'

'Yeah, tell them to turn around and come here first. They need to know what they're walking into, and we don't want to spook whoever's hacking from there. It could be a direct line of evidence to a whole lot of crime, including murder. If the cops show up now, they'll shut it down and we could lose it.'

'I will. You call Petra.'

'Oh, yeah, come to Papa!' Harley shouted suddenly. 'We've got an attack on my Bit Monster account coming from the Rado link. Roadrunner, help me track this son of a bitch down.'

Magozzi hung up and looked at Gino. 'I think the party is just about to get started. There's a Bit Monster hack coming from Club Provocateur and there's another coming from a link on the invoice Rado sent to Harley. Grace said we shouldn't spook anybody right now, just turn around and come to Harley's so we can pull this together. Petra will be there, too.'

Gino executed a sloppy U-turn and charged away from Club Provocateur. 'Did she say anything else?'

'They're calling the feds about the hacks.'

'Good. The feds can handle the computer stuff, while we handle Kelly's murder and Annabelle's disappearance. Club Provocateur is in this big-time and Rado is, too. We just need the whole story.'

66

Whatever drug had been in the water was wearing off, and at this point, lucidity was something that Annabelle dreaded. Without the numbing haze, there was nothing left but reality, and that reality was clear: she was at her captor's mercy, helpless to do anything but wait to die. And imagine how it would happen.

Don't let go, don't let go, don't give up.

She tried to focus on something else, anything else. Time. How much had passed since she'd been taken? At least a day. Her friends would have called the police by now. They would have called them when she hadn't shown up at the gallery. Detectives Magozzi and Rolseth were already working on finding a murderer, the same man who'd killed Delia and taken her. They'd already made the connection, and that was reason to hope, something to cling to in her infinite despair.

When the door opened again, she remained perfectly still, listening. The footsteps seemed different this time, lighter. Or it could have been her imagination, distorted by drugs and terror. He didn't approach her bed this time, but instead went to another part of the room. A brief silence, then a series of clicks accompanied by bright flashes of light. A camera.

Her resolve to remain lifeless evaporated and she whimpered behind her gag, flailed against the restraints on her hands and ankles, but a few moments later, she froze in terror when she heard a distorted, warbling voice echoing in the room – a voice electronically altered into a psychedelic nightmare.

'That's good. You're very photogenic, Annabelle, even better than your sister.'

And then the pain came as she felt her flesh tear beneath a torrent of lashes on her stomach and thighs, all the while the camera's light flashing. As she started to lose consciousness, she heard the modulated voice telling her that she was going to be a star.

67

Pavel watched his entire world shatter when Ty Overgaard walked through the door of his gym. The gym he'd worked so hard to build as an honest man. The gym that had fed his family well. The gym that he'd thought would keep them comfortable after he passed, which might be sooner rather than later, as things were turning out.

'Pavel, who in the hell beat the crap out of you?'

He reached for his swollen, blackened eye and felt a stab of pain in his shoulder. It was broken, he knew. There wasn't much of him that wasn't. 'Robbers. They came in when I was closing up last night. I hadn't locked the door or set the alarm yet.'

'Pavel, nobody robs a gym and you never called the police. Or me. It's about the drugs, I know it is. Talk to me.'

He put his head in his hands and promised himself he wouldn't break down. 'They brought in some boxes last night. Ecstasy. They threatened me, my family.'

'Who did?'

'I don't know them – it's just like the steroids. Men come in, they exploit my facility, they make threats. They knew I'd been talking to you.'

'What happened to the drugs?'

'Another man came later to pick them up.'

'So I'm not going to find drugs here.'

Pavel looked away.

'If you tell me who the man was, we don't have to worry about what you're holding.'

'I didn't know him.'

'You're a bad liar, Pavel, and you're in a bad situation. Let me take you to the hospital, get you patched up, and you can tell me what's really going on, who's behind this. Save yourself. You still have a future. It can be a good one.'

'I don't have a future. I've never had one.' Pavel sank down to the floor and started crying. His American Dream was now a nightmare, and what did he expect? He knew better. It was the same thing over and over, no matter where he was. The shadows of the past were long and dark and they'd followed him here. It was no better than it had been in the old country. He owed Joseph a debt, owed him his life and the lives of his family, but it would never be squared up, not with someone like him.

'I didn't have a choice,' he sobbed, hating the way he sounded, a world-class strong man, an Olympic bronze medalist for the former Yugoslavia, blubbering and weak and pathetic as an infant. 'He set me up for murder and said he'd kill my family. And, trust me, he will.'

'Your family is safe, and so are you. Do the right thing, Pavel.'

'My wife and daughter? They're safe?'

'They're in protective custody. Your wife is the one who called me. Let me help you.'

Pavel looked up at the ceiling, giving thanks to a God he had neglected for a long time. Far too long. The sudden, sharp pain behind his eyes was perhaps a reminder that he had strayed from the shepherd's path, but he would be strong again, devout in his religious convictions. Stronger than ever, as strong as his body was still. His soul wasn't beyond redemption. He'd done nothing wrong except try to protect his family the best he could. And trusted a murderer to save their lives, because there hadn't been another choice.

He let his eyes close, feeling the first sense of true calm and peace he'd had in decades. The Lord was a safe place in times of trouble, his mother had always told him. Psalm Nine.

'Give me a name.'

Just a name and this could all be over. His wife and daughter were safe. 'Joseph Koppenhöfer. But that's not his real name . . .' and then his vision started to blur and the spearing pain in his head exploded. He was vaguely aware of Ty shouting his name, but his voice was foggy, distant. At some point, there were other voices and light, so much light. He felt his body being lifted, and then the voices, the light, faded as the clot in his brain, dislodged by the beating, shut off the lights permanently.

68

The atmosphere in the Monkeewrench office was humming with nervous energy and as edgy as Magozzi had ever seen it. It was the same kind of focused human electricity that crackled through Homicide when a big case was on the verge of a breakthrough, minus the five o'clock shadows, cheap office furniture, and the persistent olfactory assault of body odor mingling with fast food.

Harley and Roadrunner gave them distracted waves before returning their attention to their computers, but Annie, all Southern charm and dressed to kill in a green suede suit, greeted them with a smile and a languid bat of her eyelashes. 'Are you two making some inroads?'

A hopeless chump when it came to Annie's attention, Gino grinned. 'We are. We just don't know where they're going to take us.'

Magozzi walked to Grace's station and placed his hand on her shoulder. The muscles beneath her soft black sweater were taut and corded with tension, and her blue eyes seemed darker today, troubled.

'Hi, Magozzi.'

'What's wrong?'

She wrinkled her nose, probably annoyed that he had spotted distress beneath the unlined face that was so expert at concealing emotion – an incontestable sign of weakness by Grace MacBride's estimation.

'I haven't been able to track James Bondage. LA did a good job, but their people had the same trouble. He knows how to manipulate Signal and his actions there mirror his actions here. From a cyber perspective, you're looking for the same killer. He took Delia Sellman's sister, didn't he?'

'We think so, but we're getting closer, Grace, thanks to all of you. We'll find him another way, it seems like a lot of avenues are opening up. Is Elizabeth in the nursery?'

She pointed to the baby monitor on her desk. 'You can hear Charlie's snoring – I think it puts Elizabeth to sleep.'

Gino wandered over, eyes busy as he absorbed the vibe of the room, the intensity of focus. 'Lots going on here.'

'Multiple things are breaking with Bit Monster and everything seems to have some connection to your case or Petra's. That's why we wanted you both to come in.'

'Is she here yet?'

Roadrunner looked up. 'She's on her way. Anything breaking for you guys?'

'Plenty. Tell us what you know about Rado. We just added him to the person-of-interest list and we need to find him.'

'We're working on that. He's targeting some customers who buy his work with crypto and hacking their accounts. We set a trap for him in Harley's fake account and he took the bait, which means we have a good chance of tracking him down. Rado also cleaned out Koppenhöfer, who purchased a sculpture last year, took him for twenty million. We think it was all part of a scheme to launch the Bit Monster heist.'

'Twenty million,' Gino mumbled in amazement. 'An account that size puts a big bullseye on your back. But it doesn't make a lot of sense that there's a simultaneous hack coming from Club Provocateur.'

Roadrunner looked pleased, like a professor with a particularly promising student. 'We don't think so, either. Unless it's some kind of retaliation. But that would make Koppenhöfer and Rado two computer geniuses engaged in some kind of a duel, and nothing about that makes sense, either.'

The ominous gong of Harley's doorbell resonated in the room, and Roadrunner sprang out of his chair. 'That's Petra.'

Magozzi watched him bypass the elevator, enter the stairwell, and by the sound of his footfalls, he was taking the steps by two or three. 'He likes this woman, doesn't he?'

That pulled Harley away from his work. 'Oh, I think he's nursing a full-on infatuation.'

Annie gave him a sharp gaze. 'Harley, behave.'

'When haven't I behaved?'

'When have you? The burden of proof is on you. Be nice.'

He gave Magozzi a smile. 'More power to him, I say. I hope they mate and have more babies to fill up this office.'

Magozzi was surprised by a petite brunette, who looked like a child standing next to six-foot-eight Roadrunner. Her dark, haunted eyes and the deep scar on her face gave the impression of some unfathomable inner desolation, but she was charming, gracious and intelligent when introductions were made. A complicated woman, he thought, one who appeared to share some common ground with Grace. And by the way she and Roadrunner were interacting, they might all find out one day.

She followed Roadrunner to his desk. 'So this is where the sorcery happens.'

'It's not sorcery, but it's where we work. We were just getting up to speed with Gino and Magozzi. Are you having any luck finding Praljik?'

She shook her head dispiritedly. 'I found Joseph Koppenhöfer at Club Provocateur. But he's not the man I'm after.'

'Koppenhöfer's not Praljik?'

'No. But he's using Praljik's Social Security number. That can't be a coincidence.'

Grace was watching her carefully, suspiciously, Magozzi thought, as she did all rare newcomers. 'Maybe they're colleagues.'

Petra's eyes sparked. 'That could very well be. Koppenhöfer, or whatever his real name is, is Yugoslavian, to use the broadest term, because I can't be more specific. He's lost most of his accent, so I couldn't tell where exactly he was from, but they may know each other from the war. Praljik was a general, and had many associates, as you would expect.' She looked at Gino and Magozzi. 'The man I met was rotten to the core. There's something very wrong with him.'

'We'll be checking him out after we leave here.'

Petra's eyes fell to the stack of papers on Roadrunner's desk. 'Rado, Syzygy of Art and Technology? Who is this?'

Harley grabbed Roadrunner's printouts of the sculptures and handed them to her. 'He's a hacker and an artist who's tangled up in this somehow. A lame artist,' he added. 'I just bought this one.'

She examined it with an amused expression. 'If you think he's lame, why did you buy it?'

'Research. It would be a tax write-off if I'd actually paid for it. It's kind of a shame, actually.'

Her eyes suddenly focused sharply on the page. 'These letters written in the margins. Where are they from?'

'Roadrunner thought the holes might be messages in the sculptures based on old computer punch tape. The various configurations of the holes represent letters using something called the Baudot Murray code.'

Magozzi noticed her face turn noticeably paler. 'You haven't finished deciphering them, have you?'

Roadrunner shook his head. 'Things started to bust wide open here when I was working on it.'

'Do you have the key to the cipher?'

'Sure.' He handed her another sheet of paper. 'Do you think there's something there?'

'I'll let you know.'

They were silent as they watched her work, converting patterns of holes to letters. 'This is a very simplistic form of encryption, isn't it?' she finally asked.

'Early stuff, but it got us to where we are now.'

She finally set down her pencil and looked up. 'Road-runner was right.'

'I was?'

'I've only finished decrypting the two you started. Balkan languages don't have many vowels, so unless you're familiar with them, you wouldn't recognize words after deciphering just a few letters.'

'So the sculptures really do say something?'

Her dark lashes dropped over her eyes, and Magozzi felt like he'd just watched a door close.

'Yes. These are names of towns where massacres took place during the war. Massacres directed by Praljik. Peter Praljik's middle name is Radovan. Rado for short.'

69

Roadrunner finally dispelled the stunned silence in the office. 'So Rado is Praljik?' he asked incredulously.

'Or someone who knows him or worships him. But the sculptures seem to be trophies. He's bragging about his exploits in plain view, which aligns with his arrogance and also makes it personal. I'm sure he never imagined anyone would figure it out. That's how egotistical he is.'

'The whole S and M thing always fit with Kelly's murder,' Gino said to Magozzi. 'Those videos at the gallery? They could be real snuff films. I don't think our killer is a twisted acolyte of his. I think he's Rado himself.'

Petra's eyes narrowed. 'Why do you think that?'

'Our victim was into S and M, and his work is filled with that kind of violence. His sculptures are only part of his show. He uses still images and live video of women being . . . Let's just say it's going to keep me in nightmares for the rest of my life.'

She recoiled and her face twisted in revulsion. 'Like Rado's rape camps. He enjoyed bondage and torture and recording it for posterity.'

Her chilling statement and the vitriol with which she'd said it affected everyone, especially those who'd been to the gallery and seen the offending material for themselves. It suddenly had very real context and that made it even more horrifying.

Magozzi glanced at Gino. 'Let's go rattle Koppenhöfer's cage. He's in a death knot with Rado. Praljik. He might know something.'

Grace rose from her chair and started walking the long, maple floor, thinking out loud: 'If Praljik and Koppenhöfer were friendly at one time, they certainly aren't anymore.'

Harley rubbed his hands together with relish. 'We'll get him. We're going to trace his hack and I'm waiting to reel him in, just as soon as he makes the next move and infects his system with our virus.'

Gino slipped on his gloves and coat. 'Give us a heads-up the second you do. Thanks for all your help, everybody. Be in touch and we'll do the same. Petra, it was nice to meet you.'

'It was nice to meet you both, too. Be careful.'

It was the right time to leave, all of them going their separate ways in the interest of achieving a single goal, but Magozzi couldn't let one thing go. 'Petra, please tell us honestly, do you think Praljik was responsible for Blanca's death?'

'I can think of no reason why he would kill her.'

'Did she know him?'

She looked away. 'We both did.'

'Then it's possible she saw him. Recognized him.'

Petra kept her eyes averted, but she nodded. 'I suppose it's possible.'

'She could have been a loose end he needed to tie up. And that makes you one, too, Petra. We're not the only ones who need to be careful.'

70

'Christ, this is even worse than I thought it was. Rado's a genius. What better way to get away with murder than not to exist?'

Magozzi shifted around on the ice cold vinyl seat of the sedan, trying to keep his rear end from getting frostbitten. 'He exists and we're going to find him.'

'I think Petra suspected Praljik killed Blanca all along.'

'So do I. That's what McLaren picked up on.'

'So why would she sit on the information?'

'Maybe she thought it didn't matter. And it doesn't really change much. Nobody had a prayer of finding him until Monkeewrench got involved, and even they haven't found him yet.'

Gino got on the freeway and headed toward north Minneapolis and Club Provocateur. The traffic was moving at a slug's pace, but at least it was sparse. 'Who's his accomplice? He might be easier to find.'

'If Koppenhöfer knew him from the old country, maybe he is. But that doesn't fit with the fact that Rado emptied his Bit Monster account.'

'Wouldn't be the first time a criminal backstabbed one of his own. There are no friendships in the underworld, just mutual exploitation and a happy arrangement that never lasts very long.'

Gino was quiet for a long time after that, which Magozzi

found pleasant, but unsettling. 'What are you thinking about?'

'The way Petra talked about the rape camps and the torture. She was there.'

'I think she was.'

They were both quiet for the remainder of the drive.

Roadrunner felt a cold-hot surge of adrenalin enter his bloodstream as he watched the status of Harley's Bit Monster account change from five million dollars to none. He was surprised by how calm his voice sounded when he spoke. 'Rado just took the bait, Harley, and our virus along with it. We can get him now.'

Joseph Koppenhöfer's office told a very different tale of Club Provocateur. In stark contrast to the derelict lower level of the place, it was laden with carved wooden furniture upholstered in velvet, thick Persian rugs, and heavy brocade curtains that looked silk and expensive. Dark, old world, and ready for a cameo in the next *Godfather* sequel. It wasn't tasteful, but it was a flagrant display of disposable income.

What didn't fit was the wall of modern art and the small-scale sculpture garden, the focal point being the Rado piece that had ultimately cost him twenty million dollars.

The man himself was dressed equally well in a fine suit, but his rough, vulpine face and soulless eyes belied the veneer of civility he was trying to project. This was not a pleasant human being.

'I'm so sorry I can't help you, Detectives,' he was saying, pushing the photo of Kelly Ramage back across his desk.

'I've never seen this woman. I spend most of my time in Los Angeles, where my operations are based, and the times I'm here I'm in this office working, never on the floor.' He smiled, showing nicely capped teeth. 'I'm not a club man. I prefer my solitude whenever I can get it, which isn't often.'

'Were you here two nights ago?'

'I was. When the club closed at two, I did some paper-work with my manager, then went to bed. I keep living quarters here for my trips from the west coast.'

'Thanks for taking a look.' Gino's eyes went back to the Rado sculpture at the center of the room. 'That's a nice piece.'

'Thank you.'

'Who's the artist?'

'Rado.'

Gino did an excellent job feigning surprise. 'No kidding?'

'I'm not. You've heard of him?'

'Yeah. A real up-and-comer, and pretty mysterious. The subject of a lot of gossip.'

'I've heard that, but I don't pay attention. I'm only con-cerned with the intrinsic value of the art I buy.'

'My partner and I think his real name is Peter Praljik.'

And there it was, the slightest tic, a flash of recognition and possibly shock, barely registering on his inscrutable face. If you weren't looking for it, it would have passed without notice. But Magozzi noticed, and Gino did, too.

'I wouldn't know anything about that, but I'm sure you're not here to share art-world hearsay, so this Praljik person must somehow be involved in your case.'

Magozzi shrugged casually. 'We'd like to speak with him about a few things. For one, he's been stealing money, a lot of it. Online fraud through a cryptocurrency exchange. The story of the day, right? It happens all the time.'

Twin blooms of red appeared on Koppenhöfer's sallow cheeks. 'Yes, it does. I've had problems myself.'

'We're sorry to hear that,' Gino said. 'Keep your eyes open, Mr Koppenhöfer. Cyber crime is the new plague.'

71

'He knows Peter Praljik, and he got really pissed off when you brought up personal finances. He put two and two together, but that doesn't get us anywhere,' Gino carped, as he piloted the car toward downtown and City Hall.

'He might lead us to Praljik. He'll go after him if he thinks he stole his money.'

'He doesn't know where he is. Nobody does. He's hoping we'll lead *him* to Praljik.'

Magozzi felt his phone vibrating in his pocket. There were two missed calls from Harley and one text that read: CALL ASAP. 'Harley's got something,' he said, pressing callback. 'Hey, Harley, what's up?'

Harley was wound up and his voice boomed over the speaker. 'We finally traced the Rado hack. That son of a bitch knows what he's doing. His onion router bounced us around the globe a few times, but our virus got him in the end. Totally disabled the encryption in the application layer of the communication protocol stack and blew out the random-selection Tor relays.'

'That sounds incredibly sexy.'

Harley snorted. 'It's better than sexy, it's fantastic. It means we got a source IP address and tracked it to a physical location.'

'You guys are rock stars. Where is he?'

'That's the best part. He's local, Circle Pines. He's

probably your killer, so it makes sense, right? It's north a little bit, but way better than Burkina Faso, which is one of the places we paid a cyber visit to, courtesy of this fuck.'

'Go ahead, Harley.' Magozzi scrawled the address in his battered pocket notebook. 'Do you know if it's a house or business?'

'We're looking at it on Google Earth now. It looks like some kind of a farm. County records say it's owned by a Violet Thorson.'

'You're the best. We're on our way.'

'Good luck and be careful. I'm guessing you won't find Violet Thorson there, but you may find a data-mining operation, and data farms have big-time security, the kind any lucrative illegal enterprise has.'

'Thanks for the heads-up. We'll keep you posted.'

'Heading north,' Gino announced. 'We should be there in half an hour.'

'Not on these roads. Don't kill us on the way.'

'I don't like the sound of goon security. Call the locals and put them on stand-by, let them know what's going on. McLaren and Freedman, too – they might want to be here.'

Magozzi did so, thinking that was a great idea: he didn't like the sound of goon security, either.

Stefan had stripped down to his T-shirt, but he couldn't stop sweating. It soaked the Metallica bandana he'd tied over his brow, and it dripped from his armpits to gather in the fleshy folds of his stomach. He was positive Monkeewrench had seen his incursion and knew where it was coming from, he'd made sure of that, but nothing was happening.

317

Of course nothing was happening. His desperation had made him delusional – delusional enough that he'd been able to convince himself that Monkeewrench would identify his attack, call the feds, and they'd come charging right over to storm the Bastille, saving his life in the process.

But that wasn't the way things worked in the real world. The FBI was a massive bureaucracy strangled by red tape and protocol. They would have to investigate and build their case before they could get a warrant and put any boots on the ground. It could take days, weeks – hell, it could take months, and he didn't have that kind of time.

A subtle SOS wasn't going to cut it. Koppenhöfer said they were monitoring his computer, but he wasn't so sure. From what he'd seen, the collective IQ in the building was double digits. Maybe he was underestimating them, but it was a risk he was going to have to take.

He turned around to look at Kirk standing mutely by the door, like a massive statue, a dumb Colossus of Rhodes. He was a formidable physical impediment to his freedom, but definitely not an intellectual one. 'Does it seem hot in here to you?'

'No.'

'I think I might have a fever.'

'Maybe you do.'

'Any aspirin in the house?'

'I don't know.'

Smart as a rock and as helpful as one. Also completely disinterested in what he did, as long as he was in his chair in front of the computer. Stefan began typing quickly, this time embedding a crystal-clear message in the code

Monkeewrench would see: BEING HELD HOS-
TAGE ARMED MEN LIFE IN DANGER NOT A
JOKE REPEAT NOT A JOKE. SEND HELP. SWAT
TEAM.

He didn't think he was being melodramatic by men-
tioning SWAT. The police needed to know how serious
the situation was here so they didn't come strolling in for
a welfare check and get themselves killed by Koppenhöfer
and his cadre of sociopaths. Twice in one day, he'd called
on the good guys to save him, and given his own almost
entirely criminal past, the irony wasn't lost on him. He
renewed his earlier vow to change the way he did things if
he got out of this shit storm alive.

He closed the tab just as Koppenhöfer burst through
the door, his eyes wild, spittle flying from his mouth as he
stormed over in a blizzard of epithets. Some were in English, others in a language he didn't recognize.

Oh, Jesus Christ. They *were* watching him, and he was
dead.

'Change in plans.' He slammed a piece of paper with a
name written on it next to his keyboard. 'Peter Praljik. You
find him no matter what. That's your only job right now.
Forget about the money.'

Stefan felt everything inside loosen, including his bow-
els. 'I will, sir,' he said, jumping out of his chair and
running for the bathroom.

Roadrunner pushed away from his monitor, riding his
chair backwards. 'We just got a message from whoever is
hacking at Club Provocateur. It's an SOS. If it's legit,
somebody is in deep trouble over there.'

Harley, Annie and Grace clamored around him. 'Maybe that's why the hack was so obvious,' Grace said. 'It was an attempt at contact, but the message was too subtle. This isn't.'

'No, it's not, and it's fucked up,' Harley said. 'Koppen-höfer and Praljik-slash-Rado are in a death knot, like Magozzi said. I don't know how, but the parallel hacking is freaking me out and so is this message, not to mention that the two of them are raging psychos by all accounts. Who knows what kind of warped pissing match they're in?'

'I'll call the feds back and tell them to scramble on Club Provocateur,' Grace said. 'Magozzi and Gino have it covered from the Rado end. This is all going to be over soon.'

Roadrunner turned a ghastly shade of white. 'Oh, my God. I just thought of something.' He banged his hand on the desk. 'Stupid, stupid, stupid!'

'What's wrong?'

'When we couldn't get a hold of Gino and Magozzi right away, I called Petra to let her know we found him.'

'Yeah, we know, we were all sitting next to you when you did. What's the problem?'

'She asked if Gino and Magozzi were on their way and I told her no. It didn't hit me at the time, but now I'm thinking she wanted to know if she had a head start.' He grabbed his phone.

Harley put his hand on his shoulder. 'Roadrunner, calm down. She's a professional. You told her to wait for the cops, and she's not going to go running into that kind of trouble alone and risk her life.'

'I'm not so sure.' He pressed his phone closer to his ear, as if that would yield a more desirable result. 'She's not answering. It's my fault. I never should have called her before we talked to Gino and Magozzi. We have to go. We have to go now.'

72

Petra didn't notice the cold as she walked the quarter-mile down the snow-covered rural road. Maybe hypothermia had deadened her nerves, made her impervious, like a human form sculpted in ice.

Her pulse quickened when she saw a split-rail fence and beyond that a white clapboard farmhouse at the end of a snow-packed driveway. Behind it were several outbuildings. There were very few trees for cover, which meant she would have to walk straight up to the house with purpose. She was glad she'd crafted some stories for different eventualities on the drive here. She was getting quite good at that.

If a stranger answered the door, she was a stranded motorist whose phone had died. If Vrag answered the door, she would kill him, regardless of the consequences. Everything in her life had led her to this moment. What happened after that wouldn't matter.

Her steps faltered. Maybe it did matter. Vrag had almost ruined her before, so many times and in so many ways. Wasn't it perverse to allow him to do it again? She wouldn't be able to do any good from a prison cell and the life she had made for herself would be gone. She knew what a psychiatrist would say about that, which was why she'd stopped seeing them.

But then there was Roadrunner. He'd been brave enough to kill his tormenter, and at such a tender age.

We refuse to be victims.

Ultimately, it was her distorted admiration of his courage that inspired her to put her head down, increase her pace, and begin the long walk down the driveway.

It was strange how life could sometimes seem like a movie – vignettes like pieces of mosaic tile, being arranged by an invisible hand while you watched in fascination from the safety of a theater seat, waiting breathlessly to see how all the pieces came together.

It was like this as Petra walked up the wooden steps, rang the doorbell, and waited while footsteps grew louder, closer. The actress in the movie was about to make a fateful discovery that would determine the outcome of the script.

The door creaked when it opened and the heroine was greeted by the villain. He didn't look the same at all, but she knew the eyes. She would never forget the eyes. He was shocked at first, then seemed very pleased.

'Petra,' he said. 'I thought you might find me eventually, but not so soon.'

Petra was suddenly back in her own body, reaching for the gun in her bag. No thought, no emotion, just purpose. But she wouldn't kill him quite yet, she deserved answers. 'How would you know that?'

'People use technology every day, all day, but they don't really understand it. They can't even comprehend how vulnerable they are, how easy it is to track somebody and listen to every single aspect of their lives. Or maybe they don't want to know. Ignorance is bliss, as they say. But you found me. Incredibly clever, Petra. I'm very impressed. I know I wasn't being careless, so it appears I have a formidable enemy.'

'You killed Martin.'

'Not personally.'

'Why?'

'I thought that would be obvious. It was a precautionary measure. I've been watching you both.'

Petra thought about the car idling outside her house last night. Had it been Moon Face or had it been Praljik? 'Why not just kill me?'

'I think you know the answer to that. We have old times to revisit . . . You know how important relationships are to me. You can't imagine how much I've missed you.' He shook his head ruefully. 'You were so special, Petra, and I was very angry when you left me. It was such a betrayal. I always fed you and kept you warm, didn't I? Most war orphans weren't so lucky.'

Petra felt a white-hot fury that she thought had died decades ago. It burned so fiercely, her skin seemed on the verge of igniting. But emotion was useless. Emotion was weakness, a mantra that had allowed her to survive, had kept her alive. 'That's why you killed Blanca, because she took me away.'

'No, not at all. I had been looking for a medium and spiritual guide for quite some time. Minneapolis is sadly lacking in skilled practitioners. I happened on her shop during a walk and the sign said "Medium and Spiritual Guide", exactly what I had been seeking. It was clearly an omen. Unfortunately, Blanca recognized me. I was as stunned as she was by the serendipitous reunion, and she did an admirable job trying to conceal her surprise.'

Petra thought about Detective Magozzi's words earlier. 'So she was a loose end.'

'Yes, one I had to clean up later.' He sighed and turned up

his hands in twisted, self-justifying supplication. 'There was nothing else I could do. I had no choice. It was an unfortunate set of circumstances and not remotely enjoyable. No death should be meaningless, and I'm afraid hers was. We had no chance to form a bond and find happiness together.'

'That's what you think? That what you do for your own sick pleasure works the same way for the people you hurt and maim and torture?'

'Happiness is very complicated, Petra. It's not the same as pleasure, and it is also not the opposite of sorrow. True happiness isn't enhanced by pleasure or diminished by sadness, but exists in spite of those things.'

Petra's mind swirled in the face of his outrageous madness, his ice cold heart. 'Who is Joseph Koppenhöfer?'

His placid expression suddenly warped in anger. 'Once my most trusted lieutenant. But, as it turned out, he was extremely disloyal, like you. That's one thing I can't forgive. Loyalty is the most important thing, don't you think?'

'You don't care what I think, and the feeling is mutual.'

He shrugged diffidently. 'I'm sorry you feel that way.'

It was time now, and the cold steel of her gun felt good and right against her fingers as she finally took it out of the concealment of her bag and aimed it at his head. He was helpless and she wasn't. A ferocious scream of triumph and heartbreak built in her throat as she gleefully anticipated the sight of Vrag's blood and shattered bone painting the room with pink mist as her bullets entered his skull.

What she hadn't anticipated was the cloth covering her mouth from behind.

BRAINSE CABRACH
CABRA BRANCH
TEL. 8691414

73

Gino slowed the car when they saw a blue Ford SUV parked on the side of the country road. In this kind of weather, you stopped at every abandoned vehicle to make sure nobody was freezing to death inside. Cell phones had eliminated a lot of weather-related tragedies, but they still happened.

Magozzi hopped out and did a check, then retreated back to the car. Sure, the heater sucked, but it felt like a sauna after spending even the briefest time outside in the evil, wrathful embrace of January. 'Nobody in there. We're good.'

Gino resumed driving. 'Do you remember that methed-out couple who broke down in weather like this, then wandered a mile, but they were so messed up, they couldn't give nine-one-one a location?'

Magozzi did, and it was a depressing memory. They hadn't been able to triangulate the call to a tower in time and they froze to death in a gravel pit. 'Yeah. Last call, the guy was saying there were people all over, but they couldn't hear him.'

'That's an American tragedy right there, and every time I see a car on the side of the road, I think about it. Maybe you should run the plates.'

'Doing it now.'

Gino parked on the road in front of the farmhouse and

they took some time to get their bearings and suss out the property. It wasn't exceptional in any way, but it was well-tended, with clean white paint and a shoveled walk. 'I don't see any security.'

'Me either. But it's the ones you don't see that you have to worry about. I don't like the outbuildings.'

Gino unclipped his seatbelt. 'Or we've got nothing to worry about. I'm hoping Violet Thorson will answer the door and offer us tea and cookies.'

'I'd rather have a glass of Scotch and a bowl of pork rinds.'

When the plates on the Ford came back, Magozzi stared at the results for a minute, a strange sensation settling over him. 'The SUV belongs to Petra Juric.'

Gino was still for a long moment, then gave the steering wheel a smack. 'Goddamnit. That's why she's been holding back. This is personal. She wants Praljik all to herself, and she didn't want the law getting in her way. She's going to kill him.'

Magozzi looked at the bleak snowscape outside the windshield. 'If you're right, it could just as easily go the other way.'

Magozzi and Gino knocked on the farmhouse door, not knowing what to expect. A little old lady who served tea and cookies? A nefarious band of cyber criminals prepared to defend their operation with lethal force? A deranged war criminal? The old Boy Scout motto of always being prepared was a timeless one, which was why they both had their hands on their weapons.

The knock on the door was finally answered, and there

was a frozen moment of shock on both sides of the door before George Bormann, dressed in a mink vest, finally broke the silence.

'Detectives! You always seem to be surprising me!'

Magozzi struggled hard to keep focused on the moment, but the past forty-eight hours were speeding through his mind so relentlessly, it was almost impossible. He admired Gino's flair for theater when he let out a friendly chuckle and pasted on a broad smile.

'Hey, George. We're as surprised as you are. Got any leftover coq au vin? I'm starving.'

'I wouldn't think of serving you leftovers! Please, come in, come in. This is my country retreat, so I really don't cook here, but I have a lovely selection of cheeses and charcuterie. And some wines, of course, although I know you don't drink on the job. And I'm assuming you're on the job.'

'We are.' George Bormann wasn't doped up or drunk today, and compared to their other encounters with him, he seemed almost subdued. There was also no sign of Petra, which was not good. 'So you own this place?'

'No, I've tried many times to buy it from Violet – she's a dear friend of mine who's moved to Arizona because of her health – but she insists on keeping it in her name. A legacy for her children. But I maintain it for her, pay all the utilities and taxes in exchange for an escape from the city.'

Plausible story, a clever one, Magozzi thought, but everything else was all wrong. Especially the tasseled red silk scarf looped around George's neck.

'In fact, I've done quite a lot of renovating as well,' he blathered on. 'Her children will inherit a far more valuable property because of my tenancy. It's actually a lovely arrangement for the both of us. Please, I'm dying to know what brings you here. It's such a strange coincidence.'

'We got tipped off that Rado might be here, and we need to speak with him.'

George laughed. 'Rado isn't here, of course he isn't! Nobody knows where he is. In fact, I have my doubts he's even still alive, but come in and tell me why you think so. Perhaps we can work on your mystery together. There's obviously some misunderstanding and I hope I can help to clear it up.'

'That would be great,' Gino said, stomping his boots on a coconut welcome mat. Magozzi noticed a nice pair of men's leather boots by the door and knelt down, pretending to pull off his own. The boots had gold plates on them that boasted they were Prada. Definitive proof that the devil did indeed wear Prada. God bless Jimmy Grimm and his crazy ideas about finding frozen footprints under two inches of snow.

'No need to take off your footwear, Detective Magozzi. This is a casual place. I like to cross-country ski here, and in the summer, I keep horses, so housekeeping isn't a primary concern.' He pressed his hands together under his chin like an excited child on Christmas morning. 'This is quite an occasion, isn't it? I think we need some music.' He walked over to a credenza that held expensive Wi-Fi speakers and cued up a classical soundtrack from his phone. 'I know, it's trite to listen to Mozart, but I happen to love his music, and there is no shame in indulging your passions, no matter what other people think.'

'Annabelle Sellman. Petra Juric,' Magozzi said.

George was a great actor. His strange pop-eyes sparked with benign curiosity. 'Are they suspects? *Women?* That would be quite a twist!'

'They're not suspects, they're missing, and we think you know where they are.'

'Oh, I assure you I don't.'

'So there's no one else here?'

'Of course not. As I told you, people are too busy nowadays to enjoy rest and relaxation, to find balance in their lives, which is such a terrible shame.'

'How about Peter Praljik?'

George made a dramatic show of placing his forefinger on his chin. 'Peter Praljik, hmm. I can't say that I know anybody by that name.'

'Just checking. See, we're thinking that Praljik might actually be Rado –'

Magozzi and Gino hit the floor when three loud booms shattered the door frame behind them. When they looked up again, George Bormann was gone.

74

Annabelle flinched, then felt a surge of hope when she heard gunshots, muffled, but distinctive. She knew the sound because she'd purchased a gun and learned how to use it after Delia had been murdered. If she'd actually gotten her conceal-and-carry permit, things might have turned out differently for her, but there was no sense regretting her procrastination now.

She strained to hear and thought she caught the distant wail of a siren. The cynical side of her, the only real side that existed now, dismissed it as an auditory hallucination fueled by desperation, but she continued to listen. If it was real, it was very far away.

'Son of a bitch!' Gino shouted. 'Are you okay, Leo?'

Magozzi was vaguely aware that he was lying on the floor and Gino was standing over him. 'I'm fine . . . Maybe got a splinter from the door.'

Gino dropped down and started moving limbs and patting Magozzi's coat. His hand came up bloody. 'You got hit, Leo. Somewhere. I'm hearing sirens, but I'm calling an ambulance. You need attention.'

Magozzi didn't feel any pain, and he didn't feel lightheaded. Well, maybe a little. He closed his eyes and listened to Gino barking into the phone, probably scaring the hell out of the 911 dispatcher. 'Wait for back-up, Gino, there are two of them. Like we always figured. Fuck that we didn't think of it . . .'

'I'm not leaving you alone until the ambulance gets here. Now just be quiet. Okay, here we go. You got grazed in the shoulder. Your shooting arm, Goddamnit, you're going to be worthless for a while. Disability, early pension, living the dream.'

Magozzi heard the sound of cloth ripping, then felt tight pressure on his right shoulder. 'What's that?'

'It's my shirt, Leo, the best one I ever owned – Angela gave it to me for Christmas, and now it's soaking up your blood, you shithead. Why did you have to stand in front of the door?'

'We were both standing in front of the door. You got lucky, I didn't.' Magozzi felt a powerful dizziness hit him and behind his closed eyes, he saw Elizabeth, saw Grace carrying their daughter down to the lake on Thanksgiving weekend. Once again, he thought of Grace's single set of footprints in the snow, Elizabeth's future footprints alongside hers, and then those tiny prints growing bigger and bigger until they walked away to find their own path.

Gino was running like he never had before, following a well-trodden trail through the snow to the first outbuilding. Circle Pines PD and some MPD arrivals, including Eaton Freedman, were covering him from behind; others had broken off to search for Bormann. 'In here,' he shouted, waving toward the barn door, then ducking for cover along with the rest of the crew. 'It's padlocked, break it down!'

MPD had a battering ram and the old wood caved

easily under the assault, splintering into shards. Four uniforms in ballistic vests ducked through the jagged hole to clear the building, their breath coming in short, fast puffs of steam.

'Clear!' one finally shouted.

Gino entered the heated, brightly lit space – it was a workshop where there were half a dozen Rado sculptures in various stages of completion. But more ominous, more evil, were the large monitors mounted on the wall that showed two bound, gagged, blindfolded women struggling for their lives. He recognized Petra from the scar on her face.

'They're on the property somewhere, next building, break it down! Break every fucking door down until you run out!'

Gino bolted out of the art barn when he heard the sound of an engine. A Porsche Cayenne burst from another building and he emptied his weapon, hitting the tires first, then the rest of the vehicle. He figured he'd hit the driver because the Porsche suddenly veered off the driveway and plowed into a snow bank. Seconds passed, agonizing seconds, and everything was suddenly in slow motion, even the man who jumped out and rolled face first onto the ground.

'Check the car!' Gino directed his back-up as he slammed a new clip into his weapon. A phalanx of cops descended on the Porsche while he ran for the man on the ground. He surprised himself, leaping through snow like a deer, like he didn't carry a gut, like he was a young man stupid enough to do beer bongs, play Broomball, and run head on into trouble.

'Don't move if you want to keep your brains,' he snarled, standing over him, gun aimed at his head.

'DON'T SHOOT! I DIDN'T DO ANYTHING! I WAS KIDNAPPED!'

'Shut up, keep your hands where I can see them, and roll over.'

Gino gave the man a good nudge with his boot and suddenly Wolfie was staring up at him. His eyes were huge, terrified, and his teeth were chattering.

'Don't sh-sh-shoot me, please!'

Gino didn't lower his gun, but he offered him a hand up. 'Tell me what the hell is going on, Wolfie.'

He stood up on shaking legs and wiped the snow off his face. 'M-M-Mr Bormann said he had work for me here, b-b-but when I g-g-got here, he locked me in a r-room, then there were gunshots and he came and g-got me, told me to take his car and get out of here.'

Gino tensed. 'Nice story, but it doesn't make a lot of sense.'

'It's all a blur – I was scared!'

'Vehicle is clear!' one of the officers shouted.

'Where is Bormann?'

'I – I don't know.'

'Turn around, Wolfie, and spread your arms.'

He did, then ducked, bolted, and started racing through the snow. His head was down, his arms and legs pumping, so he never saw Freedman until he collided with three hundred pounds of solid muscle.

Freedman grabbed him by the arms, lifted him off the ground, and turned him around so he could cuff him. 'You're running awful fast. Got someplace you need to be?

Ooh, what do we have here?' he cooed, reaching into Wolfie's parka pocket. 'A forty-five? Nice piece, well-maintained, and I'm getting the fine aroma of fresh cordite, better than coffee in the morning.'

'I don't know where that came from! You can't arrest me – I didn't do anything!'

'Glad you didn't miss the action, Freedman,' Gino said, wiping his mouth, his gun still pointed at Wolfie's head, even though he was cuffed. 'Is McLaren here?'

'He stayed back. Big bust going down at Club Provocateur he didn't want to miss.'

Gino returned his attention to Wolfie. 'So, that forty-five isn't the weapon that shot my partner, am I right?'

Wolfie's face suddenly transformed from scared to snide as he looked mildly at Gino's ruined shirt. 'I hope your partner is okay, but looking at the blood on you, that might be up in the air.' And then he started laughing. No laugh would have seemed remotely appropriate in the moment, but this was chilling, a high-pitched, maniacal giggle that didn't belong outside a mental ward. 'I have to hand it to you, finding us. You're smarter than you look, Detective.'

Gino felt something give way inside, a fragile filament connecting him to a civility that wasn't meant to withstand the level of rage he felt. He knew he had reached a defining moment in life he'd never wanted to confront, the moment of losing all control, and he didn't care.

'And you're stupider than I thought, you fuck,' he seethed, as he gave Wolfie a sharp rap in the head with his gun and put his lights out. He'd gone too far and maybe he'd get kicked off the force, publicly shunned, thrown in jail, or all of the above, but none of that mattered.

Freedman shook his head as he let Wolfie's body slump to the ground. 'Damn shame when perps resist arrest, hate when that happens.' He turned his attention to the men and women scattering around the grounds, resuming their search for Rado. 'We'll keep looking for him. You go see about the women.'

75

Petra awoke slowly and became aware of sounds – loud, confusing sounds – but she wasn't entirely certain they weren't just the pounding of blood in her brain, or part of a drugged dream. What she realized quickly, and with horrifying clarity, was that she was gagged, blindfolded, tethered to a bed, and naked. She should have pulled the goddamned trigger when Praljik had opened the door.

Through sheer force of will, she pushed back the panic, pushed back the evil memories and tried to think rationally. The detectives would be on their way. Maybe they were already here and that was the noise she was hearing. Unless Praljik had taken her somewhere else, and then they might never find her.

Suddenly the thought of all the times she'd entertained release through death horrified her. She wanted to live. She had to survive, and she couldn't rely on anybody else to help her.

She focused on her restraints, tested them. They weren't metal, they weren't rope, but some type of cloth and the cloth had give. Her ankles were fastened more tightly than her wrists; her left wrist more tightly than her right. If she tugged hard enough, she might be able to tear the cloth, but that might also tighten the knot. The other option was to try to work the knot loose and squeeze her hand together to make it small enough to slip out of the noose. As she tested both theories, she heard a door open, followed by approaching footsteps. She went still and held her breath.

Petra recoiled when a hand touched her arm and the calm she had managed to create in her mind evaporated and instinct took over. She started thrashing blindly, screaming through her gag, remembering the others, young girls and grown women alike, lined up in beds beside her, tied down . . .

'It's all right, Petra, nothing to worry about. I'm very disappointed that we're going to have to speed things along, but we already have such a strong bond that I don't think your death will be diminished much.'

She fought harder, with the inconceivable strength of a Berserker of folklore, and felt the right tether give a little more. If she didn't run out of adrenalin, she might be able to rip herself free. And then she heard the sickening screech of duct tape being torn from a roll and an emotional fissure opened, just large enough to let her hope and resolve leak away to some distant cavern inside her.

Gino's breath was ragged from cold and exertion as he ran to the last outbuilding and stood to the side of a man-sized door, his weapon raised. He gave Freedman a nod, and MPD's gentle giant splintered it easily with his shoulder. Bormann was waiting for them, gun trained at Petra's head.

'Get away from her, Bormann.'

His face lifted in a chilling smile. 'But we were just getting started.'

'Now.'

'This is Petra's gun. Isn't that ironic? She came to kill me with it, but now I'm going to kill her with it.'

'No, you're not. It's over. Drop the gun and step away.'

'I can't. Petra has to die. I wanted to do it with the tape, but you rudely interrupted me. So I'm going to shoot her instead, and then I'm going to shoot myself. That way we'll be together forever, the way it was always meant to be.'

Gino gauged his options in a split second and realized he didn't have any. Bormann was right next to her, the gun too close to her head to risk firing his own shot. Freedman was beside him, but he wasn't making a move, either. It was a stand-off, but the problem was, Bormann had nothing to lose. 'You don't want to die, and you don't want Petra to die, either.'

'You have no idea what I want, Detective Rolseth.'

'I know you want to be famous. This is going to do it.'

'I'm already famous. In many ways. Just ask Petra. Oh, that's right, she can't speak just now.' He chuckled.

Petra was lying perfectly still, listening to the exchange, gathering strength. When she heard his chuckle, something dark and primal and infinitely powerful rose inside her. All the hatred and rage and grief that had tormented her for decades seemed to coalesce and she imagined her right arm, her right fist, as the most powerful weapon of mass destruction in the history of the world. She let out a muffled scream, yanked her right arm free from the cloth, and chopped it down hard in the direction of Praljik's voice. It connected with something hard, bone, and she heard a yelp of pain, the clatter of her gun on the floor.

When Petra's arm suddenly shot out and connected with Bormann's, dislodging the gun, Gino lunged forward, but

Freedman was spectacularly fast, faster than him, faster than Petra's blistering right karate chop. In the space of a millisecond, he was on top of Bormann, a boulder crushing a pebble. Just as quickly, he cuffed him and dragged him out of the room the way they'd come in, through the splintered door.

76

'It's okay, Petra, you're okay. It's Detective Rolseth. No one else is in the room right now.'

She removed her blindfold and looked at him. He had such a kind face, the face of a good man, a sad and troubled man, and it would forever be etched in her mind. He settled a blanket over her naked body and gently removed the gag from her mouth. Her body reluctantly softened, loosened, as she willed herself back into the present, putting the past away in a separate corner of her mind, the one that vodka and tranquilizers had the power to deaden for a little while.

'Are you hurt?' he asked, as he worked to remove her remaining binds from beneath the blanket.

'I was chloroformed, but I don't think I'm injured.' She took a shocked breath when she noticed his torn, bloody shirt. 'Are you?'

'I'm fine, but my partner got hit in the shoulder. He lost some blood, but he's going to make it.'

'Thank God.'

'He's a tough son of a bitch.'

'You saved my life. That's the second time I've said that in forty-eight hours. I'm accumulating a substantial amount of cosmic debt.'

'You saved your own life with that wicked move you made. I think you probably broke his arm. And as far as cosmic debt, you can wipe the slate clean. There's another woman here in a different building. We found her first. She's been here longer than you and she needs some serious medical attention, but she's going to be okay. You probably saved *her* life.'

Petra swallowed hard, wincing at the bitterness in her throat. 'How?'

'We saw your car on the way in, so we knew you were here, and because of that, things rolled out a little differently than they probably would have.'

She closed her eyes against the sting of tears. 'There was a second man, the one who chloroformed me . . .'

'We got him, too.'

While emergency techs attended Petra, Gino walked to the other building, where Annabelle's horror chamber was. Seeing the video equipment, the various instruments of torture hanging neatly on a pegboard as innocently as kitchen utensils, the bed with its empty restraints, the rolls and rolls of duct tape made him physically ill all over again. He'd stopped vomiting at murder scenes long ago, but this was different. So outrageously different, somehow worse than any dead body.

Annabelle was lying on a gurney while paramedics worked on her, rubbing her wrists and ankles to get circulation back, taking her vitals, hooking up a saline drip. She must have heard him come in, because she rolled her head on the pillow and locked eyes with him. 'I knew you'd find me,' she whispered hoarsely.

'I'm sorry we took so long.'

Amazingly, she gave him a smile.

Gino stepped away to the corner of the room to give

her privacy and catch his breath, maybe his sanity, too, and noticed a photo tacked up on the wall. As he walked toward it, the sharp, horrible image of Kelly Ramage's crime scene came into focus, her dead body displayed like a trophy after a successful hunt. It was black-and-white except for the color overlay of a bright red tasseled scarf tied tightly around her neck. Murder as art, suitable for framing and ready for the next Rado show in some other city, the one that would never, ever happen.

He felt a frightening, consuming fury, but beyond that, and even more powerful, was deep, inconsolable sadness. His entire career, he'd seen the aftermath of the worst of human cruelty, but this was beyond cruelty: this was depravity so shocking that the only adjective he could think of to describe it was 'evil'. Pure evil. He touched the photo gently and whispered an apology to Kelly.

When he finally stepped outside again, Roadrunner was waiting by the door, bouncing on his feet like a racehorse in a gate. Freedman and Harley were by his side, probably keeping him from storming the building.

'Gino!' Roadrunner lurched forward. 'Is Petra in there? Is she okay?'

'She's in another building, but she's okay, Roadrunner.'

'Can I see her?'

'She's getting some attention now. Let's give her some time. But I'll tell you what, I'll let her know you're here.' He looked at Freedman. 'That was some move back there.'

'It's called the Body Avalanche. A pro-wrestling move.'

'Remind me never to piss you off.'

77

George Bormann was still cuffed, but sitting on a gurney next to an ambulance, his arm in a sling. His bug eyes were fixed on the gray January sky. He looked a little banged up from Freedman's crushing Body Avalanche, but he was alive and well. That was fine by Gino: he wanted him to live. For a long, long time. A life in prison here or abroad would never be penance for what he'd done, but it was a start.

'George. Or should I call you Peter? Or Rado?'

'George or Georgie will do.'

'No more dinner parties for you. No more fancy wine. No more torture. This must be a pretty bad day for you.'

'I confess it is, Detective. But I've had a full life. I have no regrets.'

'That really pisses me off, because your victims never got that chance.'

'They were lost, trapped. I set them free, and they're in a much better place right now because of me.'

'Dead is better? Well, maybe dead is better for you, too. Or for Wolfie.'

His eyes sparked, panic lighting them. 'Tell me about Wolfie. Is he all right?'

'He's alive, but maybe he wishes he wasn't. How did you talk him into being a part of this? No way was it about money. Or was he that desperate?'

George smiled and closed his eyes. 'No. I'm a very

344

wealthy man and everything I have has always belonged to Wolfie. We've been together for a very long time.'

'How's that?'

'He's the only person who has ever been loyal to me. He was the greatest gift I ever received.' His eyelids suddenly flew wide and he clawed at his chest. His mouth was moving, but no words came out.

Gino gestured to a med tech. 'This guy might be having a heart attack. Keep him alive.'

Petra felt Roadrunner's hand in hers and his touch made her glad she hadn't died and equally glad she hadn't killed. Vrag had made her a monster of sorts, but he no longer had a hold on her. Well, he probably always would to a certain degree, but he didn't have the power to manipulate her actions and make her do foolish things anymore. He was in the rearview mirror now, fading slowly away. One day, he might disappear altogether, and she would become herself again. At least, she hoped she would. 'I shouldn't have come here alone.'

'I understand why you did.'

'I know you do.' She squeezed his hand, and the knobby protrusions felt nice, comfortable, like she'd known the gnarled landscape of them her whole life. 'I think most about my dog, Mirna, and that seems so wrong.'

'No, it doesn't. That's your safe place. She's like my bike.'

'Maybe we can both find a new safe place together.'

His motions were awkward, but he reached out and tucked a loose strand of hair behind her ear. 'I think we can. You're going to be fine, Petra. We both are.'

78

McLaren was sitting in Ty Overgaard's unmarked, a rusted-out nineties Chrysler that fit his persona when he was working undercover narc. The UC guys always had to pose as the lowlifes in the trade because the people who drove the supercharged Escalades and Porsches were the ones who ran the syndicates, and they all knew each other from coming up in the business. At one time, they'd all been the guys driving rusty Chryslers, paying their dues hustling the pavement. Putting Ty in a suit and a Cadillac would be the street equivalent of installing a new CEO in a Fortune 500 company overnight without a press release.

'You did us a real solid. We've been trying to get the drop on Club Provocateur for the better part of the year, but we could never get enough for a warrant, let alone a raid,' Ty said, his gloved fingers tapping the steering wheel manically.

McLaren smiled. 'You're going to have to share the glory, buddy. There's an alphabet soup of agencies here, and they all have a stake in this.'

'I don't mind that, but I do mind the hostage part of it. That's bad news.'

'That's why we're sitting in your shitty car and letting Tac handle it. These kinds of situations are why God made SWAT, and they've been bored lately.'

'You think it's legit, this SOS?'

'Monkeewrench said so.'

'Good enough for me.' Ty tapped his earbud, listened, then nodded at McLaren. 'They're going in.'

When Stefan heard muffled but distinctly angry shouts coming from somewhere in the building, he spun in his chair and saw Kirk pull his gun and run out of the door. It was happening. It was really happening. Monkeewrench had gotten his message loud and clear, sent in the cavalry, and he was going to bust out of here faster than Usain Bolt.

He'd been obese for most of his life, but he felt miraculously light on his feet as he fled for the open door. Survival was a great motivator. The hall was empty, but the shouting was louder out there, funneling up the staircase from the room below. There was also the heavy pounding of footsteps, the rattle of heavy weaponry. Cops. Lots of them. He opened his mouth and his lungs and started screaming for help. But his screams were abruptly cut off when something heavy hit his skull, a strong hand pushed him in the back, and he started tumbling down the stairs. At the apex of each somersault, he thought he saw Koppenhöfer standing at the top of the stairs, his flat, dead eyes watching him as he fell.

I'm a fall guy, falling down the stairs! he thought giddily. *The perfect distraction. Push the fat man down, hope he dies, divert the cops' attention, escape out the back.*

But Stefan wasn't going to die, because he had enough padding to protect him. Hell, he was practically bouncing like a beach ball down the stairs, right into the waiting arms of safety – as long as they didn't get spooked and cut him into ribbons with their tactical rifles before they realized he was a good guy after all.

347

79

Magozzi had spent more than enough time in hospitals lately, but he hadn't been the one in the bed. It was a strange and helpless feeling, being dressed in a flimsy gown with needles stuck in his arms, nurses hovering around checking his vitals and the bags of whatever stuff they were pumping into his veins. One bag he knew was blood because it was red, a dead giveaway, the other was clear, and he hoped it was morphine, because the pain in his shoulder was bad.

He'd been damn lucky. The bullet had made a shallow furrow in his shoulder and exited cleanly. He was patched up, his lost blood was being replaced, and there was no way in hell he was spending the night here, no matter what they said.

Some would call this a bad day, but Magozzi didn't see it that way. He was alive and, according to Gino's brief text, they'd not only caught Praljik/Rado/Bormann, they'd saved Annabelle and Petra from horrible deaths. Kooky, farcical George Bormann, a vicious war criminal. It was going to take a while to wrap his mind around that.

Because he'd missed the show, he had a ton of questions, but the first thing he wanted to know was who'd shot him, so he could return the favor some day.

When Grace walked in, all the pain in his shoulder suddenly went away – the magic of endorphins, nature's perfect happy serum. Her face was drawn with the kind of profound worry he'd never seen her show before, but she managed a smile. 'Hi, Magozzi.'

'Hi, Grace.' He patted the bed and she sat next to him and touched his cheek.

'You look pretty good for a man who lost a couple pints of blood.'

'It's just a flesh wound, nothing the four million stitches won't fix. But you'll probably have to wait on me for a while.'

'I owe you some nursing after last year.'

'It might be more than a while, actually. The doctor said I'll be laid up for at least a year, maybe two. I won't be able to work, change diapers, or do anything around the house.'

Grace cocked a sharp brow at him. 'Really.'

'Yep. Did I mention you'll have to wait on me? Because, according to the medical professionals, pretty much the only thing I'll be good for is sitting around watching TV all day and drinking Scotch.'

'Funny. I just talked to your doctor and he gave me a very different prognosis and timeline.'

'Really? I must have misunderstood.'

She lay down next to him and stared up at the ceiling. 'We were so worried, Magozzi. When Gino called to tell us . . .'

'I hope he told you I was going to be okay.'

'Of course he did. But it's not a phone call anybody wants to get.'

Magozzi stroked her hair with his good arm. 'It's not. But it worked out okay.'

She turned over on her side and draped her arm across

his chest. 'Harley, Annie and Roadrunner are in the lounge waiting to see you, and Gino's on his way.'

'Is Elizabeth here?'

'Of course she is, but they don't let babies into ICU.'

'That's a stupid rule. I could be dying.'

'Hush. Don't even joke about that.'

'You're right. I'm sorry.'

'They don't let flowers into ICU either.'

'Really? How do you know that?'

'Because there's a bouquet of yellow daisies waiting for you at the nurses' station. You'll get them when they transfer you to a general floor.'

'Who sent them?'

'Petra brought them. She was here earlier, getting checked out. She's fine. Shook up, but fine, and Roadrunner is hovering over her like a drone.'

He smiled. 'She's special, isn't she?'

'I think so. Roadrunner definitely thinks so.'

'Good for him.' Magozzi decided not to bring up the good possibility that she had likely been premeditating the murder of Praljik. What was the point? Monkeewrench had certainly figured it out, just like he and Gino had. 'We'll be taking those daisies home with us tonight. I'm not staying here, Grace.'

'There's still a half-bag of blood that needs to get into your body before you leave. Close your eyes and rest, Magozzi. I'll be here. We all will.'

When Magozzi woke up, Grace was gone and Gino was standing over his bed, looking down at him. 'You changed clothes.'

Gino snorted. 'And took a shower. You bled like a stuck pig. Looks like they put it all back in you, though.' He gestured to the empty bag hanging from a metal tree.

'I'm good to go.'

'Nice room,' Gino said, looking around. 'Comfy-looking sofa, two chairs, tons of closet space, and a private bath. I should have waited to shower here.'

'Tell me everything, Gino.'

He pulled up a chair and sat down, then reached into a brown-paper grocery bag and pulled out two plastic cups, a bottle of Scotch, and a family-sized package of pork rinds. 'First things first. You said you wanted a Scotch and a bowl of pork rinds, so here you go.'

'I've actually never had pork rinds. Are they good?'

'They're fat. What do you think?'

'Pour me a Scotch.'

'You got it.' Gino poured two fingers into each of the cups and they toasted. 'To your recovery, buddy.'

'Thanks. Okay, now tell me who the fuck shot me.'

'Wolfie.'

'*Wolfie?* Are you kidding me?'

'Not kidding. We found nice computer set-ups in one of the outbuildings and in the house, so I'm guessing our broke Caltech grad was behind all the technology. Except I don't think he was so broke.'

'What do you mean?'

'He had some kind of long-standing relationship with Bormann, deep enough that he was willing to kill a couple cops to keep him safe, but I don't know what yet. Bormann started having chest pains when I was questioning him on scene.'

'Is he going to make it?'

'Yeah.'

'What did Wolfie have to say?'

Gino slurped his Scotch. 'Not much. He had an unfortunate accident.'

Magozzi raised his brows and, for some reason, it hurt.

'Yeah, he accidentally slammed his head into the butt of my gun. Really hard. Don't know how it happened. He's probably conscious by now, but he's going to have one hell of a headache for a few days.'

Magozzi smiled, and that didn't hurt.

'I figure Wolfie wasn't just a tech guy. He was a wingman, Bormann's accomplice, and I'll bet you anything his bootprints are going to match the second set from Dray's place. He's a good-looking kid – he was probably bait. Wolfie shows up for the encounter with Kelly Ramage and then Bormann crashes the party.'

'Is Bormann healthy enough to question?'

'Yeah, but I'm going to have to do the first round without you. You're not going anywhere.'

'I'm fine. I'm checking out tonight.'

'I see you didn't get the stubborn shot out of you. Don't be an ass, you need to rest. Bormann isn't going anywhere either. He'll be on ice waiting for you when you get out.'

'Annabelle?'

'She's going to be fine. She's actually here – I just saw her. She asked about you.'

'Koppenhöfer?'

'SWAT and a bunch of fed agencies raided Club Provocateur. McLaren was there, and they hauled out a bunch of drugs – green smiley-face Ecstasy among other things – and a Black Hat hacker who says he was being held hostage. He contacted Monkeewrench. We don't know who Koppenhöfer really is yet, but Petra says he was one of Praljik's lieutenants and something went south along the way. Pavel's dead.'

'How?'

'Somebody beat the hell out of him after we left last night, and I'm guessing it wasn't the fictitious homeless janitor. Internal injuries, maybe an aneurysm.' He dumped the rest of his Scotch into Magozzi's cup. 'Listen, I gotta stay sober and run, but I'm happy as hell to see you alive. You scared the living shit out of me. Magozzi?' He shook him gently. 'Magozzi, are you okay?'

Gino pressed the call button on the side of his bed and a broad nurse with a stern face walked in a few moments later. She was probably pleasant, most nurses he'd met were, but she looked a little scary, like a drill sergeant ready to eviscerate a new recruit.

'Is there something wrong, sir?'

'Yeah, my partner just conked out in the middle of a conversation. I wanted to make sure he's okay.'

'Detective Magozzi is fine. He's just on strong pain-management medication.'

Jesus, of course he was on pain meds, and Gino had brought him Scotch. Wouldn't that be the capper to the day, killing Leo with Laphroaig after he'd survived a gunshot wound?

Her eyes drifted to the glass on the bedside tray. 'Please don't tell me that's alcohol.'

'That? It's just some apple juice. He asked me to bring some.' Gino didn't know why he'd lied, but it was kind of fun, definitely the only fun he'd had in the past forty-eight hours.

'That was nice of you. The hospital's Food Service does have apple juice. A lot of it. It's a popular request.'

'Oh, well, he was probably confused – he lost a lot of blood. So he's good?'

'He's going to be fine. We gave him the last transfusion, his blood work looks excellent, and if all goes well, we might be able to discharge him tomorrow.'

'Great news.' Gino stood up and dumped the Scotch down the sink, like a guilty teenager.

'How much did he have?'

'What?'

'How much apple juice?'

'Oh. One small sip. Then he fell asleep.'

'Just one small sip. Are you sure?'

'I'm absolutely positive. Are liquids prohibited or something?'

'Not all liquids.' She walked closer to the bed, her shoes squeaking on the polished tile. 'As long as it was just a sip of Scotch, it isn't going to hurt him, and if I were in Detective Magozzi's position, I'd certainly want a small tipple. Smells like good stuff.'

'I'm totally busted, aren't I?'

'Yes, you are.'

'So you're a Scotch drinker?'

'A glass every night. Two on weekends. Spirits keep the spirits up. That's what my grandmother always said.'

'She was a wise woman.' Gino reached into his grocery bag and handed the bottle to the nurse. 'Enjoy, courtesy of MPD.'

Her dour expression turned wistful. 'I can't accept gifts.'

'It's not a gift. It's an official police request that you remove this bottle from the premises and put it in your car. Part of an undercover sting. You'd really be helping us out.'

'Well, anything I can do to assist the police. I wouldn't think of shirking my civic duty.' She was dangerously close to a smile.

'We'd appreciate it, ma'am. Do you like pork rinds?'

80

Gino was having a hard time containing his anger as he sat across from Bormann, who seemed as calm and content as a cat basking in the sun. He didn't seem remotely disturbed by the fact that his hands were cuffed, like his victims' had been, or that he was wearing a prisoner jumpsuit.

It was really no surprise – the man was foaming-at-the-mouth, batshit crazy, damaged beyond comprehension, and the gruesome extent of his activities was still being discovered at Violet Thorson's farm in the form of video documentation of other victims from his desolate, depraved past. Whatever his inner reality was, it had absolutely no connection to humanity or sanity.

'You've got some real problems, George. The day is young, but we already have a whole lot of evidence that ties you to the murders of Kelly Ramage, Delia Sellman and Blanca Szabo. That's on top of the two women you were holding hostage, and we're just starting. You're a popular guy – a lot of people want a piece of you. The feds and Interpol are even in line. But wherever you end up, here or abroad, you're going to rot in prison.'

He folded his cuffed hands together prayerfully, which Gino found bizarre and unsettling on so many levels. 'I'd like to go home.'

'Sure you would, but that's never going to happen.'

'Not home here, my real home. They'll want me to stand before a war-crimes tribunal.'

'Oh, yeah, they do. I know that for a fact. You make it sound like that's a good thing.'

'Oh, it is. I'm a *hero* there, Detective Rolseth. There is savagery in any war and I did my part to defend my people. They remember.'

Gino felt his temples start to throb as his blood pressure shot up.

'You're a butcher and a monster and the war was your excuse. I don't know when you started killing, but you never stopped.'

'Not everybody understands. That's why I began sculpting. It was a way for me to express myself, my unique point of view.'

'Bragging about your massacres, torturing and killing women is part of your unique point of view?'

'It's what they wanted.'

Gino turned around and looked at the one-way glass behind him, where McLaren, Freedman, and Chief of Police Malcherson stood, because he couldn't stand to look at the sociopath in front of him any longer. But he had to. George hadn't lawyered up yet, not that a lawyer had a snowball's chance in Hell of doing anything for him, but it still made things more complicated.

'Tell me about Wolfie. He's not talking.'

Bormann's mouth worked into a tender, hideous smile. 'My beloved son, loyal always. He really had nothing to do with any of this, except help me with the technology aspects. Oh, and I suppose present a handsome face to the women

357

who were anxious for adventure. I hope you'll give him leniency.'

'He's your *son*?'

'He is. Not in the biological sense – I was never fortunate enough to have children of my own. He was a war orphan, only five years old. He was filthy, very ill, and almost starved to death. But such a smart, loving boy. He is the joy of my life. He always has been.'

Gino looked away briefly, trying to imagine this soulless man feeling love for anything or anybody. He knew he didn't have the capacity for true emotion, but there was some strange bond, some narcissistic motivation in his ruined mind that approximated it. The profilers were going to have one hell of a field day with this sick bastard, and the really tragic part was, he'd been famous for the wrong reasons most of his life. And his fame was only going to grow. When the art world got rocked by the news, the price of Rado sculptures would probably shoot into the stratosphere, a truly depressing commentary on popular culture.

'Tell me about your relationship with Joseph Koppenhöfer. He used your old Social Security number to set up Vrag Entertainment. But Vrag's your name, isn't it?'

His eyes went dark and he turned away. 'We were friends once, colleagues, and also enemies, but we helped each other.'

'Some help. You and Wolfie went to a lot of trouble to set him up and screw him over – not that he didn't deserve it. He's a scumbag, too.'

'He *did* deserve it, thank you for saying so, Detective. I can barely speak about his treachery, it was so profound.'

'Is that why you hacked into his Bit Monster account?'

Bormann looked startled. 'You certainly know a lot, don't you?'

Gino remained expressionless, waiting for him to continue, which he did. He couldn't help himself. His arrogance was as great as Petra had said it was.

'He owed me, more than he could ever repay. It's hard to put a monetary figure on lost lives, on betrayal, impossible to determine appropriate reparations.'

Gino ground his teeth together, trying to stay calm and in his chair. 'And what about your reparations for the lives you took?'

'The courts will determine that.'

'What did Pavel have to do with this?'

'Pavel?'

'Pavel Kosic. You cloned his phone for your Signal communications with Kelly Ramage.'

'Oh, that wasn't personal. We knew he was working for Joseph, and by connecting him to Kelly's murder, and connecting Kelly to Club Provocateur, it would bring attention to the club and facilitate Joseph's demise without being too obvious. It was Wolfie's idea, and quite clever on his part. A masterful piece of work, modeled after chess. We enjoy playing chess together. It's a most intricate game. I wonder if Joseph — well, that's not his real name, but it doesn't really matter — has finally fallen, through our efforts. He's a very bad person.'

Gino ignored his question, wouldn't give him the satisfaction of knowing that Koppenhöfer or whatever his name was, was in bad shape himself. 'Pavel's dead.'

George's brows peaked in what seemed like genuine

pity, and it freaked Gino out almost as much as listening to him express love for Wolfie. He was like a psycho version of a shape shifter. 'I'm sorry to hear that. I've always liked Pavel. He was a good man, but he fell into the wrong side of things. But, come to think of it, he did have a choice at one point, and I suppose that makes him disloyal, too. Perhaps I'm not so sorry after all.'

81

Magozzi was watching the morning news from his hospital bed, a little pissed that he hadn't been discharged last night, but his shoulder had started bleeding again. On the bright side, he was out of ICU, on a general floor now, and would be going home later. He also had flowers to look at while he waited for Grace and Annie to bring Elizabeth – the bouquet from MPD that had arrived earlier and Petra's charming yellow daisies.

Chief Malcherson had just given an abbreviated press conference announcing MPD had a suspect in custody for Kelly Ramage's murder, one of the detectives in charge had sustained a gunshot injury during the apprehension, thoughts and prayers, but nothing more.

When this whole thing eventually blew up, like an ammo dump, and it would, Rado was going to have one of the most spectacular downfalls in media history. Unfortunately, it was just the sort of irresistibly salacious story that would be plastered on international TV screens and probably movie screens, for a very long time. The fallout would be plentiful and the bastard was going to be a celebrity.

He looked away from the news when he heard the heavy pounding of boots that always announced Harley's arrival long before he entered a room.

'Hey, Leo, good to see you bright-eyed and bushy-tailed this morning. You were pretty out of it last night. Still charming, but out of it.'

'Hey, Harley, hey, Roadrunner. Thanks for coming – you didn't have to.'

Harley placed a cardboard box on his bedside tray. 'Sure we did. We had to bring you donuts, but not cop donuts, real ones from that bakery on Selby. Gourmet stuff. Once you try these, you'll never go back.'

'Thanks. I'm going to eat them all before Gino gets here.' He lifted the lid and sucked in the heavenly aroma of chocolate and fat. A sure way to avoid protein poisoning. Life was good, getting better.

They pulled up chairs and Harley glanced at the TV. 'Man, this whole thing is going to be one magnificent shit storm when it finally hits.'

'I was just thinking that very same thing.'

'Crazy. And it gets crazier. Once we nailed Rado and had all his aliases, we were able to get deeper into his stuff. That son of a bitch was behind the big Bit Monster heist after all. We'd pegged a Swiss private-equity guy as a possible perp early on and, sure as shit, whose name popped up? George Bormann's.'

'Wow.'

'Yeah. Is that guy a mad genius or something?'

'No, but he had help.'

'He had great help, and he would have stayed richer than Midas if he hadn't decided to kill people on top of the hacking.'

'He's so deranged, I'm not sure the money ever mattered. But the killing did.' Magozzi looked at Roadrunner and smiled. 'How is Petra doing?'

'Really good. She's been looking for Praljik for a long time. She actually had a conversation with him before they took her and she's filling in a lot of blanks.'

'Gino's been keeping me posted. Thank her for the flowers.'

'I will. Yellow daisies are special to her.'

'Then they're special to me.'

A nurse walked in, holding an envelope. 'Good morning, everyone. Detective Magozzi, a gentleman just came to deliver this. He didn't want to bother you, but he asked me to make sure you got it.'

'Thanks.'

'Can I get you anything?'

'Maybe a little more coffee to go with these donuts.'

She smiled. 'Coming right up.'

Puzzled, Magozzi opened the thick, creamy envelope, lined with dark blue foil. The enclosed card was embossed with Todd Ramage's name.

I'm praying for your speedy recovery, Detective Magozzi. You and Detective Rolseth have my gratitude, and Kelly's as well. You promised justice and you kept that promise.

You were asking if Kelly had ever seen a psychic, and looking through some of her things last night, I found the enclosed business card. I thought you'd like to know, in case it ties up anything else for you.

Very best wishes, and at your service always,
Todd Ramage

Magozzi picked up the card. It read: 'Blanca Szabo, Medium and Spiritual Guide'.

'Something interesting?' Harley asked.

'Something that answers a question I had.'

Epilogue

Standing in the charming, prosperous village, surrounded by verdant hills and fields of daisies, the jagged profiles of the Dinaric Alps vaulting toward the distant horizon, it was hard for Roadrunner to imagine that this place had once been soaked in blood, leveled by destruction. The granite memorial to the massacre there was the only indication of past horrors. Bouquets of flowers, some fresh, some old and withering, lay at the base. The town had moved on, but the tragedy would never be forgotten.

He stood back from Petra, giving her space as she stood before the monument. Her dark hair shone in the sunlight, almost blue. Birds trilled, somewhere a cow lowed impatiently, and a soft breeze swept down from the hills, filling the air with the scent of flowers and grass and earth.

She finally walked forward to the foot of the monument, knelt down, and bowed her head. The light warm wind carried her foreign whispers to his ears and he heard them as the murmurs of ghosts.

After a few moments, she carefully, reverently laid down her armful of yellow daisies, kissed her hand, and placed it on the bouquet. Then she kissed the amber pendant that hung from her neck and spoke to Blanca.

Eventually, she stood and turned around. Her onyx eyes were dry, her face serene. Maybe her heartbroken soul had been mended a little. It was his greatest hope.

She walked to him and she took his hand. 'Thank you for helping me say goodbye, Roadrunner. I would never have been able to come back here without you.'

'You would have eventually.'

'No, because I would be dead. Let's take a walk. I'll show you some things.' She pulled him onto a path and they walked hand in hand toward a field of yellow daisies.

Leabharlanna Poiblí Chathair Baile Átha Cliath
Dublin City Public Libraries

Acknowledgements

Readers and fans – you're why I do what I do. Thank you for sharing the journey.

Immense gratitude to all my colleagues at Michael Joseph/Penguin Random House and Crooked Lane. You are the best. Tom Weldon and Matthew Martz, thank you both for your unflagging enthusiasm and support; to the amazing folks in marketing and publicity at both houses, past and present: Jenny Platt, Olivia Thomas, Sriya Varad-harajan, Sarah Poppe, Ashley Di Dio, and their teams; Jenny Chen, who answers emails almost before I send them; and Meryl Moss/Meryl Moss Media, Noelle Brown, and Erika Lopez. Your work is so appreciated.

In editorial, special thanks to my 'Super Editor' Joel Richardson. I'm incredibly fortunate to have his skill and keen eye steering me straight and sometimes saving me from literary burning buildings. Nick Lowndes and Hazel Orme, thanks for making my job so easy in the final stages.

To Ellen Geiger, long-time agent and pal, and Matt McGowan at Frances Goldin Literary Agency; David Grossman at David Grossman Literary Agency.

To friends and family, who offer life's rarest treasures: unconditional love and support. Ted Platz, Phillip Lam-brecht, Tim and Louise Matson, Jeff and Stacy Montgomery, Kathy and Brad Gossard, Dennis and Mary Fruetel, Mike and Jodi Clark – thank you. There are many more and you have my gratitude, but I'm trying to keep this shorter than *War and Peace*. You know who you are. Love you all.

And of course, PJ: beloved mother, best friend, mentor, and soul mate. Your memory inspires me in all ways, every day, and makes writing a pure joy.

CABR.
...ASKA URBAN
5234